THE STEEL SHARK

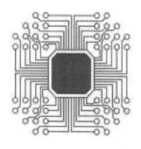

REBECCA
CANTRELL

Copyright Information

ALSO BY REBECCA CANTRELL

Joe Tesla thrillers set in the tunnels under New York:

The World Beneath

The Tesla Legacy

The Chemistry of Death

The Steel Shark

Humorous mysteries set in the sunny and glamorous world of Malibu (written with Sean Black):

A is for Actress

B is for Bad Girls

C is for Coochy Coo

D is for Drunk

Award-winning Hannah Vogel mysteries set in 1930s Berlin:

A Trace of Smoke

A Night of Long Knives

A Game of Lies

A City of Broken Glass

Gothic thrillers in the Order of the Sanguines (written with James Rollins):

The Blood Gospel

Innocent Blood

Blood Infernal

THE STEEL SHARK

REBECCA CANTRELL

DEDICATION

For my husband, my son, and the underwater heroes

PROLOGUE

Munchon naval base, North Korea
February 8

They boarded the plane as women, but they left it as men. In full naval uniform, they trooped single file down the stairs onto the frozen runway. The business jet's door closed, and the plane taxied toward a turnaround to take off again. Within two hours, the plane would be sinking to the bottom of the Sea of Japan, and they would be presumed dead.

Or actually be dead.

Laila led the newly minted men to their destiny. To do this, she had to become her brother, and she concentrated on aping his bowlegged, rolling gait. The words of a royal cousin echoed in her ears: *Always the hips are foremost, as if the cock is pulling him onward like a dog on a leash. Toes pointed out at ten degrees, and a roll of those eager hips when he lands each foot. Your brother doesn't so much walk as he fucks the air.*

She swaggered to a battered staff car parked in front of an empty bus. Cold wind snapped at a blue and red North Korean flag mounted by the car's right front tire. Next to the open door, a driver stood at attention. He was a small man, no taller than the disguised women, his dress uniform too long. He touched his old-fashioned peaked cap and started to bow, then caught himself as if unsure about the protocol.

"We are honored to welcome you to our country, General Dakkar." A North Korean accent wove through his Chinese words.

"The honor rests with me," Laila answered. Theoretically, her brother had learned Mandarin in his private schools, although in reality only she'd taken the time to study the language.

Satisfied with her answer, the driver opened the door for her and her companion while the others filed aboard the bus. When the driver drove onto a gravel road, his dim headlights illuminated only a meter ahead. Beyond lay darkness like she'd never seen.

Old leather creaked as she shifted, and her cold gun dug into her ribs. Icy clouds of breath condensed in front of her recently applied mustache. Nahal surreptitiously squeezed Laila's hand with fingers cold as ice splinters. They could do this, the pressure against her hand said.

They had been on this road together for months, after all, ever since Nahal had hacked into Laila's brother's laptop. They had discovered evidence of a wide-ranging conspiracy that ended with an email detailing a top-secret submarine transaction. That submarine might give them freedom to escape the strictures of their lives and perhaps even to prevent future injustices.

More research had revealed their government had ordered a stealth submarine from China at twice the usual price to guarantee absolute confidentiality. In trade for badly needed Western currency, a North Korean intermediary had agreed to perform the handover to further obscure the vessel's provenance and keep Chinese hands clean. So far, as the wider world was concerned, the new submarine didn't exist.

That was why she and Nahal were jolting through a deserted forest in the middle of a cold winter night.

They were going to steal that submarine.

Like something out of a film. Only a princess who had watched a thousand movies and a hacker who had hacked a thousand computers could ever have pulled it off. It had taken months of careful planning, audacious hacking, and a great deal of money, but they had come this far, and they couldn't turn back.

She stared into the cones of light, wishing she could see farther. Beyond the frost-rimed window, snow churned against a backdrop of black pines. Not a single soul to be seen.

The driver's nervous eyes met hers in the rearview mirror. She adjusted her military hat to shadow the top of her face, splayed her legs as her brother would have done, and scowled, an expression that must have been familiar to the driver because he looked away.

Several minutes later, the car rolled to a stop in a gravel parking lot. The darkness on the horizon became absolute, and she realized it must be the sea. If she reached that horizon, she would be free.

Cold night air scraped her cheeks when the driver opened the door. The smells of engine oil, steel, and fish permeated the piney darkness. Goose bumps rose on the nape of her neck. Her newly bare skin felt vulnerable without hair to cover it.

She and Nahal left the car and accepted another salute from the pair of armed men. Being a man wasn't so hard. Salutes and respect.

"Show me the vessel." The Chinese words came out rough and deep, as she'd practiced, and men scurried to follow her order. This was how her brother lived every day—men obeyed him without question.

A man barked out a word she didn't recognize, and the submarine's lights came on. She stifled a smile as she gazed upon her prize resting by the dock. The long hull was black and sinister. Gray camouflaged masts and stubby fins adorned the rounded sail fastened to the top deck. She identified communication masts, a periscope, a radar antenna, and the air induction mast. All accounted for.

Soon, she'd be standing inside that sail as captain and watching her friends go inside the submarine itself. She sank deeper into the role of her brother, pushing her hips forward against the air as she acknowledged a flurry of salutes from sailors of lesser rank on her way to her counterpart, the Chinese commander. No one else merited her brother's time.

Unlike the North Korean soldiers, the Chinese leader's uniform was stark white, and his men wore white shirts with blue-striped collars and white caps with a red star in front. Ready for the handoff, they stood in even rows on the dock next to the submarine.

"Good evening, Commander Wang," she said in Mandarin, matching her words with a salute.

A sour expression crossed the face of the young man next to the commander. He must be the now-unnecessary interpreter. Inside, she pitied him, but her brother wouldn't have, so she ignored him, enjoying having the unfamiliar power to ignore a man.

The commander returned the salute. "You speak my language well, Prince Dakkar."

"You do me a great honor," she said, aware her brother wouldn't be so humble, but suspecting the commander would respond to respect better than contempt.

He gestured to the submarine.

She walked across the dock and stepped onto the dark hull. She'd rehearsed this moment so many times it felt like a scene from a movie.

Behind her, her crew filed onto the dock. Each carried a duffel bag with the possessions she'd brought from home. Even with padded uniforms and shoes with lifts, the women looked small and slight. But their Chinese counterparts weren't much bigger. After all, submarines were said to employ small men to crew them.

Nahal stood farther back on the dock, holding a clipboard, talking to her Chinese colleague, and signing forms. So far, everything was going according to plan.

Laila climbed atop the sail and looked across the nearly deserted dock. The North Korean sailors kept a respectful distance, as they'd been ordered to do in Nahal's spoofed email. The Chinese sailors faced away from her in silent rows. She turned her gaze to the black water.

"The view is sublime when one is at sea," said Commander Wang. "Such a creature as this was not meant to be tethered in a dock."

"It is a beautiful vessel," she answered, remembering the Chinese didn't refer to ships as female, as the English did. "Sleek as a seal."

The commander smiled. Even though this wasn't his submarine and he'd only been tasked with delivering it, his pride shone through.

She climbed down into the warm control room, relieved to recognize the dials and screens. "Your simulation software was precise."

The commander inclined his head. "Your government wished you and your crew to take control of the vessel with little hands-on training."

"Indeed." Technically, that had been *her* wish. She and her crewmates might fool the Chinese sailors for the length of the handoff, but a longer training period would reveal them as women, and also reveal none had ever set foot in a real submarine.

He led her on a tour of their new home—radio room, a space for electronics, living quarters, a fully stocked mess and galley, and the captain's cabin. More cramped than she was used to, but all the more free. The lower level contained torpedoes and sea mines, sleek and deadly, reminding her that this vessel could do more than hide them from a world that treated them no better than beasts. It could fight back.

She followed her counterpart aft, struggling to understand the words as he discussed the propulsion system, generators, and batteries in rapid-fire Mandarin.

"We have built you a shadow," he said. "This is the most sophisticated diesel electric submarine in the world. No other vessel can hide under the waves so well as this. It is truly a marvel of Chinese engineering."

"It is as silent as a steel shark."

"And just as deadly," he responded.

Thus she remains free to roam the seas, Laila thought.

Her crew had boarded during her tour and stood at attention at their posts. They seemed no more nervous than any crew about to take a new and unfamiliar ship out of the harbor. The women had been through much in their lives, and they knew how to present a calm face to the world no matter the situation.

Commander Wang saluted one final time and spoke with his first officer.

Her heart pounded so hard she feared everyone in the control room could hear. Nahal had ordered the transfer of funds to complete payment on the submarine. Laila stood, back ramrod straight, and waited for the money to go through. Nahal had hacked into dozens of naval accounts to acquire the funds for this transaction, careful to create a trail back to Laila's brother. Now they waited to see if her hard work would bear fruit. Months of planning came down to the next few seconds.

A crisp nod from the Chinese soldier to his commander, and a bolt of joy shot through Laila's breast for the first time since she'd learned of her sister's death. Months of despair fell away.

"All leave," the Chinese commander ordered.

His remaining men filed out and up the sail, rubber shoes whispering across steel rungs, feet thumping on the dock.

She exhaled. The sub was almost theirs.

The commander gestured for her to precede him up the ladder, and she did. Still holding the clipboard, Nahal followed.

The three stood together atop the sail in the cold wind. She looked at the dock, the pine trees, and the rocks lining the beach. Fast-falling snow shrouded it all. By morning, they would be far away, leaving no trace of themselves behind.

"You do not wish to take a trial run with us?" The commander sounded incredulous, in spite of the orders he'd received in Nahal's email.

A foolhardy act to go out without a trial run, she conceded privately. Aloud, she said, "My men are ready. Do you not trust their skills?"

His impassive face gave nothing away. "The vessel is yours now, to use as you see fit."

"My government is most grateful to you." The money had been transferred, which was all he need be concerned about.

"As is mine," he answered.

The sound of an engine cut across the wind. Approaching headlights lanced the darkness. Perhaps their jet had been intercepted before it could crash. Perhaps the car came to arrest them. Or perhaps a North Korean delegation came to see them off, but there had been no mention of a delegation coming to see them off in the emails Nahal had intercepted.

The Chinese commander looked at her sharply as if he, too, was unprepared for the forces barreling toward them.

"We leave now," she said.

The commander wavered.

"The vessel is ours," she said. "You have received payment."

Flinging gravel, the vehicle braked to stop. A bus identical to the one parked at the end of the dock. The dark outline of twenty figures visible inside. A man with a too-familiar rolling walk burst out the front door.

Her brother had arrived.

He froze at the sight of someone standing atop the submarine in his uniform. Men in dark clothing flowed around him like oil and headed toward her. Someone had pierced Nahal's layers of protection and discovered the new meeting point. But she knew Nahal had been careful to make sure no messages could be traced back to them. Hopefully, she'd been clever enough.

The Chinese commander reached for his shoulder, but she drew her gun and clubbed him on the side of his head. Blood flowed from a wound near his temple, and he crumpled. She hoped she hadn't killed him. He wasn't part of her war.

Chinese sailors scrambled across the dock. She ducked next to the fallen commander and tried to think. She hadn't come so far to lose the women's freedom now. A bullet pinged off a mast behind her head, and Nahal pointed toward the entrance to the sub.

Laila whispered a prayer and peeked over the side. She doubted any of the men would have recognized her in her disguise, on the top of the submarine and at night. But her brother might have. He was close now, and his gun was pointed at her. He fired, but missed her. As she'd practiced, she sighted her pistol on her brother's thin chest. With a slow tug, she pulled the trigger.

His bowlegged stride faltered, and he staggered to the side. Again, she sighted, and again, she fired. He fell to the dock and lay still. Wild glee flashed through her, and she stifled a laugh.

No matter what else happened tonight, she'd won.

With a moan, Nahal collapsed against her. Red blossomed on Nahal's shoulder. She'd taken the shot meant for Laila. Laila dragged her friend to the hatch in the top of the sail. A snail trail of red gleamed on the hull behind them. Meters away, the commander lay still, white uniform bright against the dark deck.

"Hold on to me, Nahal."

Nahal's arms tightened around her neck. She half climbed and half fell down the rungs and into the control room. She eased Nahal to the floor.

"Back full!" Laila shouted.

Ambra must have been getting everyone ready, because the sub jerked as soon as she spoke. Bullets slammed the hull, but they wouldn't hurt them in here.

"Get Meri!" she called and heard her order relayed through the ship.

She left Nahal and scrambled up the rungs to secure the hatch. By the time she came down, Meri crouched next to Nahal's motionless form, a medical kit by her knee.

Laila raced into the control room. Delicate hands flew over controls. For months, her crew had practiced for this moment in their simulators, but no one had been shooting at them then. Still, they moved as well as a more seasoned crew. They were brave, every one.

They had to get away from the dock to deeper water so they could dive. In deep water, they were invisible, but right now their steel shark was a fish stranded on rocks. She must thrash back into deeper water before she suffocated.

Laila focused on the sonar screen. No other ships around.

"Dive!" she shouted.

"We're not far enough out," Ambra said.

"Drop as low as we can go," she commanded. "And keep us moving. Dive deeper the second you can."

Women scrambled to obey.

Whatever happened, they weren't going to be taken alive. She'd promised them.

1

Office of Pellucid
Grand Central Terminal, New York
March 8, early afternoon

One wall of Joe Tesla's office displayed a giant transparent brain. Red, green, and blue lines flashed as synapses fired wildly. The amygdala was overloaded. The owner of that brain had been in distress.

He didn't have to study the moving images to know, because it was his own. The footage had been captured by performing an MRI, then overlaying the 3-D representation with a visual representation of an electroencephalogram, or EEG, that showed his synapses reacting to external stimuli. In this case, his terror whenever he tried to go outside. The brain was a movie of the agoraphobia that had trapped him in Grand Central Terminal.

His company, Pellucid, created brain maps like these and used the data to help people recover from post-traumatic stress disorder, anxiety disorders, and phobias. They had an amazing track record. Soldiers were able to let go of fearful experiences. Ordinary people were able to overcome phobias. The system was working brilliantly for many people.

But not for Joe. At least not yet. The neurologist said he was making progress, but that Joe was pushing himself too hard. Baby steps or some crap like that. Joe was tired of baby steps. He wanted to take some damn adult steps. He'd been trapped inside for over a year, and he was very tired of it.

He switched to another brain, and his psychiatric service dog, a golden retriever/yellow Lab mix named Edison, rose from his bed next to Joe's desk and put his head on Joe's knee.

"It's OK, boy," Joe said, but the dog knew better.

The new brain pulsed chaotically, with intense and random streaks of light. Then it went quiet and dark. The subject had been treated with electroconvulsive therapy— electrical currents passed through the brain to trigger a seizure. The seizure was the moment when the synapses went crazy. He watched the seizure repeat and repeat in the poor defenseless brain.

"Consciousness is just electrical impulses," he told the dog. "It's an ephemeral thing—flashing and changing instantly. And stopping."

Edison licked his hand. Joe traced the frenetic movements of discharging synapses on his wall. "So fragile."

A quick knock on his door, and Dr. Gemma Plantec entered. A tiny but formidable woman, she worked as Pellucid's chief neurobiologist.

"I want to go over some data before you leave." Her brown eyes flicked to the brain displayed on the wall. "Are you finally ready for it?"

"The evidence on ECT for my type of disorder is inconclusive."

"It helps with depression, and there are preliminary indications it might help with PTSD." She moved close to the brain on the wall and scrutinized it as if it had the answers. Edison peeked around the side of the desk. "Hello, Edison."

The dog wagged his tail once, then returned to Joe's side.

"I can arrange for you to have a treatment," she said. "Bring everything you need here."

"We could." Most of his medical care was attended to at his office or his home, as he couldn't go outside. Fortunately, he was wealthy. He felt for those who were trapped in even smaller realms than he was, with even fewer resources. "But I'm not ready."

She ran one hand through her close-cropped black curls. "You're the patient."

"I thought I was the CEO."

"That, too." She conceded the point with a shake of her head. "You're making good progress, even if it's slower than you'd like."

"I feel like I'm going to spend the rest of my life haunting Grand Central and the tunnels like Erik in *Phantom of the Opera*." Even to himself, he sounded bitter. He hated being trapped—Grand Central, the tunnels, buildings he could access via steam tunnels. His entire world. No fresh air in his lungs, no rain on his skin, no true stars above his head. He was closed inside an artificial universe, his life as constrained as a player in a video game.

Her face softened, and he wanted to apologize, because this wasn't her fault, but someone knocked.

"Come in," he called.

Marnie, his executive assistant, opened the door and stuck her head through. "Sorry to interrupt. You're due at the sub in a half hour."

"Five minutes." He had synesthesia and the color for five (brown) appeared in his mind. This brain quirk often came in handy in his mathematical world, helping him to find patterns in massive arrays of data.

The brain on the wall pulsed, and Marnie looked over at it. "What's happening to that brain?"

"Electroconvulsive therapy," Dr. Plantec said.

"Like in *One Flew Over the Cuckoo's Nest*?" Marnie's eyes never left the convulsing brain.

"Kind of," Joe said.

"It's come a long way since that unfortunate depiction." Dr. Plantec pursed her lips. "And it wasn't even accurate at the time."

Marnie glanced between them. "Just say no."

She stepped back and closed the door.

"She makes a compelling point," Joe said. "Succinct, too."

"Shall we review the data?" Dr. Plantec set her tablet on his desk, and they spent the next few minutes discussing her latest results. She was brilliant, and he was lucky to have recruited her.

And she was usually right.

Nothing else *was* working fast enough—drugs made him stupid and slow and still didn't help, talk therapy made it worse, and his Pellucid desensitization was proceeding by only millimeters at a time. His condition was caused by an untested drug, not an actual memory, and it responded differently than other people's phobias.

Maybe ECT was the answer. But a side effect of that treatment was amnesia. Sometimes, the patient just lost memories from around the time of the treatment, but other times, longer-term memories disappeared, too. He wasn't ready to part with those. He'd lost too much already.

2

Jack's Dive Locker, Brooklyn
March 8, afternoon

Vivian wanted to quit her job. She liked Tesla well enough, and she still felt guilty she'd lost track of him on the night he was dosed with whatever it was that gave him agoraphobia, but she hated this underwater crap. His fault she was standing in a cold swimming pool in a wetsuit that leaked at the sleeves, trying to overcome a fear of water she'd carried around since a near drowning on Coney Island when she was eight.

"We only have one more thing before we can finish up and go home." Chad the instructor talked like a chipper preschool teacher. He also looked fourteen years old, and had a series of chakra tattoos along his left side. He was one centered dude.

She looked at her watch. Chad had started class a half hour late and was running fifteen minutes beyond that. One more thing to go, and she was already late. Maybe Tesla would take the sub and leave without her. Not that she ever got that lucky.

"Face your partner and smile from your inmost being." Chad smiled, presumably in case they didn't know what that kind of smile looked like. Near as Vivian could tell, it looked patronizing. "Open up and make your world bigger."

She faced her dive-training buddy. His name was Guy. She'd seen his driver's license. Not even a nickname. Just a noun of generic manliness. Guy gave her a reassuring smile. He'd picked up on her nervousness. They'd probably picked up on her nervousness from space.

"Now, you're going to put your regulator in your mouth," Chad chirped. "Then dive down to the bottom of the pool and adjust your buoyancy to stay there. After that, swim across the bottom all the way to the other end."

So far, so good. Swim underwater for one pool length. She could do that without breathing if she had to.

"But you're not going to use your own regulator. You're going to buddy breathe," Chad said. "Share air."

Buddy breathing meant your buddy took the regulator out of his mouth and gave it to you to use. Which meant that half the time he was using it, so half the time she wouldn't have access to air. Vivian looked over at Guy. If she had to, she could take him down and steal the regulator. She smiled for him, and Guy looked uneasy.

Chad was finishing up. "Take it nice and slow and easy. You can always surface and start over. There's no time limit. No pressure. You're just getting the feel of using someone else's regulator if you have to. Nowadays, every tank has two regulators—a primary and a spare—so if you do run out of air, you can always use your partner's spare. We only practice buddy breathing so you can get a feel for it."

Then Chad exhaled and blew it out as if he were teaching them yoga and not scuba. "Ready?"

Half the class nodded in a gung-ho fashion and the other half in a resigned one. Vivian was resigned.

She drew in a deep breath of chlorine-scented air, then stuck the regulator in her mouth. It tasted like rubber, and she hoped they'd cleaned it since the last user. Across from her, Guy did the same. He waggled his eyebrows and pointed his thumb down at the water. That was the first step in the five-point descent they'd just been taught. Step two was to orient yourself. Pretty straightforward in the pool. Hard to get lost when you just had to follow the line of blue tiles inlaid into the bottom of the pool. Step three was to put the regulator in your mouth. They'd both done that one out of sequence. Step four was to check your timing device to calculate the start of the dive. Both looked ostentatiously at imaginary watches. The last step was to let the air out of the buoyancy compensator device, or as Chad called it, 'the BCD,' and sink.

Face-to-face, they sank to the bottom. Vivian fought back panic as soon as her head went underwater. Bubbles shot out of her regulator. She was breathing too fast, and she brought it under control by inhaling to a count of five, exhaling to a count of seven, then waiting for a count of five. Tesla did something similar when he had panic attacks. She wasn't pleased to think they had random panic in common.

Guy made the OK sign, hand on his head.

She nodded. She was OK enough.

A special dive pool, the bottom twenty feet down. She messed with her BCD at the bottom, trying to set it up so she would hover. Air in, bounce up, air out, sink. Repeat until it was just the right amount of air. And repeat.

Out of the corner of her eye, she saw Guy doing the same.

Eventually, they were both kind of hovering with just a little bit of kicking. Close enough.

Who was the buddy in this scenario? Should she take out her regulator and use his, or make him use hers? Guy hung nearly motionless next to her. His buoyancy was under better control than hers.

Fine. She pushed down her unease, took a deep breath, clenched and released her jaw, and took out her regulator. A few bubbles drifted up. She reached the regulator across to Guy. He took a breath and gave it back. So far, so good.

She took another breath and slowly kicked forward. Guy was level with her, everything was fine. She wasn't going to lose it. She had a spare regulator if she needed it, and the surface was only seconds away. She could do this.

Then Guy's eyes widened as if he'd suddenly realized he was underwater without an air source in his mouth and the insanity of that.

He grabbed the regulator out of her hand and yanked it up to his mouth so hard she smacked into his chest. His blue eyes were wide and panicked, and he sucked on her regulator like he hadn't taken a breath in an hour.

She gave him a couple of seconds to get it together, then tapped him on the shoulder and pointed to her regulator.

He handed it back, and she took a long breath. Before she could give him the regulator, Guy panicked.

He pushed himself away and flailed, clearly trying to find his own regulator. They'd practiced leaning forward to let the regulator fall forward and then sweeping to the right to retrieve it. Chad had insisted they do it three times, and they'd humored him.

Clearly, Guy didn't remember any of his training. He wasn't sweeping. He wasn't leaning. He was thrashing. He nearly clipped her face with a fin, and she backed away to give him the space to recover.

But he didn't.

He floundered. Air bubbles popped out of his mouth and headed up for the surface. Following them would have been a good idea, but he wasn't doing that either. In his panic, he'd zeroed in on one thing—finding his regulator. Which clearly wasn't going to happen.

Deciding she'd been standoffish buddy long enough, she swam in front of him and tried to catch his eyes, to make a calming gesture or hand him her spare regulator.

No go. He didn't seem to see more than a few inches in front of his face. Poor guy was in a bad spot.

Trying to get inside his flailing arms, she darted toward him, grabbed his regulator with one hand and slammed it against his mouth. He ducked his head back in surprise and clocked himself hard on his tank valve. He opened his mouth, probably to swear, and she plopped the regulator in like a mother stuffing a pacifier into an angry baby's mouth.

He sucked in one long breath, then another. She threaded a hand through his BCD and slowly started to ascend.

He shook his head. He took the regulator out and mouthed, *Sorry.*

His heart thumped so hard she could see his carotid artery flutter with each beat, and he was shaking. She hated to think of what he'd discharged into the water in his panic. Still, she stopped ascending and they hung there for a long minute. Slowly, his breathing stabilized.

She pointed to his regulator, and he nodded. Let him be in charge of the air. Staying face-to-face, only a few inches apart, they traded off the regulator. Gently, she kicked them toward the end of the pool.

Eventually, they got there and surfaced. Half the class was already gone.

"I'm sorry," Guy said.

"It's fine." She was going to switch him out for a new dive buddy for the next class. She had more than her share of neurotic men in her life already. In the water, she was supposed to be able to be the weak link.

"How are we?" Chad asked. "A little rocky at first, but you two came together like a team."

"Yup," Vivian said.

"I panicked," Guy said. "If Vivian hadn't been there, I don't know what would have happened."

Drowned, she thought.

"That's what a dive buddy does," Chad said in his irritatingly calm voice. "That's why we never dive alone, bro."

Vivian hauled herself out and started stripping off gear.

"Slow down," Chad said. "We've got the pool for an hour."

"I'm late." Vivian set the weight belt next to the pool, took off her BCD, and closed her tank valve.

"I'll carry your stuff back," Guy said. "It's the least I can do."

"Thanks." She stripped off her wetsuit and left it in a pile on the floor. "You got it together, and that's what counts. Don't focus on the bad moment. Everybody has a bad moment."

"I bet you don't," Guy said.

She snorted. "You have no idea."

"Do you want to switch out for a new buddy?" Chad asked. "No harm in that. Gives you a chance to meet new people. Learn their styles."

Guy looked at her. He had giant blue eyes and long black eyelashes. He wasn't going to put any pressure on her, but he clearly wanted to keep her around.

Knowing she'd probably regret it later, but feeling sorry for him, she said, "I'll stick with Guy."

Story of her life.

3

Off the coast of Montauk, New York
March 8, evening

Joe Tesla had found freedom in the silent green sea. He loved how the blue shafts of his navigation lights illuminated the murky darkness. He loved the old-fashioned sonar ping that displayed the underwater world on a green screen in his cockpit. He loved the sight and sound of water rushing past the half bubble of thick acrylic that served as his window to the undersea world. He loved the sense of infinite possibility. His crippling agoraphobia had stolen the outside world, but it hadn't stolen the sea.

Edison was latched into a safety harness in front of him, and he gave him a quick pet. Edison's tail thumped in response. Joe angled the submarine down. "Just a little deeper, boy, and then the fun begins."

"Are we rated for that depth?" Vivian asked. His sometimes bodyguard, she was usually fearless.

"This baby can go even deeper. She's a work of art."

"Sure." She tightened her seat belt.

"All the safety money can buy." His facial-recognition software had earned him millions, but because his agoraphobia had trapped him into an indoor existence, he didn't have much he could spend it on. Unlike his peers, he had no use for cars or houses or private jets.

But he could use a submarine.

There was something else he'd like to have—someone he trusted to be his eyes and ears in the world above. "Speaking of all the safety money can buy, have you thought about my job offer?"

"You receive great protection via Mr. Rossi and his team. And I'm on call there. You don't need to hire me full time."

"You're better than the others," he said. "And if you worked for me, you'd have benefits and a much higher salary."

"That's very kind of you, sir, but I work for Mr. Rossi. He pays more than enough."

Mr. Rossi didn't pay her enough. Joe had checked. "My door's always open if you change your mind."

"If your door opens right now, we'll drown."

"It's a figure of speech." He was hurt she wasn't taking his offer more seriously, but he didn't want her to see it. Instead, he reached down and patted his dog. Edison licked his hand. He sensed Joe's disappointment.

"Are we close to the marker?" she asked.

That was the end of the discussion for today and a not-so-subtle reminder to get back on task. They were on a submarine scavenger hunt. Sponsored by an organization called Blue Dreams and limited to ten private subs, it had an entrance fee of a half million (brown, black, black, black, black, black) dollars. The proceeds were to go to the winner's charity.

If he and Vivian won, the funds were earmarked for a facility that trained service and guide dogs. He wanted to shorten the average six-(orange)-year wait for these dogs so everyone who needed a helper like Edison could get a dog right away.

A shipwreck took shape in the darkness. He swiveled his navigation lights over an algae-covered hull. Silver fish with big round eyes darted away from the beams.

"I hope the crew got off safely," Vivian said.

"She's been down here for five years."

"Still."

Even though the shipwreck wasn't their goal, he eased the sub in sideways for a closer look. His propellers kicked up algae, and he nearly knocked against the wreck. When he pulled back on the stick, she tensed up but didn't say anything.

"I know," he said. "But I got this."

He was still learning to control his craft. A submarine wasn't like a car—a sub was slow to accelerate, slow to turn, and hard to stop—but it had been so long since he'd driven anything, he could forgive the small yellow craft a lot of flaws. He hoped it could forgive him his.

"What's it called?" she asked. "The ship?"

"According to my map, she was called the *Aronnax*. Maybe named after Pierre Aronnax from *Twenty Thousand Leagues Under the Sea*?"

Barnacles crusted the ship's surfaces, and anemones softened the sharp edges of her broken hull. Her mast had snapped, and the stump listed to the side, rotted lines undulating like tentacles in the current.

"Doesn't look like it worked out for old Pierre," she said.

Slowly, Joe circled her. The *Aronnax* wasn't the most famous wreck down here, not even close, but she had a desolate charm. Someone had loved this pile of rotting wood once—painted her hull, varnished her spars, coiled her lines on her shiny teak deck. Until the ocean swallowed her and left her rotting in her grave.

Edison gave a sharp bark, and he followed the dog's gaze.

A gray shadow had slipped from the sailboat's hull and eased into the navigation lights. Triangular dorsal fin, powerful vertical tail, and sleek gray skin.

"It's just *Jaws*," Joe said. "Nothing to worry about."

A calm dog, Edison rarely barked, but he knew a predator when he saw one, and he growled.

"I'm with you, Edison," Vivian said.

"You're such a badass on land. But underwater—"

"Before you finish that sentence, remember we'll be back on land soon."

He grinned, tipped the sub upright, and followed the shark. If the animal chose to evade him, he'd never keep up with it, but the shark didn't seem to mind. It glided through the water with tiny flicks of its fins, more maneuverable and free down here than he would ever be. He envied the beast more than he could say.

The shark headed for a line of algae that looked like a bump on the ocean floor. The line extended out past his vision in both directions. Longer than any snake or eel. The shark had found what Joe was searching for.

The animal opened its massive jaws impossibly wide. White teeth flashed as the creature lunged to bite the line. Brown muck exploded upward, clouding the water and obscuring the shark. He waited. The ocean rewarded patience.

Slowly, the muck settled, and the shark came back into view. It must not have liked what it had tasted when it bit down, because it let go of the cable. After another glance at the strange dark line, the shark swam until the green darkness swallowed it from his view.

He slowed the sub and drifted down. The cable gleamed black where the shark had scraped away the algae, brown otherwise.

"Following a shark is cheating," Vivian said.

"Nothing wrong with natural inspiration." He maneuvered closer to the bottom. "That's definitely a transatlantic communications cable. Maybe the cable we're looking for."

People had been dropping cables under the sea since 1858 when the first telegraph line connected Ireland to Newfoundland. That cable had long since gone silent. This one, too, might not be active anymore, but he suspected it was. If so, he just needed to follow it to the marker and the first part of the scavenger hunt would be over.

"Why'd the shark bite it? And will it bite us?"

"It can't get a grip on the sub." He hoped. "But it bit the cable because it could detect electric current running through. It happens so often that modern cables are specially designed to withstand periodic bites."

"Great," she said. "We're cruising right next to something sharks like to attack."

"Bite, not attack."

"A distinction that doesn't matter much if it takes off your arm." Vivian rolled her shoulders, as if preparing to fight to hold on to her arms. She'd definitely land a few punches if a shark tried to eat her.

He followed the cable east into deeper water, and an octopus swam into view. The mollusk danced in his lights, then draped itself over the bubble cockpit.

"Wow," Vivian said.

Round suckers tasted the outside of his window, and an alien silver eye looked in. He'd read octopi were at least as intelligent as dogs, and he wondered what the creature thought about these strange intruders in its realm.

He let the sub drift forward, not wanting to scare the octopus away before it finished its examination. After all, he was down here looking around himself. The least he could do was let the octopus satisfy its curiosity, too.

Edison's brown eyes followed each movement, and he leaned forward and licked the inside of the plastic where suckers pulsated inches from his face. Even Vivian seemed enthralled. After a few minutes, the octopus dropped off and glided out of sight.

He followed the cable. According to his interpretation, the clue for the first flag referred to an active transatlantic cable, which meant the flag should be somewhere close by. The sub's electric engine vibrated under his feet as he increased speed.

"Flag at three o'clock!" She pointed to a row of yellow banners. The first markers in the scavenger hunt.

He aimed for them. "How many?"

"Ten!" she crowed.

The color for one (cyan) flashed in his head, followed by the color for zero (black). Cyan, black meant he'd gotten here first.

But there was another challenge. Blue Dreams' sponsor was a bowfishing company, and they'd specified the flag had to be shot with an arrow and reeled in. He looked at his depth gauge. They weren't too deep, about a hundred (cyan, black, black) feet. He could put on scuba gear and go outside to shoot the flag instead of trying to shoot a bow with the sub's grabber arms.

"Unbuckle," he told Edison.

The dog leaned down and bit the release button in the center of his specially constructed harness. He wriggled out of the restraints and turned to face Joe.

"Dang," said Vivian. "Smart boy!"

Edison ducked his head as if the compliment made him bashful.

He unclipped his own harness and climbed out a lot less gracefully than the dog.

The sub dipped upward. If left to its own devices, it was designed to surface—a fail-safe to keep an injured or unconscious submariner from sinking into the depths of the sea.

"You have the bridge," he told Vivian.

"Aye aye, sir." She took hold of her controls and leveled the sub.

He maneuvered past her, foot catching on a red emergency suit stowed under her seat. He'd equipped the sub with four (green)—one for each potential human passenger and an extra for the dog. If the submarine got stuck underwater, the passenger had to climb into that suit, exit the sub, and pull a tab. The suit would inflate automatically and send the wearer rocketing toward the surface. Or at least that was the theory. He hoped he'd never have to test it.

Edison squeezed past him to the stern, where the designers had installed the wet exit. The feature had cost a fortune. Worth it.

First, he had to get Edison ready. After he bought the sub, he'd assumed he would have to leave his best friend inside when he went diving. Instead, he'd discovered dogs could be taught to scuba dive. When he'd first stumbled across videos on the Internet of dogs paddling around underwater with bubble helmets and special vests, he hadn't believed his eyes.

But after he'd run down the source and contacted the dogs' owners, he'd discovered he was wrong—dogs could and did dive. He'd been surprised at how easily he'd collected the gear: a yellow buoyancy compensator tailored to Edison's furry form, a bubble helmet that made him look like a space dog, and a miniature air tank. After that, it had been a simple matter to train the dog to swallow when his ears hurt, to stay close to him, and to follow hand signals when they couldn't speak. Edison was a smart dog.

He waited while Joe hooked everything up, regular thumps of his tail betraying his excitement. They both loved being out in the water together. They'd been on many dives, and Edison knew what was coming.

Joe shrugged on his bulky buoyancy compensator and attached his weight belt. The extra lead around his stomach made him clumsy as he checked and turned on his tank, put his mask on, and slipped into long fins. Ready to go. He put his regulator into his mouth and took a quick breath. All good. Then he folded himself into the airlock and snatched up a dive light and the bow and arrow. The arrow was connected to the boat by a long line, usually used to haul in fish. He angled it carefully to the side so it wouldn't hurt him or Edison.

"Here, boy!" he called.

Edison climbed awkwardly into his lap. Joe triple-checked the dog's air lines before closing the inner door. A hug to reassure Edison, then he pressed the button to flood the compartment. Cold ocean water seeped in around them as the pressure slowly equalized. In a few minutes, the pressure in their little chamber would match the pressure outside. Once it was done, they could exit at current depth without damaging their ears.

Edison bonked his helmet against Joe's snorkel mask, and he patted the dog's yellow suit. *We're fine*, he told Edison silently. The dog seemed to agree and relaxed to wait it out.

Joe checked his dive computer. At this depth, they had about twenty-two (blue, blue) minutes of dive time before they had to worry, but it'd still be best to do a safety stop at a higher depth before they got back into the sub if they spent much time out there. Vivian could bring the sub up to twenty (blue, black) feet and wait for them to finish the safety stop before they climbed back inside.

Eventually, the airlock filled with water, and the outer door opened. Joe uncurled into the sea. Edison doggie-paddled next to him. His wet tail waved from side to side like a tentacle, and his furry head swiveled back and forth to follow the flashlight beam.

Joe loved it out in the ocean, too, but today he had to hurry. His competitors might arrive at any moment. The clue had been complicated, but they were smart, or had smart teams. He didn't have time to be complacent if he wanted to win this thing. And he liked winning.

He pointed the light at his chest and touched the top of his head with his glove to indicate he was OK. Vivian returned the signal from her position at the controls inside her illuminated bubble. His sub was in good hands.

Formalities out of the way, he headed straight for the flags, long fins lending him speed. Edison couldn't keep up when he went all out, so he pulled the dog under his belly and towed him along.

The dog's bubble rubbed his chest as Edison turned his head from side to side to take in the underwater world. Visibility was about twenty feet (blue, black), so the dog couldn't see far through the green darkness. But it seemed to be enough for him.

Joe stopped about five (brown) feet away from the fluttering yellow marker. That was the official maximum distance, probably to make bowfishing look easy. He let go of Edison and pointed to his heel. Obligingly, Edison doggie-paddled there.

His buoyancy was solid. Joe nocked the arrow, aimed at the flag, and let fly.

And missed.

Bubbles shot out of his regulator as he swore.

Hand over hand, he reeled the arrow back in. He'd practiced this before, and he ought to be better. First-day jitters.

He set up, aimed, fired, and was rewarded by seeing the flag jerk forward. When he reeled the arrow in this time, the bright yellow flag was attached.

Edison bumped his heel, and he swiveled around to make sure the dog was all right. His mouth opened and closed in a silent bark. Joe played his flashlight around the water, searching for whatever had caused the dog to bark. He hoped it wasn't a shark. Even though sharks were rarely dangerous, he didn't want to meet a predator that size out here with Edison. He'd read that sharks didn't usually attack people, but there wasn't a lot of literature about how sharks would react to a dog.

A flash of artificial light cut through the water, and his stomach dropped. Not a shark. Worse. A competitor.

He recognized the submarine the second he saw it. Although it looked green down here, he knew it was Ferrari-red at the surface and tricked out with features even he couldn't afford. The sub belonged to a foreign prince who had outspent him by a factor of ten (cyan, black) and had a team of fifteen (cyan, brown) men working round the clock to maintain his craft and figure out his clues—Prince Timgad.

Joe'd already had an argument with him when the prince had tried to have women formally banned from the competition, even though no women had signed up as competitors. To spite him, Joe had added Vivian to his team as the lone female competitor. He doubted he'd have gotten her into the water if the prince hadn't been so abrasive, but she wasn't about to let the prince ban women and get his way.

And he, Vivian, and his tiny yellow explorer had beaten the prince to the first flag. He'd win the first round, so long as he got the flag back to shore first. And he damn well would.

Vivian's sub hovered a few yards from the prince's sub. She looked between that sub and Joe and waved at him, her gesture making it clear he needed to hurry. She didn't want to lose either.

Joe grinned. He could do this. Edison must have been watching his face, because his butt moved in a tail wag. He drew the dog in close and swam toward Vivian as fast as he could. They'd been out in the ocean only a few minutes. They could skip the safety stop and hightail it back to shore. Then the woman's team would defeat the prince's.

A shadow loomed out of the water behind the red sub. Impossibly big. Bigger than a shark. Bigger than the subs in the contest. A whale?

He kicked harder, keeping a tight hold on Edison. Whatever it was, he'd feel safer once he had the dog back in the yellow submarine. Edison wasn't the kind of dog to panic, but he didn't want to take chances. Too dangerous out here.

The shadow was blacker than a whale. Bigger, too.

It bore down on the green craft as if it meant to engulf it.

Joe took in the sleek lines, the stubby fin at the top, and the sheer size. A submarine. A military submarine. No military subs should be in this water, not this close to New York City. His blood turned as cold as the seawater around him.

The small sub looked like a remora tucked under a shark's belly. The pilot's startled face stared up at it. His hands yanked at his controls, but he couldn't escape the relentless shadow.

The military sub settled to the bottom, crushing the little submarine under its massive hull. A brown cloud spread around it. A wash of white bubbles shot up its sides and escaped toward the surface. The cockpit must have been breached. The man must be dead. A single dark ribbon threaded through the brown murk.

A victim of its own momentum, the shadow crept forward. It aimed straight for his little yellow submarine.

And Vivian.

4

Time slowed to a crawl as it used to when Vivian was in combat. Her mind flipped through possibilities, trying to find one that would save everyone. She could do an emergency surface with the sub, but she'd have to leave Tesla. That was a no go.

Someone in that giant submarine had murdered the pilot of the tiny sub, and maybe they were gunning for Tesla next. Not that she could do a damn thing from her little bubble. Her sub didn't have defensive weaponry. A rich man's toy. The most she could do would be tap on its hull with one tiny explorer arm.

Several yards out, Tesla was swimming hard, hauling along the dog. He'd never reach her before the sub rammed her. Even if he did, it wouldn't matter. He'd never get inside in time.

Get her craft out of immediate danger. If worse came to worst, he and the dog could surface and get picked up by a passing ship.

But they wouldn't. Tesla couldn't go outside, and the surface of the ocean definitely counted as outside. Conscious, he'd never be able to reach the top of the water, and Edison would stay next to him until they both ran out of air and drowned. His fear of going outdoors was why she always carried a hypodermic needle in her shirt pocket, ready to knock him unconscious in case of emergency. Like this one. Fat lot of good it would do.

The black sub advanced. It couldn't stop any more easily than she could, and it'd run her over if she didn't move. But her damn sub handled like a horse mired in mud. She'd never be able to dodge.

Surface. She'd get away, come back for Joe and Edison. She pulled up on the stick, expecting the sub to shoot up like a champagne cork. Instead, the little yellow sub crawled upward like a snail. It wouldn't get clear in time.

She turned the engine to full and steered at a right angle away from the oncoming danger. Her sub started the beginning of a slow arc.

It'd be close.

Abandon the sub. Put on the emergency suit and surface. But then she remembered Tesla had gone outside through the outer hatch door. The outer hatch was open, the airlock flooded. She couldn't open the inner door until she pumped it out, and she didn't have time. She might open the bubble, but that took time, too.

Whatever happened to her, it was going to happen inside.

Her sub inched to the side, every millisecond bringing her closer to safety.

But she ran out of time.

The black sub crashed against her side. The little yellow sub tumbled in front of it. Green water and brown mud flashed across the cockpit bubble.

She fought to control the crash, but the stick kicked sideways in her hands. A sickening snap. Bone-deep pain. Broken wrist.

A grinding screech and her sub finally lay still at the bottom of the sea.

A navigation light had been knocked around, and its beam spotlighted an immobile black wall. The giant sub had ground to a stop, too.

She was pinned. The safety harness cut into her shoulders, and her hips and arm ached. The harsh smell of melted plastic stung her nose. She coughed. Something was on fire.

A jagged silver line raced across the bubble like a lightning bolt. Water seeped through the crack and trickled down to the floor. Another crack. Then another.

She stabbed the quick release for her safety harness and stood. The sub creaked and shuddered. Pain shot from her arm when she moved, and blood dripped to the floor from a cut on her temple, but that didn't matter.

The only thing that mattered was getting out of the submarine.

Alive.

5

Inside the submarine *Siren*
March 8, evening

Laila lay on her side in the narrow tube with her cousin Ambra squashed against her. Theoretically, two people at a time could get out through the escape trunk, but in practice it was a tight fit, especially since Ambra was the largest woman on the sub. But the escape tube was the only way in or out of the *Siren* when submerged, and Laila had to verify the prince was dead.

Cold seawater rushed into the tube. Since the first time she'd used it, she'd had nightmares about drowning in this tube. She held tight to her rebreather. If it got blown out of her mouth, she might not recover it in time.

"Did we have to kill the prince?" Ambra's rebreather dangled next to her cheek.

Laila had to remove her rebreather to speak, and she didn't like it. "The sub was only part of his plan. So long as he's alive, he's a danger."

"Considering how you feel about him, that seems pretty self-serving." Ambra's body was tense next to hers, either with anger or fear.

"As soon as we verify it's him, we can check the hull for damage and meet up with the *Pearl* and go our separate ways. The hard part is almost done."

Laila shifted the rifle digging into her side. The Chinese-made QBS-06 had been in the submarine's armory. The weapon had been designed for use underwater. It fired fléchettes—pointed steel projectiles with fins on the end. The fins stabilized the fléchette as it traveled through the water to its target. Each projectile looked like it'd tear through anything it hit. She hoped to watch one go through the prince.

Ambra stuffed her rebreather into her mouth and ended the conversation, but her dark eyes were still uneasy.

Relieved to stop talking, Laila bit down on her mouthpiece. Although she and Ambra used sophisticated rebreathers designed for Special Forces frogmen, she hated to rely on them. The specifications said their devices were foolproof. They scrubbed carbon dioxide from each exhalation and recirculated oxygen. But the oxygen generators in the sub itself were faulty, so she didn't trust these either. They were having to surface ventilate to replenish their atmosphere in the sub, but that obviously wasn't an option with the individual rebreathers.

Ambra wiggled, probably searching for a more comfortable position, and her hip pressed Laila's. Laila wished she hadn't had to bring anyone out with her, but the other women had insisted, pointing out the safety protocol of diving in pairs. So she'd relented and chosen Ambra, because she was a strong swimmer and good in a fight.

The walls threatened to close in on her, and Laila concentrated on her breathing. She didn't dare hyperventilate and pass out. She held her nose and blew to clear her ears and felt Ambra do the same. They needed to equalize the pressure in their ears so they'd be safe to go when the door opened. If it ever opened. If they didn't drown in the narrow tube.

She forced herself to visualize the clean white around her bunk, the blue wool blanket covering the narrow bed, her beloved Kindle resting on the pillow. Her new home. Inside the sub, for the first time since early childhood, she felt safe.

It felt good not to be frightened all the time, to not be vulnerable because she was a woman, because a man could do what he wanted with her and to her. But it wasn't enough to run away.

She had to stop the cycle of violence, or at least stop Prince Timgad from escalating it further. She'd taken his tool, and she would use it to fight him.

After an eternity, the outer door opened. She swam out and cleared her ears. They were deep for diving, about thirty meters, which was why it had taken so long for the pressure in the escape trunk to equalize.

No sunlight could reach down here. She turned on her flashlight and shone it around. Tiny bubbles ran along the ship's bow, farther forward than she'd expected. The *Siren* must have dragged the prince's sub with her as she'd slowed, his vessel caught on the front like a camel hit by a train.

Faint light silvered the rising bubbles. The little sub must still have power. The prince must be sitting in his underwater prison, as helpless as her sister had been, as she had been. Let him marinate in his fear. Let him understand what it felt like when a larger will was imposed upon him. Let him die in pain and terror.

Ambra touched her elbow. She bobbed like a seal and pointed down toward the source of the bubbles. Ambra wanted to examine the sub's hull. As did she.

Laila kicked off and descended. Neither woman had known how to dive before they took the sub, but one of their crew, Ambra, was a trained dive master. She'd brought training materials aboard and taught the women two by two, everyone practicing until they were as comfortable underwater as they had been above. Ambra was adept at spearfishing, and she supplemented their meager food stores with fresh fish. This was vital, because the Chinese had left them underprovisioned.

Her gun jostled her back. She was grateful to have a powerful weapon, something more than the knife sheathed at her ankle. She hoped she would be able to use it, that the prince was still alive and that she could watch the life leave his eyes by her own hand.

Ambra grabbed her arm, then pointed to her flashlight. Ambra turned hers off, and Laila followed suit. Darkness pressed against her with even more weight than the water. She felt helpless and longed to turn the light back on.

Ambra tugged on her chin, pointing it down and away.

Laila peered through the dark water ahead, unsure what she was looking for.

Slowly, she made out a faint light shining from below. She slid forward, one hand brushing the cold, smooth side of the sub so she wouldn't get lost. Ambra rested a hand on her shoulder, and they swam forward together, silent in the sea, without even bubbles to give them away.

As she rounded the side, she spotted the light and the gangly man who held it. Long black fins flickered at the ends of his slim legs. He was swimming through the water toward the trapped sub.

She unslung the automatic weapon and touched the extra fléchettes in her wet-suit pocket.

Ambra yanked her arm, and Laila almost lost her grip on the rifle.

Another figure had slipped into view behind the swimmer. Too small to be an adult. But what would a child be doing down here?

The figure wore a bright suit, and something was odd about its outline. It took her a second to recognize it because the creature didn't belong in the deep sea.

A dog.

The prince hated dogs. He'd thrown her sister's puppy out of a moving limo because it had nipped at his rough fingers, and because he hadn't wanted her to have something to love. Such a man would never go scuba diving with a dog.

Perhaps the animal belonged to one of the prince's bodyguards. But that made no sense. She couldn't think of a single man in the prince's orbit who owned a dog. He would never have allowed it. Maybe someone else had been on the submarine, someone she didn't know.

Ambra pointed back the way they'd come with an arm a shade darker than the water. If they went back, they wouldn't be seen. A diver and a dog weren't a threat to the *Siren*. They could check their submarine for damage somewhere safer, and she could find out the prince's fate from the news. But she had an absolute need to verify personally that he was dead. She had to deal with this new threat.

She swam on. The man and the dog reached the submarine pinned under the *Siren's* bow. They dove to it, and the dog's thin legs dug up mud and silt. The silt rose in a cloud of brown, but before it obscured the tiny craft, she saw the pilot imprisoned inside the clear plastic bubble.

Not the prince.

A woman.

Laila reeled backward and jolted into Ambra. She'd hit the wrong submarine. All her work and planning, and she hadn't even killed the prince. He wouldn't dare to venture underwater again. She wouldn't see him die today. She'd put them at risk for nothing. Even worse, the survivors could call for help and give their account. The *Siren* had to be well away when that happened.

She banked the rage and looked back the way they had come. Bubbles floated up around the middle of the sub, and a blue light flickered there, fainter than starlight. The light didn't come from the *Siren*. Another craft was pinned beneath her. A second submarine.

Surely *that* was the prince's gaudy craft. If so, the *Siren* had hit him fair and square, as planned. The submarine with the woman and the dog must have come along at the wrong moment and been struck by accident. That was their tragedy.

Not hers.

She'd found her target. The prince must be buried deep under her hull. She would check to be certain after she dealt with the new threat.

She started to swim toward the submarine with the woman and the dog. If the man could free the trapped woman, they could surface on their own and wait for help. It was a busy part of the sea. Someone would probably pick them up. But then they would know about her mystery sub, about her crew. She couldn't allow that to happen.

Oblivious that Laila was deciding his fate, the man gestured to the woman inside and tugged on the bubble covering her as if he could yank it open on his own. Doubtful. Especially if she didn't give him time. Laila swam near the *Siren*'s side, darkness an easy camouflage.

Ambra yanked on her arm and pointed back to the escape trunk. Ambra wanted to get back inside the *Siren*, probably to distance themselves from the crash, then check the hull for damage. Logical, as far as it went.

But the man and woman had seen the *Siren*. They couldn't be allowed to escape. She shook free of Ambra's grasp and swam down toward the trapped submarine, feeling the rifle bump her spine. She would shoot the man and watch the woman drown. It didn't much matter what happened to the dog.

Ambra grabbed Laila's neoprene-covered calf and pulled her up short. Ambra gestured back toward the escape trunk with exaggerated and angry motions. Laila shook her head and pointed to the little sub. She was the captain, and she must be obeyed. She pointed more forcefully.

They could argue about this inside, talk about the terrible accident, how they felt so responsible for the death of the woman and the dog and the tall man. They could do all that after the crew of the unfortunate tiny sub was dead.

Ambra hesitated, then shook her head. She took a dive slate out of a pocket in her buoyancy compensator and wrote, *Must go.*

Laila rubbed out the words with her neoprene sleeve. *Must kill. They saw our sub.*

Ambra scowled and wrote her own message underneath. *Innocents.*

Unfortunate they were innocents, true, and she promised herself she would grieve them later, but for now she had to be firm. The lives of the women under her command rested with her. She wrote, *Sad, but necessary.*

Ambra cleaned off the slate completely and tried again. *We're not killers. The others will back me up.*

Of course they were killers. It was just luck that Nahal had survived. The Chinese commander was probably dead. Her brother was dead. The prince was hopefully dead.

They had taken the submarine to prevent thousands, maybe millions, of deaths. The loss of these few civilians would be regrettable, but was necessary. How could Ambra not understand? She wrote a single phrase, *Collateral damage.*

She turned back toward the trapped submarine. She didn't have time to argue. The inhabitants of the submarine might surface at any time and give them away. She couldn't let them put her entire crew in danger.

Ambra grabbed her leg, and Laila tried to pry Ambra's fingers off. Ambra dug her nails in deep and dragged her backward. She was strong, Ambra, and she had weight on her side.

Laila kicked out, and a flipper slammed Ambra's cheek. The rebreather popped out of her mouth. Salt water rushed in to take its place. Ambra fought to keep from coughing and flailed with her arms, trying to get the rebreather back. Even in the faint light, Laila could see Ambra's wide eyes.

Laila caught Ambra's rebreather and pushed it back to her. Ambra put it on and drew in a shuddering breath.

Laila patted her cousin on the back. Ambra wasn't going to give this up. Maybe Ambra was right. They weren't unfeeling assassins. Nahal always said that if they had to kill, they would, but it would be with a purpose. They had founded this operation on that precept.

Even if the man and woman talked about a giant submarine, it was unlikely anyone would believe them. The prince was dead, and his deadly plan had died with him. She and her crew had accomplished what they set out to do and they could stop.

Ambra touched Laila's shoulder. She looked calm but determined.

Laila nodded. She'd nearly let her hatred of the prince and her paranoia overwhelm her. Good that Ambra had been there to be a check on her.

Laila pointed toward the escape trunk.

Together, they swam quickly back the way they had come.

6

Joe pointed to the red emergency suit under Vivian's seat, but she gave him a puzzled look. She must not know exactly what he was pointing to. Maybe her head wound was more serious than he'd thought. He pointed again. She followed his gesture and found the suit.

Relief bloomed across her face as she took it out. Clumsily, she began to put it on with her good hand. Not that it would help if he couldn't get her out of the sub.

He studied his yellow submarine. The bastard piloting the giant sub had crushed his ship into the mud. Hopefully, the door release remained intact.

Blood ran down Vivian's face and splattered onto the floor. Head wounds always bled a lot, right? It didn't mean it was serious. Not really.

He anchored himself on the ocean floor and yanked on the hatch. The sub remained as immobile as a building, the weight of the ocean anchoring it. He'd expected that, but he had to try. He couldn't let Vivian die in the sub. Not on his watch. Not Vivian.

Frantically, Edison dug. The dog couldn't dig the sub out. He was fouling the water and making it hard to see.

Joe swam over to him, grabbed a handle sewn onto the top of Edison's BCD and hauled him away. Edison looked at him, brown eyes wide with anxiety.

Joe tugged the dog back to the front of the sub. That was the only part not buried, and the only place they could extricate Vivian. He would figure it out.

She still struggled with her emergency suit. He was glad it was loose-fitting. She'd never be able to get into an ordinary wetsuit with a broken arm. He wished he'd sent her off to get the flag and stayed in the sub himself, but he'd mistakenly thought she would be safer inside than out.

She finished and gave him a thumbs-up sign. In the regular world, that meant you were OK, and in the diving world, it meant you wanted to surface. Both interpretations were accurate.

She pointed up at hairline cracks in the bubble. Water dripped through and pooled on the floor. It wouldn't be long before the cockpit was full. That would equalize the pressure and make it easier to open.

Vivian wasn't going to wait that long, and he didn't know how to tell her to. She lay down on her back, positioned both feet against the bubble and pushed. Fresh blood ran down her face inside her hood. The bubble didn't budge.

If those jackasses could reverse the big sub, she could get out. How could he tell them? He couldn't exactly knock on their front door. He didn't have a radio and, even if he did, he had no idea what their frequency might be, or if they were even listening.

The other sub was, in fact, ominously quiet. It had to be some kind of equipment malfunction. Otherwise, they'd have seen the two tiny subs before they hit them.

Unless it was deliberate.

Dull thuds vibrated below his hands. She was kicking the crap out of the bubble. With the pressure above, she'd never get it open.

He took the dive knife out of his pocket and worked it under the mud into the hatch release. The knife slipped from his numb fingers. He grabbed it with his other hand and accidentally cut a dark line in his palm. He was so deep underwater his blood looked green instead of red, like Vulcan blood.

Her kicks seemed to be losing steam. She must be getting tired. He hoped she wouldn't wear herself out. She'd need to save something to get to the surface.

But the surface was a long way away.

First, he had to open the hatch release. A thread of blood drifted up from his palm. Hopefully, the great white shark they'd followed earlier had better things to do than circle back and eat him.

He worked the knife blade into the broken hatch release and levered. The hatch moved. He thrust the knife in farther, turned it. The hatch moved again.

She'd stopped kicking.

He slid the blade around and pressed down on the release. The hatch creaked.

He braced his back against the giant submarine's hull and lifted with his legs. She strained from the other side, bloodied face inches away.

The hatch cracked open, and water rushed in. She dropped back. Together, they watched the cockpit fill with seawater. It wouldn't fill all the way—the air inside would prevent that—but it ought to fill enough that they could open the hatch once the pressure had equalized. He held up his hand, palm out, to tell her to wait. Her eyes were wide, and she looked like she was hyperventilating. Vivian was the toughest woman he knew, solid under pressure. Except underwater.

He was making her worst nightmare come true.

Once the bubble was as full as it looked like it was going to get, he forced the hatch open wider. It moved much more easily now.

Her hand came through the edge of the hatch, then her arm.

She pushed through the small opening, and he pulled from his side. A tight fit. Bubbles rushed out of her suit as she exhaled. For a brief instant, he thought she wouldn't make it, but then she popped free, and they both shot back almost a yard.

Edison swam up close to her, and she reached down to pet his back. Edison was best in the world at comforting panicky people. As Joe's psychiatric service dog, he'd had plenty of practice. Vivian hugged the dog hard, and Edison licked the inside of the bubble surrounding his head.

With a visible effort, she let go of the dog and turned to Joe. He pointed toward the surface. She probably couldn't see much in this darkness, but up was where they wanted to go.

Slowly, he kicked off from the side of the sub. He tugged on her suit while holding on to the handle on Edison's suit. Joe's flashlight dangled from a strap on his wrist. He had everything he needed.

He spared a glance toward the black sub. Tiny bubbles drifted up along the sides. The prince was probably already dead, and he felt torn. After he got Vivian to safety, he'd check.

Vivian had found a flashlight and turned it on. He guided her hand so the light shone on his face. He pointed to her suit, to the surface, and blew out air in a steady stream. He held his breath and waited for the bubbles to disperse, then shook his head.

She nodded. Hopefully, she remembered the briefing he'd given her on the emergency suit: *Once you pull the tab to go up, don't hold your breath, instead breathe out in a steady stream to avoid an embolism or a collapsed lung.* Or at least he hoped she remembered, because he didn't have any other way to communicate with her. He had to get her to the surface as soon as he could, in case the black sub had run into him on purpose.

Carefully, he pushed her, turning her around so her back was to him. He reached across her and pulled the tab. Her suit headed toward the surface. In a few seconds, he couldn't even see her boots, just the tiny speck of light on the back of her suit rising toward the surface.

He wished he could have hung on and ridden her suit's momentum to the top, but he worried Edison might hold his breath, and the dog's lungs or ears might be damaged. As smart as he was, Edison couldn't understand the safety briefing.

They'd have to go up the old-fashioned way, slowly. If someone from the large sub had bad intentions, he'd do the best he could. At least Vivian was out of danger.

He turned toward the smashed submarine. A light flickered, and he aimed for it. Unlikely the pilot was alive, but Joe had to check. Vivian had survived the initial impact. Maybe the prince had gotten lucky, too.

Edison swam nearby, yellow legs paddling hard. He was part Labrador, a water dog. He'd always been a strong swimmer, but had become even stronger since they started going out diving from the yellow submarine.

The giant sub hadn't stirred. Was it disabled? If so, ought he try to rescue the people inside? He had no idea how. They probably had an adequate air supply, and no giant bubbles indicated a hull breach. He'd send someone down after he got to the surface. They'd nearly killed Vivian, and he wasn't feeling too kindly toward them.

He looked in the direction where he'd first seen the prince's submarine. A light sputtered, but there were no more bubbles. The little sub must have been crushed under the giant hull.

Joe swam toward the trapped submarine. Shattered plastic glittered under the beam of his dive light. The impact had broken the cockpit bubble. The flashlight blinked off. He banged his light against his thigh, and it came back on, but who knew for how long. Quickly, he swept his light over the remains. A pale hand stretched out from the mud.

Joe swam down to touch it. The hand felt so cold he almost dropped it. Gritting his teeth, he peeled back the man's diving suit to feel his wrist.

No pulse.

How could there be? The body was crushed under the hulking black submarine. Joe wished he could bring the body to the surface. If he left it here, it might never be recovered. The visibility was low, and it was a big ocean. A dive team could search for a long time without finding something so small as a human body.

He held up a hand to tell Edison to stay still, then descended until he was eye level with the hand. A slow examination in a grid pattern revealed no way to extract the corpse.

He'd have to leave the body for someone else.

7

Vivian blew out her breath in a long exhalation, trying not to think about her lungs exploding, bubbles boiling through her blood, embolisms seeking out her brain, all the nightmare scenarios from the safety briefing. She had a lot of sympathy for her panicked scuba buddy right this minute. She was trying very hard not to have a bad moment. Because she wasn't in a pool with a buddy and instructors and a world-class hospital minutes away.

She was alone, and if she messed this up, she would die. In the water.

Hoping he'd left nothing out, she followed the instructions from Tesla's safety briefing to the letter and forced herself to keep exhaling. She wasn't going to run out of air and suffocate in her suit. Plenty of air up there. The suit bore her upward.

A sheet of silver as bright as a Mylar balloon shone above her upturned face, and her heart leaped. The surface. The silver wasn't flat like a table. Instead, it rose and fell like a sheet flapping on a clothesline. Waves.

She burst through the silver sheet into the sunlit world. With her uninjured hand, she fumbled to unzip her hood. Once it was down, she took a long breath of salty sea air. It tasted better than any air she'd ever breathed. She took another breath.

A wave knocked her in the face, and she coughed. The air might be friendly, but the sea sure as hell wasn't.

She bobbed around like a cork, the air inside the suit keeping her afloat. So long as she didn't inhale a wave, she'd be fine. Tesla had told her the suit had an emergency beacon that would activate when exposed to salt water. Even now, hers was calling rescuers. She hoped.

Tesla. And Edison. She hadn't expected them to surface with her. They didn't have suits, and she wasn't sure what would happen to a dog during a rapid ascent. But they'd be along any second. Tesla must have had a plan to get to the surface on his own, or he wouldn't have sent her up. Right?

A minute passed, then another. She learned to anticipate the waves, to hold her breath, and dive through. Her mouth tasted of salt, and blood ran down her cheek from the cut on her head. On land, she wouldn't have cared about it. But here she wondered if she was sending out messages to every shark in the sea: Come get your wounded prey! Shop here for a tasty and vulnerable treat!

Hoping to see bubbles from a scuba diver, she scanned the sea. Nothing. Maybe Tesla was a slow swimmer. Maybe he was doing a safety stop. Maybe he wasn't coming. Or maybe he was stuck down there.

She searched for a rescue ship. No one had heard her transponder's pleas for help. Did the damn thing work? She didn't even know where it was supposed to be on her suit. For all she knew, it might not even be there, and it wasn't calling in the cavalry.

First things first. She had to find Tesla. Cradling her wounded arm, she paddled in a wide circle, searching for bubbles. If he didn't surface soon, she might drift away. Already, she wasn't sure where she'd first come up. She kept circling.

A plastic bubble popped to the surface. Inside, a dog barked soundlessly.

"Edison!" She swam toward him.

As soon as he saw her, he dove back underwater. He'd lead her straight to Tesla, if she could keep up. She angled her body downward and tried to dive. Her emergency suit bobbed to the surface. It wasn't designed for this. But if she took it off, she might drown. She was a lousy swimmer with two arms, let alone one. She was a land-based bodyguard, not a lifeguard.

Edison surfaced again. He looked at her sternly. He knew her duty.

She would have to take off the suit. One-handed, she struggled with her zipper, but her cold fingers slipped off the tiny metal tab. Edison paddled over and bumped the handle on the back of his vest against her uninjured hand. Automatically, she grabbed it.

The second her fingers closed around the handle, the dog dove. She took a deep breath before he dragged her underwater. Once her legs were under, she kicked as hard as she could to help the poor dog. Her broken arm had gone mostly numb before, but it began to throb.

The dog towed her to where Tesla hung about twenty feet down, face pointed toward the dark water below. The silver sheet of light she'd so longed to reach had probably triggered a panic attack.

When she reached him, she let go of the dog and latched on to Tesla's shoulder. His head shot up, and his arms wind-milled just like Guy's had. She nearly lost her grip before he recognized her. His eyes were so wide they seemed to fill his snorkel mask, like an anime character. He was terrified, but he calmed down once he recognized her. One up on Guy.

Her suit lifted them both, and he stiffened. Movements frantic, he peeled her hand off his shoulder.

She fought to stay level with him in her buoyant suit. Her lungs burned. She held up one finger, hoping he'd guess that meant she'd be back soon. She needed air.

She headed back to the surface and took deep breaths until Edison arrived to pull her back down. This time, she knew how far to go, and she was in better shape when she reached Tesla.

He seemed calmer, too, and he took her good arm to stabilize her. She slid out of his grasp and moved his hand to her belt. They hung face-to-face in the water, slowly ascending. She had only a few seconds before he started to panic. Edison spotted the problem and pushed the handle on his vest into Tesla's hand, then tried to pull them down. It slowed their upward movement and bought her time. Good dog.

Tesla released his hold on her belt long enough to hand her his spare regulator. She shoved it in her mouth, exhaled, and drew in a long breath. Already putting her buddy-breathing training to good use. Together, they could do this.

She drew her good arm out of her sleeve so it rested against her side. Then she stuck her hand in her warm armpit. That ought to get feeling back in her fingers. If she fumbled this, she wouldn't get a second chance.

Tesla's eyes were growing wider, and bubbles shot out of his regulator way too often. He was hyperventilating, barely holding it together. She was impressed he'd lasted so long so close to the light and the outside world. All things considered, he was actually pretty damn strong.

She reached into her pocket and took out the syringe. She'd been carrying the fast-acting sedative for months in case of an emergency in which Tesla needed to be taken outside whether he wanted it or not. This definitely counted.

In one quick movement, she stuck him in the shoulder, needle going right through his neoprene wetsuit and into his muscle. She pressed the plunger. He jerked back, and the syringe tumbled into the depths. Another piece of unappetizing garbage in the Atlantic.

His eyes went glassy. Wincing, she used the elbow of her broken arm to hold his regulator against his face. If it fell out, he'd drown. She started kicking toward the surface.

Tesla let go of her belt.

Edison sensed he was needed. The dog swam up past her to look at his master's face. He bonked Tesla's head with his bubble, and Tesla's eyes moved to the dog's. He smiled around his regulator and patted the dog's back.

Without Edison pulling them down, they were heading up. She hoped the drug would keep Tesla calm. If he thrashed around, she couldn't do much with one arm. On land, she'd choke him out, but the water put her at a disadvantage.

Tesla's eyes rolled back, and she pressed the regulator hard against his mouth. She gritted her teeth against the pain in her arm. Nothing to do but wait out the ascent.

By the time they broke the surface, Tesla was completely out. She inflated his buoyancy compensator, and he tipped over to float on his back. The suit was clearly intended to keep unconscious wearers alive, a good thing as she couldn't have held him up long with one arm. Edison paddled next to his master, nudging his limp form. Clearly, the dog didn't like to see his master out cold. She didn't blame him. It creeped her out, too.

But things were looking up. They were above the water breathing real air. She could hold on to Tesla and keep them together. And nobody had drowned. Except for that guy in the other sub. Unless he got crushed to death.

She tried not to think about that. She focused on the next minute, and the one after that. Eventually, those minutes would stack up, and the situation would change. Just stay alive for one more minute. That's how she powered through stressful situations.

Edison huddled between her and Tesla. The dog didn't have a wetsuit, and he'd started to shiver.

"Good boy," she said, and realized he probably couldn't hear her through his scuba bubble. She wanted to reach over and pet him, but couldn't let go of Tesla. Her hand was a frozen claw, and she was afraid if she pried her fingers loose she'd never get them wrapped around the suit, and Tesla would drift away.

It had been several minutes since she'd first surfaced, although she refused to let herself count how many. Their transponders must be sending out signals like crazy, so each minute was bringing them closer to rescue. They weren't going to die here.

Edison looked over at her, doggie eyebrows bent with worry.

"I hear you," she said. "But we're going to be fine."

Edison probably couldn't hear her inside his bubble, but he watched her lips. Maybe he could read lips. It wouldn't surprise her. That dog could do just about anything.

"Good boy," she said clearly and loudly. "You did a great job!"

The dog had done his best. She'd done her best. So had Tesla. Now they had to hope someone else was doing their best to find them. She hadn't been so helpless in a long time, and she hated it.

Together, they drifted, an island of three in the vast blue sea.

Cold and exhaustion got to Vivian, and she dozed off. A sound jerked her out of her exhausted trance. Familiar, but she couldn't place it. A thumping. Then she knew, and she practically wept with relief.

She tugged Tesla around to face the source: a blue and white helicopter with NYPD written on the tail—New York City Police Department's Harbor Patrol.

She uncurled her clawlike fingers from Tesla's suit and waved her good arm back and forth like a metronome. Their bright red suits and Edison's yellow body were visible targets against the green water. Surely they'd be easy to spot. She waved again.

The chopper came in fast and low, and she waved. Edison made barking motions, but no sound came through his bubble.

The helicopter came right for them. The rotors kicked up water. Salty droplets stung her face, but she didn't care. The cavalry had arrived.

A ladder dropped from the helicopter's side and splashed into the water a few yards away. She pointed to Tesla and shook her head. He wasn't going to be climbing that ladder, and she couldn't drag him up. Awkwardly, she started to tow him toward the ladder, and the dog followed, tugging on Tesla's suit. This was going to take a while.

Someone understood the problem, because a floating basket stretcher and a diver landed in the water less than a minute later. The diver swam over so quickly he looked like a movie on fast forward. He wore a full wetsuit, but a curl of black hair had escaped the hood and was plastered to his forehead.

He grabbed hold of the back of Tesla's BCD.

"There's another sub," she yelled. "One guy still on the bottom."

The man tapped his ear. He couldn't hear her over the sound of the helicopter.

She'd have to wait until she was on board. The other guy was probably long dead at this point anyway.

The diver heaved Tesla into the basket and started clipping him in. He darted around easily. She held on to the basket's metal side with one arm and wished for dry land. Every so often, a wave slapped her in the face to remind her exactly why she hated the ocean.

Edison struggled to climb in with his master. She put a hand on the dog's back and looked to the diver to make sure Edison could get into the basket right now, or if he needed to wait for the next one. She wasn't getting out until the dog was safe. No man or dog left behind, that was her new motto.

The diver scooped up Edison and dumped him on Tesla's chest. Edison nudged Tesla's shoulder with his bubble head. She'd have to get that bubble off him once they got aboard. He was a patient dog, but it had to be driving him nuts.

The diver clipped Edison into the basket. Then he moved her back and gestured to someone in the helicopter. They started lifting Tesla and his dog. Her job was done.

Now her arm throbbed in earnest. It had been waiting for the adrenaline to clear. She shivered. Water had leaked into her suit when she'd been bringing Tesla up, and she was drenched. Her teeth chattered.

She paddled one-handed back toward the ladder. The diver drew up even with her and pointed at her arm.

"Broken," she yelled.

He grabbed hold of her collar. Ordinarily, she'd never let herself be towed around like a toddler in a pool, but she hurt too much and was too cold to stand on pride.

Once they got to the ladder, she dragged herself onto the lowest rung. She hung there like a drowned rat until they dropped the basket again. With the diver's help, she flopped in. She lay flat on her back and felt the rotor wash pummel her face while the diver clipped her in. Every beat meant she wasn't alone, and soon she was going to be on dry land.

Her basket dangled from a silver cable that moved steadily upward, swinging from side to side as the helicopter fought the wind. She focused on the pontoon skids that must let the machine land on water. Just over those pontoons was an open door. It would be a minute, and then another minute and another after, but she didn't sweat it. Tesla was safe. Edison was safe. She was safe.

Now, she was starting to get angry. Someone had smashed into them, nearly killed them, killed the guy in the other sub, and then done nothing to help. The giant sub must have had an exit, if Tesla's sub did. Probably full of fit young sailors and medics. But not one of them had come out to try to undo the damage they'd caused. They couldn't even be bothered to back off Tesla's sub so she could get out. If he hadn't been there with his knife, she'd be dead.

Hands guided the basket into the helicopter's belly, and the basket came to rest on a metal floor. Tesla was flat on a stretcher with Edison strapped in next to him. A redheaded man started unfastening the clips that held her in. A familiar dark head appeared, and the diver hauled himself up next to her.

As soon as he was inside, the sound of the rotors changed, and they rose and headed for shore. She sat. Her arm reminded her it was broken, and she needed to be more careful with it. Another thing the driver of that giant sub had to answer for.

She leaned forward and ripped off Edison's helmet one-handed, so the dog could breathe regular air. He licked her hand, clearly to say thank you, then went back to cuddling up to his master. She wished she had a big warm dog. She wouldn't even mind the wet-dog smell.

"There are subs down there," she yelled. "Three. A big one and two little ones."

"We'll have ships here soon to investigate, ma'am." The diver helped her out of the basket and into a seat. Her knees had gone rubbery, and she shook too much to fasten her own seat belt.

The diver fastened straps across her shoulders, and the medic with bristly red hair gently touched her injured arm.

She gasped. "Broken."

Red took a splint out of a white box.

"The guy down there won't last long," she yelled. "If he's even still alive."

"I understand that, ma'am." The diver finished buckling her in. "Help is on its way."

"What happened to your friend?" The medic slipped the splint over her forearm and pointed at Tesla.

"He might have hit his head," she said. He might have, and she couldn't tell them he was drugged to the gills.

"Is he under the influence of any medication?" he asked.

She closed her eyes and leaned back. Her teeth chattered so hard she decided she didn't have to answer.

8

House under Grand Central Terminal
March 9, morning

Joe moved his head and decided he never wanted to do that again. Each heartbeat slammed painfully inside his head. He started to count each throbbing beat, but that caused the corresponding colors to flash across his mind, which made everything so much worse. He worried he would vomit.

Nails clicked on the floor as Edison approached the bed. He brought with him the smell of a fish market at the end of the day. Joe stumbled into the bathroom, relieved to be home safe and sound with Edison. Vivian had been with him before he lost track of what was going on. So, they were all three (red) safe and sound. Unlike the driver of Prince Timgad's sub.

A damp nose nudged Joe's hand before a cool tongue lapped his cheek.

"Hey. Good boy."

Edison stopped licking him.

He wobbled, but managed to stay upright, so he was counting that as a win. He opened the old-fashioned medicine cabinet and took out a bottle of aspirin. He knocked back a few and cup after cup of cold water. Edison's brown eyes followed every movement.

"I'm fine. But *you're* not going to like what comes next."

Edison cocked his head.

"Bath."

Probably thinking of escaping, Edison looked toward the door.

"Nope. Sorry."

Joe turned on the shower and filled up the antique claw-foot tub, adding a dollop of oatmeal dog shampoo. "You first."

Edison gave him a long-suffering look before he jumped in, and Joe grinned. Life was back to normal. By the time he'd washed the dog, washed himself, brushed his teeth, and gotten dressed, he felt almost human.

He grabbed the laptop from his nightstand and booted it up. He wanted to identify the sub that had hit him while the memory was fresh in his mind. First, he sketched it out, trying to remember the dimensions, the outline, and the shape and location of the crow's nest thing perched on top. He had a good visual memory, and the sketch came easily.

Then he brought up a list of current submarines. At around two hundred feet (blue, black, black), the sub he'd seen was too small to be nuclear, but it had looked fairly modern. Pattern recognition was his superpower, and he quickly identified the vessel that had run him down: a Swedish Gotland-class submarine.

A little more time online and he learned a submarine of that type had been lent to the US government for practice war games, but was currently supposed to be back in Sweden. He even found a photo of it patrolling the Baltics dated a few days earlier. So, the ship he'd seen couldn't have been that one.

According to the Internet, the Saab Group had built three (red) subs of that class at the Kockums shipyard in

Malmö. If the sub hadn't been the *Gotland*, it could have been the *Uppland* or the *Halland*. They sounded like IKEA furniture names. He'd nearly been killed by an IKEA submarine. That didn't seem likely. Why would the Swedes be hanging around off the coast of New York running over civilians?

He dug deeper and discovered a news story about a hacking at a Swedish military installation. Details were sparse, but it looked as if a foreign entity might have stolen the design for the Gotland-class submarines. Searching told him the culprit hadn't been identified, but suspicion had fallen on China. China was notorious for hacking classified military documents, so it wasn't farfetched. If China had obtained the plans, maybe they had built the sub that had run him and the prince down. They could have sold it to anyone. Made more sense than angry Swedes.

Eventually, Edison whined and looked at the door, and Joe realized he was starving. The dog must be hungry, too. Shame on him for ignoring Edison. Edison was a hero and ought to be treated like one.

"Let's see about food." He ruffled Edison's damp ears. "We've got steaks in the fridge."

Edison's tail wagged at the word *steak*. He'd earned that treat and more.

"Steak?" Joe said, heading down stairs carpeted with a red Persian runner older than he was. "Who wants a steak?"

Edison ran ahead. His toenails were muffled by the rug as he bounded down the stairs and through the hall. Joe followed a lot more slowly, a hand on the wall. His head ached, he was dizzy, and he felt weak. Overall, though, better than he'd expected. While the knockout drug had a lot of unpleasant aftereffects, none was as bad as being dead.

"Are you feeling better, Mr. Tesla?" Mr. Rossi, his lawyer, stood at the foot of the stairs. As usual, his salt-and-pepper hair was immaculate, his Italian suit perfectly pressed, and he looked like George Clooney. His tie was embroidered with tiny anchors. Joe had seen enough anchors for a while, but he smiled.

"Why are you here?" he asked. "Is Vivian OK?"

"She suffered a cracked ulna, but is otherwise fine. She wished to be here until you awoke, but I sent her home to rest and took her place."

"Thank you for both." Vivian never accepted you-saved-your-boss's-life bonuses, but he knew her mother needed a new refrigerator, so he'd have a fridge delivered to her house. It might bother her, but once it was installed, she couldn't send it back.

"Some gentlemen from the New York Police Department's Harbor Patrol Unit are here to speak to you about the accident."

As if on cue, two (blue) cops came out of his parlor. The older cop looked to be in her early forties, with the leathery skin that comes from being outside in all kinds of weather. The younger was maybe late twenties, his potato nose peeling from a recent sunburn.

"Thank you for pulling us out of the water. I'm Joe Tesla."

"Detective Bellum." The woman stuck out her hand, and he took it. She had a strong grip, as if she were proving a point.

"Detective Hap." The younger guy had a strong handshake, too.

Both were asserting their dominance already.

He wouldn't be dominated in his own home, so he turned away and headed for the kitchen. He'd promised Edison a steak, and he needed food himself.

"Mr. Tesla." Bellum's voice sounded like she'd smoked a pack a day for twenty (blue, black) years. "We need to talk to you."

He didn't slow his pace. "In the kitchen."

Mr. Rossi didn't voice an opinion.

Joe took steaks out of the converted icebox, cut one up, and dropped it in Edison's bowl. Edison finished eating before Joe finished washing his hands. "Hungry, boy?"

Edison wagged his tail.

"Mr. Tesla," said Bellum. "Tell us what happened out in the water."

"Our sub got sunk." He dropped the remaining steak on a cookie sheet, drizzled olive oil on it, rubbed in coarse salt and pepper, and dropped a handful of frozen green beans next to it. He walked over to his stove. An elegant piece from the 1920s with gently curving legs like a table, a trio of burners, and an oven that opened at waist height all painted with a glossy white enamel. He'd rewired it himself. He slid the tray into the oven and set it to broil. "Anyone want a drink? I have—"

"Sunk? By whom?" Bellum moved to stand in front of him.

"I'm sure Vivian Torres gave you the details." He stepped around her and went over to the pantry, where he got out dry food for Edison. He didn't remember exactly how he got to the surface. Based on his headache, she'd knocked him out somewhere, but he wasn't going to talk about that part.

"And now we'd like to confirm her details." Bellum again. Apparently, the other guy was just there for decoration.

He gestured to his kitchen table. Once everyone was sitting, he gave them a rundown of events, including his recent research, ending with, "Who does the giant submarine belong to?"

"There's no record of a submarine of that type being in that location," Bellum said.

He looked over at Mr. Rossi, who gave an almost imperceptible nod. That's why they were here. They hadn't believed Vivian's story. Or they hadn't wanted it to be true.

"I saw it. Miss Torres saw it. There has to be physical evidence. The ocean floor is pretty muddy there. It must have scraped a trench along the bottom when it took out our two subs."

"Did it leave a trench?" Bellum asked. "Exactly where?"

"I have the GPS coordinates..." On his sub's computer, at the bottom of the ocean. "Near where we were picked up by the Harbor Patrol. Right by the contest flags. Blue Dreams had the GPS coordinates for the flags. I'd say start there."

"We found a body there."

"I'm sorry to say I'm sure you did." He'd seen it, after all.

"The body recovered was of the bodyguard of Prince Timgad. The prince himself was not aboard."

Lucky for the prince, not so much for the bodyguard. "And the sub?"

"We found the remains of Prince Timgad's sub in that location, as well as yours. But no larger submarine."

"It seemed very mobile," he said. "It probably didn't wait around."

"The US Navy assures me they would know if a submarine of that description were anywhere near New York, and if there was one, such a thing would be a matter of national security, and we'd appreciate you not disclosing it to anyone outside of law enforcement."

Someone was clearly covering his ass. He got up and fetched his steak from the broiler. His stomach growled.

"The Harbor Patrol officer says you were impaired when he brought you on board," Bellum pressed.

He swallowed a bite of steak. "I hit my head."

"Are you certain your condition wasn't alcohol- or drug-related?"

"Yes." Not exactly. His head ached. Definitely drug-related. He forced down another bite of steak.

"Maybe you saw the shadow of a boat passing overhead and mistook it for a submarine." Bellum wanted him to agree with her scenario.

"A shadow couldn't smash up my sub. Or the prince's."

"Maybe your subs collided, and you're misremembering." She didn't sound like she believed the maybe part of that sentence.

"Nope," he said.

"Maybe you were driving while impaired."

He looked over at Mr. Rossi. "My head hurts. I need to have a doctor look at it."

"I'll call Dr. Stauss," Mr. Rossi said. "You should go lie down."

Joe dumped the remains of his steak into Edison's bowl. A couple of gulps later, it was gone. Double steaks. Edison's lucky day.

"I'm sorry I can't be more helpful," Joe said to Bellum and Hap.

Bellum rose, too, and handed him her card. "Call me if your memory of the incident returns."

Face unreadable, Hap stood next to her.

He set the card on the table. "And I'm certain my account tallies with that of Miss Torres."

"How can you be so certain?" Officer Bellum asked. "Did you collaborate?"

"It'll tally because it's the truth." He looked into Bellum's gray eyes. "I hit my head underwater and was taken aboard the helicopter in a semiconscious state. As you can see, I just woke up. So, when would we have had an opportunity to collaborate?"

"Maybe before you left home in the first place," Bellum said.

"I think you need to go," Joe said. "I'm done talking."

She walked down his old-fashioned hallway, tanned hand nearly brushing the ashes-of-roses wallpaper. Hap trailed behind like a puppy.

Joe opened the wood and glass door and showed them out onto the porch of his Victorian house. They were buried over a hundred (cyan, black, black) feet below the surface. Built long ago for the designer of Grand Central Terminal, the house had everything he needed. His refuge, and he wanted the police out of it.

"Thank you for stopping by. And for the rescue," he said.

"I'll see them out," Mr. Rossi said.

Joe stepped into his underground garden and watched the group head to his elevator. It'd take them straight up into the middle of Grand Central Terminal and out of his life, at least for a while.

Then he looked at his front yard. He'd had an opera-set designer named Maeve Wadsworth turn the cave in which his house sat into a simulacrum of a summer garden—a blue sky that changed colors throughout the day to end in an orange sunset on the western edge, a seagull flying endlessly toward the sun, and a soft blanket of real plants on the floor. She'd set up LED lights to keep the plants alive. It had worked perfectly, and his garden grew year-round.

He took a deep breath, drawing the fresh green smell into his lungs. It made him feel better. His head still felt like it had been smashed against the wall a couple times, and he winced. Again, having a headache was better than being dead.

Vivian must have injected him when they got close to the surface. It had been the right thing to do, as he hadn't been able to make himself go up any more. The thought of bobbing around on the face of the ocean in the sun still made his heart race.

He sat and leaned against the schist wall of a cavern bored out a century before. Edison rested his head on his lap, and he ruffled his ears. "You smell much better, boy. You were pretty ripe when I first woke up."

Edison gave him an injured look, and he laughed. "You like the odor of rotten fish better than lavender?"

Edison wagged his tail in agreement.

Mr. Rossi emerged from the elevator, walked across the old wooden walkway, and stood nearby. "How's your head?"

"Been better." But it had been worse, too.

"You were combative with them."

"They were combative with me." He petted the dog. "Are they going to investigate the sub, figure out why it rammed us?"

"Seems unlikely."

"If they find something, it means a sub turned up right off the shore of New York and they didn't even notice until it ran into someone." It was in the government's best interest to pretend Joe was lying and investigate quietly. He understood, but he didn't want to let it go.

"It could mean that, yes," Mr. Rossi said.

"What's your advice?"

"Lie low. Don't cause any trouble and see where this goes. It might get swept under the rug and not present a problem." Mr. Rossi fiddled with his gold cuff links.

"Someone killed the pilot of that sub, either accidentally or on purpose."

"There's talk that someone was you," Mr. Rossi said. "I suggest you don't aggravate the situation."

Joe sighed. Edison bumped his shoulder. "Let someone get away with murder?"

"It's not your place to investigate these kinds of things."

Answer enough, he supposed. "If I do it anyway?"

"I shouldn't meddle if I were you," Mr. Rossi said. "They're thinking of filing charges."

"What kind of charges?"

"Boating while intoxicated." Mr. Rossi flicked an invisible speck off his suit. "Manslaughter."

"If they're willing to go that far, there must be a good reason." Joe stood up. His head throbbed with pain and anger.

"Maybe."

"I can't undo what happened to the prince's bodyguard, to Vivian, to me, to my sub." He reminded himself not to shout at Mr. Rossi. "But I can make damn sure it doesn't get swept under some political rug."

Edison nudged Joe's palm with his nose.

"It's OK, boy," Joe said. "I'm not upset. I'm angry, and I intend to do something about it."

"I advise against it."

"Noted," Joe said. "Now help me figure out the next steps."

9

**Vivian's apartment, Brooklyn
March 9, morning**

Heart pounding, Vivian bolted upright. Daylight pierced her bedroom curtains. A quick glance at her sister's rumpled bed. Thank God Lucy wasn't there. She didn't want to explain herself to her snotty teenage sister.

She leaned against her pillow and willed her heart to stop pounding. She'd been having a nightmare about being trapped inside the submarine. When she'd started to drown, she woke up. She shuddered, then slowed her ragged breathing. She was home. Lots of things could happen to her here, sure, but drowning was pretty damn unlikely.

The painkillers they'd given her at the hospital had started to wear off, and her arm ached. She touched the cast with her other hand. She wouldn't be able to work until her ulna healed. And she wasn't the only one who depended on her income—her mother and Lucy did as well.

"Vivian?" her mother asked softly from the other side of the door. "Are you awake?"

She debated pretending she wasn't, but her mother would know, even through the door. She always knew. "I'm fine."

Her mother bustled in and handed her a cup of coffee. "The police are stopping by soon to have you sign your accident report."

Vivian took a small sip of coffee. Strong and black, it tasted like heaven. "It wasn't an accident. That sub meant to ram us, or ram the prince."

"Murder by submarine?" Her mother gathered a pair of socks from Lucy's bed and smoothed the bedspread down flat.

"Something like that." The caffeine was already clearing her head. "No one gives a rat's ass about me, so they must have been after Tesla."

"Or the prince or his bodyguard." Her mother sat on Lucy's newly made bed. "After all, his bodyguard is the one who's dead."

"And he was rammed by a submarine. That'll be an international incident."

"Assuming it's not swept under the rug." Her mother was on her feet, tidying Lucy's dirty clothes into the empty hamper. Vivian's side of the room was, of course, spotless.

"What do you mean?" Vivian asked.

"My goodness." Her mother stopped long enough to give her the look she used whenever Vivian was being unbelievably stupid. "Weren't you in the military long enough to know the easiest thing to do is to pretend nothing happened?"

"But something did happen. I told them about it in my accident report." Someone from the Harbor Patrol had taken her statement in the hospital. Sadly, not the cute guy who'd performed the rescue. "Plus, they have a dead guy to explain."

"Just a bodyguard," her mother said. "And you hit your head, dear. You were probably imagining things."

Vivian touched the stitches in her scalp. "I didn't hit my head hard enough to imagine a giant submarine."

Her mother's piercing eyes stared into hers. "Maybe you did."

Vivian didn't answer.

"Get up, take a shower," her mother said. "You told me that cast on your arm is waterproof."

No lying around in bed at her mother's house, near-death experience or not.

An hour later, Vivian had showered and gotten dressed. She was already tired of having a broken arm. She followed the smell of Portuguese sausage into the kitchen.

"Let me make you a plate. Sit right there," her mother said.

Usually, she hated it when her mother fussed, but today she was grateful for the food and attention. Something felt off, though.

She looked around the kitchen. "When did you get a new refrigerator?"

"While you were sleeping. From Mr. Tesla. They took away the old one, and we're not sending it back." Her mother put a plate of eggs, sausage, and toast in front of her.

Vivian didn't even know where to start on the refrigerator thing. Maybe she ought to take Tesla's full-time-job offer. Then she could pay him back for the fridge. But he'd offered her a big raise, and it made her uncomfortable. Plus, she didn't like the idea of having a single employer. Too much like the Army. She tugged on her sling.

"It hurts, doesn't it?" her mother said. "They gave you pills. Take the pills."

"They make me stupid."

"You think maybe you're going to cure cancer today without them?" Her mother glared up at her, hands fisted on her round hips.

"We won't know if I take them, will we?" She knew she was being contrary.

Her mother held out two pills. Vivian hesitated before scooping them up and washing them down with a sip of coffee. So she wasn't going to cure cancer today.

The door buzzer rang.

"We can't keep the refrigerator," Vivian said before going to answer the door.

Just as she opened the door, her mother yelled, "If your Mr. Tesla wants to give us a refrigerator for saving his life, we're keeping it!"

A woman in a worn navy blue pantsuit stood in the doorway. "Vivian Torres?"

"How can I help you?"

"I'm with the New York City Harbor Patrol. Officer Bellum." She showed Vivian her badge.

"I gave a full statement." The pills were making her too tired and slow. She needed to wake up. "And please also deliver my thanks to the officers who rescued us."

She motioned for Officer Bellum to step inside.

"I was going over your statement." Officer Bellum held up a sheaf of papers. "So, Mr. Tesla has a history of drugs."

"He got slipped a mickey once, and I injected him yesterday. That's not much of a history."

"A refrigerator is a pretty big bonus."

Thanks, Mom, Vivian said silently. "He gave it to my mother as a gift."

"It might not be seen as a gift."

"No?" Vivian asked.

"It could be seen as a bribe."

"Is there anything else you need to go over in my statement?"

Officer Bellum walked her through her statement again. They stood in the hall—Vivian didn't want her in the rest of the house. By the time it was over, Vivian was ready for another nap. She wanted to be angry about the whole situation, but she was too tired. Once she woke up, she planned to make trouble.

Big trouble.

She'd been run over, nearly drowned, and now she was accused of taking a bribe for who knew what reason. She was going to find out what was going on and kick someone right in the ass.

10

Siren's bridge
March 9

Laila glanced over at Ambra, who was the Chief of the
Watch. Ambra sat at her station near the diving officer, the
helmsman, and the planesman. They looked at home
working the rudder and diving plane controls. Hard to
believe that a month ago they'd been living as humble wives
and daughters and sisters.

"We've completed our regular sonar sweep," said
Ambra. "All clear."

No one had followed them from New York yesterday.
Laila had hoped they'd get out clean, even as she'd worried
the survivors from the wrecked sub would alert the US
military, which would start a wider search. Maybe there had
been no survivors.

Ambra rose and took a few steps to where Laila stood
looking down at maps on the plotting table. The blue
lighting made her look drawn. "On course to intercept the
Shining Pearl."

"Show me."

Ambra took the yellow pencil from behind her ear and
used it to point out their position relative to the _Pearl_'s on
the paper maps. The _Siren_ had electronic maps, and the GPS
took her position when she surfaced, then tracked her course

relative to that point when she was submerged. The computerized system was supposed to be foolproof, but Ambra created backup plots on paper, too. A trained mathematician, she had a good head for such calculations. Ambra's parents would be horrified to know how she was using her expensive degree.

Laila pretended to study the map unfurled across the plotting table, but she was really thinking about the *Pearl*. The *Pearl* belonged to her beloved Aunt Bibi. Her husband had died young and left his wife a sizable fortune. She'd used it to purchase a yacht and perpetually travel the world, out of sight and control of the rest of the family. All the women envied her.

Bibi kept a small, intensely loyal crew. She paid them well, and they said nothing about what took place out on the open sea. Bibi was free in a way none of them would ever be. Her husband was dead, and she'd borne him no children. No one had a claim upon her obedience.

Every summer, Laila and her mother and sisters had spent a few weeks with Aunt Bibi on her yacht. Freed from the strictures of everyday life, they swam and fished and watched forbidden television, played games, and ate whatever they wanted. Aunt Bibi's carefree existence had inspired Laila and Nahal to dare the unthinkable and take the submarine.

Aunt Bibi had known about parts of their plan since the beginning, and she'd pledged to help them. She didn't know why they were taking the submarine, or what they would do with the submarine now that they had it, and Laila would never tell her. She hoped Aunt Bibi thought they would use it as she used her yacht—for freedom and peace.

"Think of the food," Ambra whispered.

"Chocolate and black tea," Laila said. The Chinese had left only a few weeks' worth of supplies and hadn't included anything indulgent. The crew had eaten nothing but rice, fish, and canned cabbage since they stole the *Siren*. Their supplies of soy sauce and hot mustard had been exhausted the first week.

"And fresh figs," said Ambra. "And baklawa."

"And new oxygen generators, so we can finally dive and stay under for a long time, like a proper submarine."

And gossip. She wanted to know what the family thought about the plane crash that had supposedly taken her life and the lives of the women in her crew. Had the plane gone down as planned, and was their secret safe, or had the pilot taken her money and betrayed them all?

Had the prince died in the wreck? She didn't see how he could have survived it, but she had to be sure. Aunt Bibi would know. Bibi had remained in close contact with her sisters, never needing to care about the cost of satellite-phone calls as she crisscrossed the seas.

"How long?" Laila asked.

"In an hour," Ambra said. "We'll be eating figs."

"*Ex abundanti cautela.*"

"An abundance of caution," Ambra translated. "I took Latin, too. We'll be careful."

"We must become shadows in a pitch-dark night. No one can know we have come and gone."

"The darker the better, I know."

"If it's too bright, we can't surface." If the man and woman in the tiny sub had made it to the surface, authorities might be searching for them.

Ambra tightened her lips. "So we stay down here eating pickled cabbage? You're jumping at shadows. How could anyone know to look for us?"

"Even so."

"Our risk assessment should be based on a consensus," Ambra said. "Not fiat."

"That wasn't the agreement. A ship needs a captain."

"Does it?" Ambra straightened her blue uniform. "Isn't that the kind of hierarchy we're trying to escape?"

Jenna looked over from her station as helmsman. Had the crew talked about this among themselves?

Laila drew herself up to her full height, several centimeters taller than Ambra, although Ambra weighed more than she did. "I am captain. We all signed the oath. You, too." She was glad Nahal had thought to force each woman to sign a blood oath to serve Laila directly. Nahal thought like a chess master, several moves ahead.

Ambra, too, must have remembered the candlelit room where she'd so eagerly pledged herself, because she turned back to her charts, shoulders stiff with pride. Laila had promised to take them away from their lives, and she had. Once she was certain the prince was dead, they could vote about what to do next—travel the seas with the submarine, or go their separate ways.

She wondered if Ambra's opinions were held by the rest of the crew, but she didn't want to force the issue and have to face them down. It would be over soon enough. She stood quietly on the bridge as they sped toward the rendezvous point.

"Here, Captain," said Ambra. "Dark enough?"

Laila strode over to the periscope, pulled down the handles, and looked through the eyepieces. They'd surfaced to periscope height, eighteen meters, a few minutes before, but she'd been restraining herself from looking until now.

The *Shining Pearl* rode proudly in the water. She was a long boat, more than sixty meters, with sleek lines and sides white as pearls. She'd been owned by an American real estate tycoon before Aunt Bibi, and no luxury had been spared. Laila's heart jumped, as it always did when she saw the ship. Since she was a little girl, that familiar shape had meant freedom.

Lights gleamed from the yacht's windows. Bibi had turned them down, but not off, as Nahal had told her. Per the instructions Nahal had sent out weeks before, Bibi's yacht slowed. She was expecting them.

The sonar revealed no ships for miles around. They matched pace with the slowing yacht.

"May I see, Captain?" Ambra used the world *Captain* in a tone Laila could describe only as insolent, but she couldn't chastise her without seeming petty.

Instead, she took one last glance and stepped back. Ambra had to maneuver around her to look, but they'd gotten used to the close quarters, so she barely noticed.

"It looks clear."

"I see fifteen men lined up on the bottom deck," Ambra said. "They're backlit by the windows, so I can't see if they're armed."

"Aunt Bibi wouldn't put out armed men to greet us." Laila was outraged.

"She's not my aunt." Ambra swiveled the periscope, taking in the entire length of the ship.

Not too long ago, Ambra had been advocating less caution, and now she was being paranoid. She just wanted an argument, but Laila wasn't going to be baited.

"What's the usual crew complement?" Ambra asked.

"Thirty. Each loyal to my aunt."

"Doesn't make them loyal to me."

"Do you want your figs, or don't you?" She tried to lighten the mood.

"They don't look like soldiers," Ambra conceded.

"It's not like we have a choice. We need food. And news."

Ambra didn't step back from the periscope.

Laila checked her watch. Astronomical twilight was over. They'd reached the darkest part of the night. "Prepare to surface and come alongside the *Pearl*."

Women scrambled to obey, even Ambra.

Laila looked back through the periscope. "Take us up."

The figures on deck caught sight of them, and a round woman in a flowing green dress waved from the port side. Aunt Bibi.

The sub maneuvered next to the yacht. Laila was first up the sail. Being captain had its privileges, and she needed to start insisting on them. Once topside, she took a deep breath and let it out. It smelled fresh and clean, a relief after the close, cabbage-scented air inside the sub. It felt wonderful to be outside in the cool night air, with the sky above stretching out to the stars.

Many of Aunt Bibi's crew were women. She often said that, since men controlled the Navy, women could control her boat. Her captain had a rigorous training program for new recruits, and they performed well. For the first time, she wondered how Aunt Bibi dealt with discipline problems.

The seas were relatively flat, but it was still tricky. Both vessels dipped up and down. Anyone who fell between the vessels could be crushed to death.

Aunt Bibi's crew had tied fenders to the side to keep the sub from scraping the yacht. Her crew helped to tie the sub to the yacht, then lowered a gangplank between the two vessels. Rope railings ran along both sides.

Laila took hold of the wet ropes and walked across the bobbing surface to her aunt.

Bibi swept her into a hard embrace, enveloping Laila in her spicy signature scent. Her perfume was custom-designed in Egypt, and she smelled like safety. Laila leaned into her and felt herself relax.

"You look so beautiful," Aunt Bibi said. "Hair like a pixie."

"We can't stay long." Her voice caught.

"You could," Aunt Bibi said. "Of course you could."

They had to be gone long before the sun rose, in case they might be caught by satellite photos. Nahal had developed the protocol during their planning, and Laila believed in caution more than ever. "I wish we could."

"My crew will start loading your supplies." Aunt Bibi gestured to the row of retainers standing patiently behind her.

"My crew will do it. No one comes aboard my vessel but my own crew."

Aunt Bibi raised an eyebrow theatrically. "You don't trust my crew?"

"Ambra will come with me. Everyone else will load supplies."

"I hope you let them off duty to eat." Aunt Bibi put her arm through Laila's. "We've prepared a feast."

Laila's stomach growled, and Aunt Bibi laughed.

"I think you will be pleased," she said.

An hour later, Laila had eaten so much she could barely move. Ambra had come and gone. The other women were rotating through the polished wooden dining room in groups. Some women loaded supplies, others stowed them, and the remainder got to eat. If she hadn't eaten so much herself, she never would have thought they could put away so much food.

Aunt Bibi had hidden treasures in with the food and diesel fuel she'd requested, and Laila knew they looked forward to seeing what gifts awaited.

But first she needed the Internet. Aunt Bibi had a satellite connection. She held Nahal's laptop under her arm. Nahal herself was still on the sub, recovering from the gunshot wound she'd sustained when they first took the submarine. Nahal had forced Laila to memorize the procedure for activating layers of virtual private networks to cover her tracks before she logged on to the dark web. Nahal's enthusiasm for the dark web and the hacker culture had always been a mystery to Laila. In college, she had always teased Nahal that her idols were shadowy hackers instead of film stars and musicians. But she couldn't deny the usefulness of Nahal's obsessions now.

Laila had brought her a giant plate of food, but there was little she could do for her.

"I would like a private space," she told Aunt Bibi. "For computer use."

"The library is best." Aunt Bibi gestured in the direction of the library and returned to her conversation with the submarine's doctor, Laila's cousin Meri.

Laila rose and hurried out of the dining room. She knew the corridors of Aunt Bibi's ship as well as she knew the *Siren*. A few minutes later, she turned on the light and closed the library door behind her. Aunt Bibi's library was a thing of beauty. Floor-to-ceiling bookcases covered outboard walls curved to match the shape of the ship. Slender golden ropes strung across the middle of the shelves held the books in place during rough seas. One wall contained classics, another scientific and nautical books, another religion and philosophy, and the final wall held popular books augmented at every port. She hurried to the gleaming table, slipped into the chair, and opened the laptop.

The work of a few minutes showed that the prince was still alive.

Alive.

The man she'd killed had been his bodyguard. The entire trip had been for naught. The prince was still alive, so no one was safe.

She read more. The man in the other submarine had been Joe Tesla, a software CEO. Nahal had mentioned him in the past—she thought he was some kind of genius, but Laila hadn't ever really listened when Nahal talked about him. She'd have to remedy that.

The websites didn't mention the presence of the *Siren* at the crash. Tesla must have told someone, but the news hadn't been published. Perhaps she could use that silence to deflect the prince's suspicion from herself and the *Siren*. A long shot, but better than nothing.

She followed another set of protocols and entered the dark web. With Nahal's recent instructions sounding in her ears, she was able to find the correct exchange, set up her deadly request with the right code words, and transfer bitcoins to an underground escrow account.

She had just paid for a hit on Joe Tesla. When Tesla turned up dead, Tesla himself might look like the target of the undersea attack, not the prince or his bodyguard. It was a desperate act, perhaps, but she could think of no better solution.

Then she ordered two oxygen generators for the *Siren*. She'd written down the information, but it took a while to find a source, even on the dark web where seemingly everything was for sale.

A quick rap on the library door caused her to jump.

"Come in," she called.

Aunt Bibi entered. She looked tired and old, but her smile was still warm as ever.

"I know you must leave soon, but let's stroll along the top deck before you go." Aunt Bibi hooked her arm in Laila's, and together they made their way to the topmost deck. The boat glowed in the soft golden light.

"It looks peaceful, does it not?" Aunt Bibi asked. "And safe."

"You won't sway me."

For a moment, they walked together in silence, and she remembered the many times they had walked alone on the deck together, all the years of her childhood.

"Your mother was devastated by news of your death," Aunt Bibi said quietly.

"I'm sorry." Her mother had made her alliances clear long ago—to her husband, her sons, and then her daughters. Only when nothing else remained would it be her turn.

"I couldn't ease her grief," Aunt Bibi said. "Secrecy was my promise to you. But I wish you would tell her. She suffers."

"Does she?" She didn't think her mother could have let herself care about her worthless daughters.

"And." Aunt Bibi chewed her lower lip as if to bite the words in half before she spoke them. "She has also lost your eldest brother."

"Has she?" Laila tried to look surprised. Not a simple task, since she knew of her brother's death because she'd shot him herself.

"A training incident," Aunt Bibi said.

"Much for my mother to bear. But she has my father to hold her up."

They both knew her father wouldn't provide support to her grieving mother. He had other wives, other children.

Aunt Bibi squeezed her arm. "Someone tried to kill your future husband, Prince Timgad, but he was spared. It's said a careless billionaire ran into his submarine while they vied for some worthless token in a submarine race."

Suspicion had fallen on Tesla. Good. "He has nine lives, like a cat."

Aunt Bibi stopped at the railing and looked across the starlit waves. "You could end it now. You could rejoin your family. You could send your crew home to theirs."

"And marry Prince Timgad?" She looked down at the top of her submarine, where women in blue uniforms carried brown boxes across the deck and into the sail.

"It is said now he will be the next king, and you would become his queen."

She'd known of Timgad's favor with the current king. "I would become his slave, not his queen."

"We all must serve a master." Aunt Bibi shrugged. "We who were born to the House of Dakkar. This time shall pass, and we shall be rewarded ever after. It is our duty."

"I serve a higher duty." Laila had struggled against her duty all her life, but leaving it behind hadn't made her happier.

"Is there a higher duty than the one we owe to our family? Our mothers? Our sisters? Our daughters? Our house?" Aunt Bibi took her hand. "I know it's difficult to be a woman, but we can help each other to endure."

"I don't want to endure." Anger rose in her, not only at Aunt Bibi, who had been spared a lifetime of servitude by her husband's death, but at the world that had made her believe it was the fate of others to endure such things. "I don't want those women down there to endure. They shouldn't suffer because they were born women. Our house is built upon the suffering, the blood and bones of its women. I won't let them *endure* it a moment longer."

Aunt Bibi leaned away. "Then take them away. Abandon your family and your duty. But stop whatever it is you're doing on this submarine."

"If I run away and hide, take them away to hide, then I turn my back on the millions who are enduring unspeakable horrors in the name of the family. In my name. What of them?"

"You cannot change the ways of the world with only a submarine." Aunt Bibi leaned closer, and the scent of her perfume mingled with the smell of the sea. "A single craft of steel and courage isn't enough."

"You've changed much with your single ship." She smiled at her aunt. "You gave us a place of safety, a place of joy. A place where we could bloom in quiet and freedom, if only for a few weeks a year."

"You can give the same to the women under your care, either on your submarine or with new identities on land," Aunt Bibi said. "Your actions won't change the world, but they will change the lives of all your crew. Such actions can be enough in a well-lived life."

"Not for me." She started back up the deck, ready to return to her tiny enclosed world and the women who would help her to carry out her mission. "Not anymore."

Aunt Bibi said nothing for a long time.

"Where will the royal family vote on the succession?" Laila asked.

Aunt Bibi stared at the submarine bobbing behind her ship. "The celebration will be in New York City."

That was where Prince Timgad had planned to take the submarine and the weapon he'd intended to mount on it. She'd hoped that stealing the submarine and killing the prince would stop him from starting a war. But he was still alive. He couldn't use the submarine now, but he still had the weapon, and he would be looking for other ways to deliver it.

"Where will the vote take place?"

Aunt Bibi watched the stars.

"Aunt Bibi?"

Her aunt sighed, then spoke in a voice so quiet Laila could barely hear her. "On Prince Timgad's yacht, the *Roc*."

"The *Roc*?"

"It's the largest superyacht in the world, one hundred and eighty meters long. Commissioned five years ago and launched on Tuesday."

"The largest yacht named after the largest bird," Laila said. "Not a subtle man, the prince."

Aunt Bibi smiled.

"When do the men gather together for the vote?" Laila asked.

"I don't know when they come together, or where they leave from."

"When do they arrive in New York?"

"On March 22. Their arrival is timed to coincide with an Israeli vessel full of protesters against American policy."

The yacht and the scapegoat would arrive at the same time.

That was her timeline, too. She had twelve days.

11

Grand Central Terminal, New York
March 10, morning

Joe closed the iron scrollwork door and lifted the elevator's
lever. The elevator shuddered into life. He'd looked into
replacing the outdated thing, but had come up against a wall
of bureaucracy so high even Mr. Rossi had given up and told
him to learn to love the elevator he had. Serviceable. It had
been for more than a century. Even attractive, with a square
Persian rug on the floor, a small chandelier in the ceiling, and
elaborately worked scrollwork sides and door. It was also
open beyond the scrollwork so he could see raw stone
sliding by as the elevator creaked up over one hundred (cyan,
black, black) feet from the formal entrance to his house. The
elevator felt rickety and unsafe, no matter how many city
elevator inspectors certified otherwise.

The elevator stopped, and he hurried out. Edison
followed at a more leisurely pace. The dog wasn't afraid of
elevators. A quick trip up the spiral staircase and Joe and
Edison stood inside the information booth at the center of
Grand Central, under the famous four-faced clock.

"Good morning, Mr. Tesla," said Evaline. She worked
the information booth and was probably the only person in
the world who knew as much about train schedules as Joe.

"Morning, Miss Evaline," he said. "Are the trains running on time today?"

"Always, Mr. Tesla," she said. "Except the Harlem Line. It's about two minutes late."

"They'll catch it up," he said.

She bent to pet Edison, and he gave her a tail wag. He didn't respond to most people petting him while he had on his vest, but he made an exception for her.

"You're looking fine this morning," she told the dog, like she did every morning, and Edison wagged his tail.

Joe had missed work yesterday because of his hangover after the accident, and he was glad to get back to his routine. He opened the brass door, whistled for Edison to come to heel, smiled at Miss Evaline, and stepped out into the bustle of Grand Central on an ordinary workday.

"Mr. Tesla?" A man in a business suit thrust a microphone in front of his face. "How do you respond to allegations you were playing chicken with Prince Timgad? And that led to the death of his bodyguard?"

Joe stumbled back against the door. Miss Evaline reached to open it for him, but he wasn't going to turn tail and run. He was going to work.

"No comment." He pushed past the reporter.

A woman in a white power suit kept pace on his left. "You didn't mean for him to die, did you?"

He walked forward. He wasn't even going to dignify that question with a 'no comment.' Edison stuck close to his heels.

Mr. Suit closed in on his right. "How long had you and the prince been feuding?"

A crowd of people in neon green T-shirts milled around in front of Joe. Their shirts proclaimed *Proud to be a*

Minnesotan. He wished they said *Proud to Know Where the Hell I'm Going So I Can Get Out of the Way.* But they didn't.

Miss White Suit crowded so close he felt her breath on his cheek. Her cameraman jockeyed behind her. "What does this mean for your security clearance?"

He hadn't thought about that. If he lost his security clearance, he might have to step down from Lucid, his first company, and the one that had brought in most of his fortune. He pressed his lips together and plowed through the Minnesotans.

The reporters and cameramen were better at moving through crowds, and they kept pace. He thought about an owl he'd once seen out during the day and how it had been mobbed by crows, hectoring and yelling, knocking feathers off the poor bird as it searched for cover.

"So, you're saying you did mean for the bodyguard to die?" White Suit said. "Are you being charged with murder?"

He walked on.

"Did you know the royal family is demanding your head?"

He didn't turn to see who was yelling what questions. He wanted to get inside his office. Behind him, Edison yelped.

He whirled to face the person who had hurt his dog.

"Sorry," mumbled Mr. Suit's cameraman. "I didn't see him there."

Edison leaned back against Joe's leg. He scooped the dog up in his arms and hugged him against his shoulder.

He glared at the cameraman. "Don't touch him. Not ever. Is that clear?"

The cameraman stepped back a pace and kept filming.

Edison nuzzled Joe's cheek, reminding him to stay calm and focused. His first priority was to get the dog somewhere safe. He hefted Edison so the dog looked over his left shoulder like the world's furriest baby and strode forward. He was in a crowd of New Yorker businessmen, and the reporters lost ground. The businessmen didn't give way like the polite Minnesotans. He slowed. He didn't want to be filmed sprinting away.

"It's OK," he whispered to Edison.

The dog swiveled his head back to look at him and let out an encouraging bark.

Joe didn't look back. He marched up the stairs, ignoring the questions shouted from behind. It sounded as if a third reporter had joined the fray, but he didn't look.

The woman in the white power suit somehow caught up and was at his elbow as he reached the office doors. She was thin and small, adept at cutting through crowds, although how she kept pace in her high heels he couldn't imagine.

"Were you piloting the sub at the time of the accident?" she asked. "Or was it your lover, Vivian Torres?"

He was so taken aback by both assumptions that he almost answered, at least to deny he was sleeping with Vivian. He was sure she wouldn't want that lie out there. But he was afraid that anything he said would make things worse for her.

He slid sideways through Pellucid's front doors without a word.

"Close and lock!" he yelled.

"Ahead of you." Marnie was next to him and already locking the door.

The woman in white knocked on the glass like she actually expected them to let her in. A sprightly little tattoo of denial. He turned his back on her.

"They've been calling all morning," Marnie said. "You might want to get ahead of this. Draft a statement, run it by Mr. Rossi, and give it to one of those sharks."

He lowered Edison to the ground, and the dog shook himself.

"You OK, boy?" he asked.

Edison wagged his tail to say he was, but Joe checked each leg to make sure. That cameraman had big feet.

"Should I call a vet?" Marnie asked.

"He's fine. No thanks to the reporters."

"I canceled our clients," she said. "Patients with anxiety issues shouldn't run that gauntlet before their screenings."

"Thank you." Efficient as always was Marnie. "Let the reporters stew."

"Don't forget you have that gala tonight," she said. "The press will probably eat you alive if you don't give them something."

Joe groaned. She was right. "I'll be out in a minute to draft something."

He walked past the giant glass brain in the lobby. It was laced with fiber optic cables that lit up to correspond with the EEG results of past patients, including Joe. Ironically, a lot of activity pulsed through the amygdala—the center of the brain that processed anger—which suited his mood.

He closed his office door. This call was going to be tough enough to make without an audience. Edison curled up on the dog bed next to the desk, his scuffle with the cameraman apparently already forgotten. He hoped the reporters wouldn't hassle the dog when he went out with his dog walker later. With any luck, they'd leave Edison in peace.

But right now, he had to call Vivian and warn her about the reporters, their questions, and the headlines she might have to deal with. As mad as she was at him already, this wasn't going to make it better. And that mattered, because he sure as hell wasn't going to let this go, and he needed her help.

Vivian didn't answer.

12

Apartment, New York
March 10, afternoon

Avi put on his white dress gloves and picked up two
cardboard boxes. One box contained a drone, the other a
camera, batteries, and a tiny tripod. Perfectly normal devices
for a photographer to possess. And that's what he was
posing as—a photographer. Not just any photographer
either, but one who had been hired to use a drone to film
tonight's gala at the Natural History Museum hosted by Blue
Dreams.

To get the job, he'd had to locate the original
photographer hired by Blue Dreams and kill him. Now he
would take the man's place. Simple.

Avi had trained in up close and personal combat, but
had lost his taste for it. Now, he preferred to work remotely,
to avoid the touch and the smells and the cleanup. He'd
made an exception for the photographer, because Avi had
no time to set the job up properly. It must be done quickly.

The contract had come via standard online channels.
He'd not been surprised by the job. He'd been expecting
someone to be contacted from the moment he'd heard of
the attempt on the prince's life. Perhaps Tesla had been
trying to kill the prince and had accidentally killed his
bodyguard, and this contract was in revenge for that act.

Perhaps someone had been trying to kill Tesla and had failed. Either way, Avi would complete his task.

Still holding on to the boxes, he rotated his left shoulder. A bullet had damaged his rotator cuff. Surgery and physical therapy had never put it right. He'd spent the previous day in Calvert Vaux Park hunched over a remote control, becoming familiar with this type of drone and its limitations, then thrown that drone into a dumpster so it couldn't be traced to him. He would use the original photographer's drone—covered with the man's fingerprints and DNA.

His shoulder ached from the unaccustomed position and tension. Weight training kept his wounded shoulder strong, but nothing stopped the pain. Painkillers would have helped, but he'd forbidden himself from ever taking them. Drugs were a weakness, and he abhorred weakness in himself, even as he expected it in others.

He stepped out of his room at the Grand Central Hyatt and let the door fall closed behind him. This room was close to his quarry, expensive enough it would seem an unlikely place for a man like him to stay and not so expensive he needed a complicated cover identity. His driver's license had an address in Lincoln, Nebraska, and his credit card bills went there, too. No one ever asked him about Nebraska. In fact, most people's eyes glazed over when he mentioned it, making Lincoln the perfect cover city.

He wore a nondescript gray trench coat over a black suit. His shiny shoes were forgettable, as was his face. He'd made himself even more nonthreatening with a blond wig, a straw fedora, and round hipster glasses. People looked right through him, and they always had. As a young man, he'd hated it, but now it was his greatest gift.

Footfalls silent against the thick carpet, he walked to the elevator. With one white-gloved fingertip, he pressed the down button. A woman in a red cocktail dress breathed out alcohol fumes next to him, and he held his breath as he waited for the car. She looked like she wanted to talk, then took in his glasses and his bland expression and changed her mind. That boded well for his disguise.

A few minutes later, he was walking briskly uptown toward the Natural History Museum. A yellow cab honked, and car exhaust fouled the air. Other pedestrians jostled by with their own odors. He walked past Grand Central Terminal without sparing it a glance, his straw fedora tilted down to shadow his face from its surveillance cameras.

Based on the instructions emailed to the photographer he'd murdered, he needed to be at the event a half hour early to set up his camera and drone. He had plenty of extra batteries and an external charger, plus a special item he'd secreted in a flat gray box next to the emergency exit the day before, when he'd mapped his methods of egress from the building.

He tripped up the stairs where, with a smile, he presented the dead man's credentials, submitted to wanding with a metal detector, and allowed his boxes to be opened and searched. He was just a simple geek come to film the event, and he had nothing to hide. The bored security guard bought into that theory, too, and barely looked at him.

No one even looked at him twice as he walked up to the second floor, behind the tail of the giant blue whale. He was here to film the event, to watch Tesla, and to search for his moment. No one needed to worry about him.

Until he wanted them to.

13

House under Grand Central Terminal
March 10, evening

Joe knew he should be getting dressed for tonight's party, but instead, he sat in his parlor and tried to catch up on his email. He'd taken a day off after the sub accident, and things were still piled up. Pleasant down here, with the electric fire lit in the hearth, Edison curled at his feet, and a warm cup of Earl Grey steaming on the antique side table.

He loved the room—thick Persian carpet, floor-to-ceiling bookcases filled with leather-bound books, carved mantel over the electric fire, oil painting of the builder's daughter in a yellow dress, and original Victorian furniture. This room had survived nearly unchanged for a century, a time capsule from the days of Jules Verne, HG Wells, and Nikola Tesla himself. The only thing from the modern era was Joe's laptop.

But he still felt out of sorts. He'd heard nothing about a further investigation of the crash and was starting to worry they were either treating it as an accident, or they weren't even trying to find another suspect beyond him. He'd tried to hire another submarine to go out and look at the crash site, but even Marnie hadn't been able to find one. He could rent a dive boat, but he'd have to go outside to board it. He needed a submarine, something small enough to make it up the pipes to his dock, something he could get in and out of without going outside. He'd already ordered another one, but the company was backed up and it would take months to be delivered to New York. So, he was stuck.

A ping told him he had another email.

"Last one," he told Edison.

The dog didn't even twitch an ear. He was used to false promises.

The email was from Alan Wright, a billionaire involved in the scavenger hunt. Joe had known him a long time, but he wouldn't call him a friend. Still, he clicked on it. He could practically hear Alan's voice as he read the words.

You mucked it up for all of us. I know you didn't run down Prince Timgad's sub, but public opinion is running against you. Blue Dream's video of you swimming in to get the flag with a dopey grin on your face has gone viral. I figure your people are too kind to send you the link, but here it is.

Will you show your face at the gala tonight or hide away in your hole?

- A

Joe hesitated before clicking the link. Footage from the scavenger hunt. Probably embarrassing, but maybe there would be something useful. Either way, he'd better see it before he left. Someone was bound to ask about it.

The video started off pretty innocuous—ten flags drifting from side to side underwater. He'd forgotten they'd been so well-lit. So peaceful looking.

Then a dark form some distance away came into view—him with Edison tucked under his stomach. The dog looked calm, glancing around with his eyes relaxed and his tail wagging.

"You love being underwater, don't you, boy?"

Edison lifted his head.

"Sorry." Joe's stomach tightened at the thought of going out in a submarine. But he would, as soon as the new sub arrived. He wasn't going to let his world get any smaller. "We're going to stay on land for a while."

On-screen he advanced on the beckoning flags. He looked so smug and self-satisfied. He'd never really understood before that moment what people meant when they said someone looked punchable. *Dopey grin* was actually a kind characterization. The figure shot, missed, then nailed the flag right in the middle, and mercifully turned away from the camera. At least it had been a good shot.

A shadow appeared in the frame behind him—too large to be his sub or the prince's. He leaned forward. This might be worth the embarrassment of having watched the rest of the video.

He downloaded the video and enhanced the shadow, but the ocean's visibility was so low he couldn't get a clearer view no matter what he tried. The police were right—the shadow could have been a boat passing overhead. But he knew it was something else.

Deciding he needed more information, he hacked into the contest site, accessed its database, and got a longer version of the video. He hadn't known it, but the organizers had had an underwater camera set up by the contest flags. Which made sense. They wanted to show the flags being taken and had to verify the order in which the submarines arrived.

He fast-forwarded through the footage. Nothing of interest happened before his arrival, but after he took the flag, a giant shadow went by and stopped. That must have been the larger sub passing by and crashing into the prince's submarine. Unfortunately, the crash was off camera, or that would have solved all his problems. The shadow wasn't definitive enough to be identified as a submarine either, but he knew it was.

Time passed with nothing happening. Then the camera caught a faraway figure in a black wetsuit and long fins. It wasn't him, because Edison wasn't nearby and Edison had never left his side down there. It wasn't Vivian, because she'd been wearing the emergency suit and hadn't had fins. It wasn't the bodyguard, because he was already dead.

At this distance, he couldn't tell much about the figure. He compared the swimmer to the gait-recognition videos he had on his computer that he'd been analyzing for Pellucid, his first company. They'd started with facial-recognition software, still their bread and butter, and moved into gait-recognition. Easier to identify someone at a distance from their walk than their face, and walks were harder to disguise. He didn't have much data on swimming recognition, but something about the way the diver moved at the hips and shoulders looked feminine.

His phone buzzed. A text from Maeve Wadsworth. She'd designed his underground garden, and they'd been seeing each other for a while. She was his date for the gala tonight, and he was late.

Will I be alone here all evening? she asked.

On my way, he texted back. Not exactly true yet, but it would be soon.

He closed the laptop and jogged upstairs to put on his tuxedo. It was just back from the cleaners. He took off the plastic covering and put the tux on as fast as he could. He even remembered to dress up the dog. It didn't take too long.

He fiddled with his bow tie. Easier to memorize the schedule of the trains going into Grand Central than to tie a simple tie. Why was that?

He stepped back and looked at himself in the cheval mirror as he imagined the previous owners had been doing since the turn of the last century. They probably hadn't looked much different than he did now. His tuxedo was cut in a classic style. Simple black with a crisp white shirt, no tails.

"I look like a penguin," he told Edison.

The dog looked handsome in his black service vest with a bow tie attached to his collar. He didn't look like a penguin.

"And not a cool-looking emperor penguin either, more like a goofy macaroni penguin."

Edison wagged his tail, hopefully appreciating the joke.

"It won't matter because everyone will be looking at you, and you look very dapper." But that wasn't true. Everyone would be looking at Joe. He was attending a gala at the Museum of Natural History arranged by Blue Dreams weeks before to celebrate the team that captured the first flag. The contest was to take place over several weeks, and they had plans to celebrate each stage.

Now the celebration was to remember Prince Timgad's bodyguard and the accident that had killed him and spared Joe. They were going to discuss whether the contest should continue. It would, of course, continue. It involved too much money and had too much momentum to stop. But many attendees would probably blame Joe that the discussion had to come up at all.

He'd dropped out of the race. After that, he'd wanted to donate his entrance fee to the bodyguard's family quietly, but Mr. Rossi had convinced him to announce his intentions publicly. He was even going to have to give a speech. He touched the notecards in his pocket, and Edison nudged his knee. The dog knew how much he hated public speaking.

"Let's get moving. We'll walk to the Bryant Park Station, then take the B to the museum station. Does that sound good?"

Edison padded across the marble floor and into the hall. He was ready to go.

Joe took another last look at himself, tilted the mirror to check out his newly polished shoes, and gave up on any more preening. He looked as good as he was going to, and Maeve was already irritated. Best to get moving.

He hurried down the stairs and made a quick stop in the front hall to take a few keys off the ring hanging there and to pick up a flashlight from his collection. He never left the house without a flashlight these days. As well-lit as most tunnels were, he didn't want to get stranded if the lights went out.

Edison waited by the front door. He looked striking—yellow fur bright against the red door, black bow tie gleaming.

Joe opened the door and stepped out into his garden. The rich green smell of plants greeted him. The ceiling lights had dimmed to indigo. In the world above, the sun had long since set and night had settled.

Edison followed across the soft carpet of green to the back door. Joe entered his security code and pushed open the thick steel door. It always reminded him of opening a vault. He reset his alarm codes. He'd upgraded his security after a break-in and was pretty sure it was easier to break into Fort Knox than his house.

Edison went out first. Joe went second and closed the giant door. The difference between this raw tunnel and his finished and cheerful home tunnel was stark. Out here, the air smelled of rock, mildew, and rust. He grinned. Some people hated the tunnels, but he loved them. They were his backyard.

Edison sniffed an unused train track gone rusty with time, probably tracing the footsteps of a rat. He looked back as if to signal an all clear. That was good enough for Joe.

He and the dog set off up the unused track. This track would connect with other tracks where trains still ran, so they'd have to stay on their toes, but the subway station they were after wasn't far, about half a mile. He fell into the gait he'd developed for the train tracks—shorter than his usual stride, measured by the distance between train ties, and not his natural pace. He ought to film it for his gait-recognition database.

"Feels good to be out, doesn't it?" He took a glow-in-the-dark tennis ball out of his pocket and tossed it along the unused track.

Edison ran for it.

He felt himself unwind. He kept up a quick pace while playing fetch. He bet he'd be the only person with a wet tennis ball in his tuxedo pocket.

Eventually, they reached an in-service track, with a live third rail, and that was the end of their game of fetch. They'd gone this way so many times before that they were both on autopilot.

He and Edison walked to the Bryant Park Station at 42nd Street (green, blue). The station felt homey. He liked the dark orange pillars and the gleaming white tiles. Edison liked the smells. He stayed close—as soon as he donned his vest, he was all business—but his nose swept back and forth along the platform until the train came and they got on together. The subway riders, as always, smiled at Edison. A little girl wearing a Batgirl costume told him his tie looked sharp. Edison's tie, not Joe's. He wondered why she was dressed up as Batgirl, since it wasn't Halloween, but it was New York, so he didn't ask.

At 81st Street Station (purple, cyan), he exited the train and waited for the crowd to disperse, then headed to the stairs at the end of the platform. He and Edison had unlimited access to the tunnels under the city—a perk of his underground house. The house came with access to all the tunnels for the designer and his descendants. While he wasn't technically a descendant, he'd procured the house from one, and his security clearance made it easy for him to receive the keys to the kingdom.

Several yards down the tunnel, an old metal door had been set into the wall. It had been placed there a century before and been well maintained ever since—the surfaces were regularly painted and the hinges oiled. The door opened onto a steam tunnel. Many buildings in New York City ran on steam, including the Museum of Natural History. He had keys for all of them, at least for their steam tunnels.

He unlocked the door using a key from another era— long-barreled with a hexagonal head.

Insulation-wrapped pipes ran along the right-hand wall. Little dust had gathered on the insulation, so the pipes had been changed recently. Con Edison worked constantly on the system, and he often met their workers in his wanderings in his giant backyard.

Edison crowded up next to him, and he petted the dog's head. "It's OK, boy. Just us."

He walked faster. Although he usually liked being underground, Edison hated the hot and humid steam tunnels. He'd had a bad experience in a steam tunnel, and he clearly remembered it.

The door at the other end of the tunnel stood open, and a woman in a black and silver evening gown beckoned. "Come on, Edison! Don't you look fancy?"

The dog broke away and hurried toward her. Maeve. She'd dyed her hair silver and swept it upward. Black stripes ran down her silver dress, curving across her breasts in toward her waist and back out across her hips. Joe wanted to run his hands along those lines.

"You look fantastic." She always did. He leaned in to kiss her, and a long time later, she stepped back.

"We could skip the first part of the party and come back later." His voice was husky.

"Tempting." She kissed his neck above his collar. "But I'm not letting you out of your speech."

He kissed her again. "You sure?"

She pulled away. "Nice try."

Someone cleared his throat from the shadows behind her, and Joe jumped.

"It's Mr. Karpenko," Maeve said. "The museum sent him to keep an eye on us."

"Thank you for taking the time." As part of his steam-tunnel life, he had to get special permission and an escort to enter many buildings from the basement door. He knew a lot of security guards.

"Just doing my job." Karpenko stood only a little taller than Maeve and was small-boned. He seemed like an odd choice for a security guard, but maybe he had ninja skills.

Maeve took Joe's hand and led him up a set of utility stairs, her glamorous dress out of place against the raw concrete. "You wouldn't believe who is up there."

Karpenko locked the door behind them and traipsed a foot from Joe's heels. His proximity made Edison uncomfortable, and Joe motioned for the dog to go farther ahead.

"They're even filming it," she said. "They have drones flying around the museum."

Films with multiple angles of his humiliation. Great.

14

Museum of Natural History
March 10, evening

Vivian wished she were anywhere but at a fancy gala at the museum. She'd been here on field trips, and she'd loved the exhibits of fish and polar bears and crabs, and the life-sized blue whale hanging from the ceiling. If she remembered correctly, it was ninety-four feet long and weighed twenty-one thousand pounds.

But the vast room felt too much like the ocean. Dappled blue light shone down on the whale and lit up partygoers. It reminded her of her time in the submarine.

She did a quick circuit to get a feel for her surroundings. Blue Dreams had brought in a catering company and set up buffet tables in the corners. Waiters circulated through the crowd carrying silver trays loaded with Champagne flutes. A platform had been erected underneath the whale's tail and a blue curtain hung at the back. That was the makeshift stage where Tesla would be speaking later, assuming he showed up.

A woman in a black dress that looked like it was made from garbage bags sneered at Vivian. She sneered back. She knew she looked like a poor relation in her black pants and jacket and fancy white shirt. Her sister, Lucy, would have been able to list her sartorial shortcomings in detail, but this woman had no right to.

People's eyes slid right past her. Not a bad quality in a bodyguard, even a one-armed one. A warm hand touched her elbow, and she turned to her partner for the evening, Dirk Norbye. An old friend from the Army, he was currently in the NYPD but often moonlighted as a bodyguard for Tesla. He looked fine in a tailored blue suit that probably cost a month's salary.

"Did you see Tesla?" she asked. Dirk had looked on the second floor, and she'd taken the first floor.

"Nope," he said. "But I did spot a guy you might want to talk to."

He pointed, and she knocked down his pointing hand because it looked too obvious. The hottest guy she'd seen in a long time stood near the buffet. He had curly black hair and pecs she'd like to bounce a quarter off. The errant lock that had fallen out of his wetsuit hood arched above his forehead. The diver from the police harbor unit who had rescued her and Tesla.

"Wishing he'd had a reason for mouth-to-mouth?" Dirk asked.

"He is way too hot to be single."

"You'd be surprised," Dirk said.

"Would I?" she asked. "Tell me details."

The man headed toward them.

"Hey, Norbye." He shook Dirk's hand and turned to her. "You look a lot better than the last time we met."

He remembered her as a drowned rat. Great. "Thank you."

"Officer Baxter," he said.

She cleared her throat. "I'm Sergeant Torres."

That wasn't even accurate, since she wasn't in the Army anymore. Smooth, she thought. Very smooth.

He shook her hand. No wedding ring. Nice eyes, green.

Dirk herded them toward the buffet. Crab cakes, oysters, and who knew what other kinds of seafood were calling his name. She could go a long time without eating seafood again.

"That submarine you were in was quite a mess." Baxter looked her up and down. "But you look great."

"I got lucky. Just the arm and a cut on the head."

"The other guy wasn't so lucky," Baxter said.

Dirk had found paradise. He loaded up a plate and disappeared into the crowd. She'd eaten at home. With one arm, she wouldn't be able to hold a plate to put food on, let alone eat it.

Baxter picked up a plate.

"Were you able to bring up the body?" She moved down the food line next to him. He picked only vegetarian items. Interesting.

"Not me personally, but I was part of the team that went down to get his body."

She shuddered. "Not sure I ever want to go back."

"You'll go back. There's something enticing about water." He pointed to her sling. "And even injured, you had nerves of steel when it counted. I've done a lot of rescues, and you were the most together person I've ever plucked out of the water."

She shrugged away the compliment. "Did you bring up the submarines?"

"A retrieval isn't in the budget. Someone will probably turn them into dive destinations. Not a lot of crashed submarines around here."

"Don't you need them to determine the cause of the crash?" If they were threatening to charge Tesla with manslaughter, didn't they need to do a thorough investigation first? Unless the charges had been a bluff to get more information out of him. You never knew with cops.

"Pictures are plenty. Looked like you guys smashed into each other." Behind his head, a sperm whale and a giant squid battled to the death in a diorama. She sympathized.

"We were smashed *into*," she said. "You can't believe those two tiny subs could do that kind of damage to each other, even in a head-on collision."

"I can believe a lot of things." He put two oysters on his plate. "But not everything."

"You don't believe my statement?" Her arm throbbed, and she knew that meant she was getting too upset, but she wasn't going to back down.

"Here's what I know." Baxter looked certain in what he knew. "Something went wrong down there. You broke your arm, the bodyguard died, and your driver was high as a kite when we fished him out."

"Mr. Tesla wasn't driving in that condition. As I made clear in my statement."

Baxter held up his free hand in a pacifying gesture. "I'm here for the food and the entertainment."

A flash of silver caught her eye from across the room. Maeve. She and Tesla were easy to recognize—Tesla looking suave in a tuxedo and his tiny girlfriend in her super-fashionable dress and silver hair. They were turning heads all the way down the hall.

"I'm here to work, Sergeant Baxter. But thank you for coming to our assistance."

She turned her back on Baxter and his gorgeous green eyes. He'd gotten a lot less attractive after he'd said he didn't believe her. Funny how that worked.

15

Museum of Natural History
March 10, evening

Joe paused at the crowd's edge. He hated crowds almost as much as Maeve loved them. As soon as he stopped, Edison sat. Joe looked at a pod of dolphins swimming with a school of tuna, frozen in place for the exhibit. He remembered piloting his sub in the middle of a pod of dolphins once, how they'd practically danced around him, and clicks and whistles had come through his hydrophone. It'd be months before he got a new submarine and joined them again.

"I see Vivian." Maeve was already waving. "She looks great. Really butch. She totally has the legs to pull that suit off."

Mr. Rossi must have hired Vivian to be his bodyguard at the event. He was surprised she'd agreed. He suspected she'd be happy to kill him herself over the refrigerator, not to mention the recent headlines blaring that they were in a relationship.

Vivian came over. She did look good—tall and fit and angry. He got ready to apologize.

"Mr. Tesla." She gave him a frosty smile.

"Uh-oh," Maeve said. "What did you do to make her so mad?"

"I was trying to be nice."

Maeve tilted her silvery head. "I see a client on the other side of the room. Far away from you guys. Really far."

Quicksilver fast, she darted into the crowd.

"Your mom likes the fridge," Joe said. "I'm sorry it caused you problems."

"Yes." She clearly wasn't going to talk about the refrigerator. "They're not bringing the subs up."

"What?" His answer came out louder than he'd intended, and Edison leaned against him. "Someone probably murdered the bodyguard."

"You know, murders seem to happen every time you go outside. Have you thought of staying home?"

He laughed. "I basically do. I just have a large home—especially if you count the swimming pool in my backyard."

"I count that as the ocean. And I'm not swimming in it again until you get rid of your pet sharks." She smiled when she said it. A good sign.

"It's the hit-and-run drivers you need to worry about," he said.

That prompted another smile. Eager to capitalize on her good humor, he filled her in on his findings with the video from the contest.

"I want to hire you to keep going with the investigation," Joe said. "Are you in?"

"I'm in. I've been hassled by the police and mocked in the newspaper as your arm candy. I want to sort out this damn crash already."

"Which was worse?" Joe asked.

"Interrogation while doped up on painkillers while trying to stop my mom from accepting the fridge, or the public perception we're dating?"

She looked pretty mad about both scenarios.

"You don't want to know," she said.

Answer enough. "Sorry about the press. I didn't tell them that, and I thought if I denied it, it might make it worse."

"Let's get this over with," she said. "And nail whoever is putting us through this."

Maeve was back. "They're loaning us watches!"

"Watches?" Vivian said. "Gee whiz."

Vivian wasn't a gadget person.

Maeve held out her wrist to display a bulky watch with a screen on the front instead of a clock face. The screen displayed a moving aerial view of the hall. "It shows footage from the drone flying around in here. You can see everything on these!"

"So. We can spy on our fellow partygoers?" Vivian asked.

"There's no audio," Maeve said. "Can you believe how dusty the back of that whale is? Really breaks the illusion."

She fastened a watch around Joe's wrist and handed the third watch to Vivian.

"Could be useful," Maeve said. "For increased situational awareness."

"If you can't beat 'em." Vivian fumbled to put the watch on her wounded arm. It looked awkward, but Joe knew better than to offer to help.

Alan Wright appeared at his elbow. "You look pretty fit for a sub-crash survivor."

"Assuming they don't drown, sub-crash survivors usually look pretty good," Maeve said. "They're like canned fruit in syrup."

Alan snorted and gave Maeve an appreciative look. Joe remembered, again, why he didn't like him.

"I heard they're considering manslaughter charges against you," Alan said.

Maeve shot him a worried look. They hadn't talked about that.

Joe glanced down at the scene on his wrist. The drone hovered a few feet over their heads for a few seconds, then flitted off like a hummingbird, showing a shot of a walrus.

"I'm sure the investigation will exonerate us," Vivian said. "Since we're blameless."

Alan snorted again. Joe hated that sound.

"I'm taking my sub out tomorrow to have a look-see, Joe," Alan said. "I suppose you're too freaked out to join me."

"I could manage." Joe worked on his poker face. He didn't want Alan to know how desperately he wanted to go down and look at the crash site himself.

"No dogs allowed," Alan said. "But I can bring it to your dock through that old water outflow. You won't even have to step outside."

"I'm in." Now he'd owe Alan. He hated that, but it would be worth it.

Vivian stared at her wrist, as if transfixed by the drone's-eye view. She looked nervous, probably worried she might have to go back out in the sub. He didn't blame her. He wasn't looking forward to his first time back in a submarine either, but he wasn't going to let his fears shut off another part of the world.

He couldn't.

16

Museum of Natural History
March 10, late evening

Avi flew the drone back for its last battery change. The doughty black and white device came straight for him, as loyal as a falcon returning to the leather glove of its master. Light caught the dust motes around it, and they swirled in a dance both ancient and modern.

His shoulders were tense from working the remote control all evening while he'd waited for this moment, but soon his mission would be over and he could take a long soak in the fine bathtub at the Hyatt with Epsom salts.

He reached out his arm for his flying machine. Its weight settled into his outstretched palm, and he drew his hand back from the railing. Using the joystick, he swiveled the tiny camera around to study the people around him, including those above and below. No one watched the anonymous man with the drone. He was simply a fixture at the whale's tail, like the museum exhibits they no longer bothered to look at. He was the invisible help, not worth these fancy people's fancy time.

Still, he did a second pan with the camera to verify that he was unobserved. With a practiced motion, he took out the spent battery with one gloved hand, added the battery to the box next to his black shoes, and slipped in a fresh one. The drone was ready for action.

Instead of releasing it into the air as he'd done all night, he fitted a small tripod to the drone's belly. He'd modified an off-the-shelf tripod to make it sturdier and to build in a specialized frame for its new cargo. Carefully, he lined the tripod up with the camera's view. He checked the tripod with a tiny level to make sure it was perfectly straight.

Again, a slow camera pan to make sure no one cared about his actions, then he casually drew a 9 mm Ruger from the gray box he'd stashed near the emergency exit. The gun was clean. He'd purchased it from his long-term weapons supplier, one of few men he trusted with his life, and he'd been assured it couldn't be traced.

The modified grip fit easily into his gloved palm, and he tightened his fingers around it, whispering a blessing before fitting the gun into the tripod. Far below, a man in a navy blue tuxedo stepped onstage to a smattering of applause and began to introduce Tesla. Avi had to be quick.

He cupped the drone in a gloved hand to hide the gun from view as long as possible, then used the controls to have it lift off his palm. The drone staggered and dipped next to the railing like a baby bird on its first flight. He adjusted for the extra weight. He'd spent hours practicing with the drone with the gun and without, and he knew it could carry its deadly cargo as far as needed.

Stabilized, the drone soared along the back of the whale, across the crowd, toward its destiny.

17

Vivian wanted to go home. Her arm ached, the view from the little drone made her dizzy but she couldn't seem to stop watching it, and Tesla was about to go onstage. The only worse thing for a bodyguard would be if he stepped into a war zone.

Mr. Rossi had hired her and Dirk to watch over Tesla, but Dirk was off chatting up some blonde over by the whale's tail. Meantime, she was by the whale's head, standing behind the curtain on a makeshift stage, basically just a raised platform. She looked across a sea of overdressed partygoers. The attendees seemed focused on each other. The waiters busily serving overpriced appetizers and Champagne she couldn't drink on duty. Nothing threatening.

But her gut told her something was off.

Maybe she was still keyed up from the sub accident, and it didn't mean anything. She wished Dirk was down here and that she had two arms. And that Tesla wasn't about to step out in front of the crowd and become a giant target.

Tesla fiddled with his tie. The dog had picked up on his nervousness and leaned against the knee of his expensive tuxedo. Yellow dog hairs clung to the black fabric.

"You're pulling it off center." Maeve reached up and straightened his tie, smoothing it into a credible bow. "You'll be great."

"Why can't I make the announcement via email?" Tesla asked.

"Maximum impact," Maeve said. "It's kind of a PR gesture, so you have to do it publicly."

"I'm not doing it for PR." Tesla shifted from foot to foot, like he was about to sprint away. He touched his jacket pocket, where Vivian bet he kept a couple of index cards with notes for his speech like some kind of security blanket. She knew he had it memorized. Tesla memorized everything.

Maeve gestured for him to bend down and whispered something in his ear. Tesla gave her a wicked grin, and Vivian was glad she'd missed whatever that was about.

She glanced down at her wrist to give them privacy. The drone flew along the back of the whale toward them, ready to film Tesla's speech. Maeve was right about the dust. Vivian's mother would have insisted on climbing up there and riding the whale with a feather duster to clean it before the party.

That image made Vivian smile. They'd get through this. She was probably just keyed up because the last time she and Tesla had gone out anywhere, it had ended in a submarine crash and they'd both nearly died. Just an echo of worry.

Tesla stepped into the spotlight, and polite applause greeted him. Vivian stood next to Maeve, who peeked through the curtain to watch Tesla. Vivian ignored her boss and scanned the crowd. Everything looked fine. So why did she feel like it wasn't?

"Thank you all for turning out tonight." Tesla held on to the podium in the same way she'd grabbed on to the escape ladder. Not a natural performer. "Tragedy has touched our event, an endeavor of exploration and charity."

She checked the drone's view. Pretty handy having eyes in the sky. Nothing to worry about from the drone's point of view either—most people were listening, a few checking their watches like she was. Nobody tense or reaching for a weapon. The drone seemed sluggish. Maybe it was running out of battery power. It had been circling them all night.

"...and so, I'm withdrawing from the competition," Tesla announced.

Of course he was. His submarine lay in pieces at the bottom of the ocean. But the crowd still looked surprised. Maybe they had two submarines for this kind of emergency and couldn't believe Tesla didn't.

"And I'd like to donate my entrance fee to the family of Hector Connelly."

That was the first time Vivian had even heard the bodyguard's name. All part of the bodyguarding job—live and die anonymous. At least Tesla had found out his name and mentioned it in public. That was something.

Vivian studied the applauding crowd. Nothing amiss. A waiter stood next to the buffet table by the stage holding a tray of Champagne flutes, probably for Tesla when he finished. Maybe he was going to drink a toast to Mr. Connelly. If she died, would he drink a toast to her? Donate money to her mother? Probably.

She glanced back at her wrist. The drone lumbered along the sweep of the whale's head and dropped straight down. On her watch, Tesla's form grew larger. The drone was coming in for a close-up.

Doing a close-up made sense, but instinct propelled her out from behind the curtain. She shielded her eyes from the spotlight and searched for the drone. She heard it—its tiny engine sounded like a hive of angry bees. It had to be close.

Tesla spotted her and half turned. He had a puzzled expression, but she didn't have time to explain. She squinted at the drone.

White, with two sticks hanging from the bottom and four rotors keeping it aloft. As expected, a camera was tucked under its belly. Below the camera a familiar black shape lined up with the lens.

"Gun!" Vivian was halfway across the stage. "Down."

Tesla dropped behind the podium. The only cover on stage. Edison streaked from backstage straight to his master's side.

She swore. She hadn't been allowed to bring a gun into the museum. She had exactly zero weapons. She had a sling for her arm. A jacket. Sensible shoes.

The drone shot the podium. Splinters flew. The recoil knocked the drone back, and the next shot went wide behind the podium. A scream echoed around the hall. The drone rose up to go over the podium so Tesla would be in the gun's sights.

She sprinted past Tesla, snagged the waiter's metal tray, and winged it right at the drone. A person might have seen the movement in his peripheral version, maybe ducked. But the electronic device could see only what its camera saw, and it stayed still, firing more rounds at the stage.

The tray clipped a rotor. The device slewed to the side. The tray fell, cracking some guy in a tux right on the head. He folded to the ground. Hopefully he'd be OK.

Like a fool, Tesla had come out from behind the podium as soon as the gunshots stopped. He ran for Vivian, probably thinking he could help. The dog followed close behind.

The crowd was shrieking and ducking and running. No way she could get through that scrum to get to the drone. And the drone was lurching closer to Tesla.

Tesla had almost reached her. Right out in the open like a target. She was about to get very fired, but there was nothing for it.

She shouldered him off the stage, and he hit the carpet hard. But at least he wasn't such a target. The dog leaped after him. She was glad Edison hadn't decided to bite her for knocking his master around.

The drone tried to rise, but couldn't. It looked like the rotor she'd hit wasn't turning. Score one for the tray.

Still, the drone wasn't fully incapacitated. It wobbled toward Tesla as he tried to sit up. Edison stood between his master and the gun, growling. Too high for the dog to reach, but she bet he'd have snatched it out of the air if he could have.

She jumped off the stage and landed next to Tesla, bending her knees to take up the shock. The drone dropped another foot.

"Get under the stage," she yelled. "Underneath."

Tesla rolled under the stage, but Edison stayed next to her. He was a warrior, that dog.

She snatched the tablecloth off a nearby table. Glasses and shrimp cocktail crashed to the floor. The drone dropped down almost to floor level, going after Tesla under the stage, as she'd planned.

Flaring the tablecloth like a matador, she whipped it around and dropped it over the drone. Before the drone had a chance to move, she jumped on top. Something made a satisfying crunch. The machine struggled under the tablecloth, and she stomped on it until it was still, then a couple more times because she was mad.

She spotted Dirk by the exit, helping people through, looking calm and unruffled. A quick glance at the whale's tail confirmed the drone operator was gone. She scanned the crowd, but nobody seemed suspicious. If only she'd taken more notice of the drone operator, but all she remembered was a black suit and a white shirt, rounded glasses, and a mop of blond hair. Probably a wig.

Tesla climbed out from under the stage.

"Are you OK?" Tesla asked.

Her arm hurt like hell. "Fine."

"Thank you," he said. "Again."

Edison licked her sore arm.

"Don't send me any more kitchen appliances," she told Tesla.

He was already over by the wreckage, stomping on the drone. She was pretty sure it was out of commission, but she hated to stop him. She liked hearing the sounds of the damn thing breaking.

But there might still be danger. She grabbed Tesla's arm and hustled him toward the door. She wouldn't feel better until Tesla was someplace secure. Dirk jogged over.

"We have to leave, sir," said Dirk.

"Maeve!" Tesla shook free of Vivian's grasp and jumped back onto the stage.

Vivian flanked Tesla on one side, Dirk went to the other, and they ran next to him. Her arm twinged every time she moved. She hoped she hadn't knocked something important loose. Time for that later. First, they had to get Tesla and Maeve to safety.

Faster than they were, Edison had reached the blue curtain. He howled. The hair on the back of her neck rose.

Tesla sprinted to him, and she and Dirk kept pace. Tesla yanked the curtain back so hard it fell off and dropped onto the stage, blue material mounding up behind him. She looked up for a threat. Nothing. Dirk looked behind them.

Tesla let out a moan and dropped to his knees. Maeve sat with her back against the wall. Her face was paper white, and one hand touched a wet wound in her chest. Red blood ran across the sparkly silver beads on her dress.

Tesla tore off his jacket and balled it up before pressing it onto the wound. Maeve groaned.

"It's OK," he said. "It's OK."

"I'll get a doctor." Dirk hightailed it off the stage.

Vivian applied direct pressure to the makeshift bandage so Tesla would have his hands free, and also because she wasn't sure he knew how. Warm blood soaked into the shirt and wet her fingertips. She gritted her teeth and kept the pressure on.

Tesla wiped the blood off his palm on his pants and stroked Maeve's face. Her eyes drifted closed, eyelashes casting shadows down her ashen cheeks.

"She can still hear you," Vivian said. "Talk to her."

She'd read that hearing was the last thing to go when a person died, but she didn't tell Tesla.

Tesla murmured something to Maeve, and her lips twitched into a tiny smile.

Dirk was back with a white-haired woman in a floor-length green satin gown.

"I'm a doctor," she said. "Let me see."

Vivian stepped back, and the woman bent over Maeve. Vivian flicked another look around the room. Everyone was heading away from them, the drone operator long gone, probably halfway to New Jersey.

"Let's get her lying down," the doctor said. "On her side."

That probably meant she was afraid Maeve would choke on her own blood. Vivian hoped Tesla didn't understand. She helped the doctor ease Maeve flat on the stage. Maeve's eye makeup glittered in the overhead lighting. She was so pale. Tesla held her hand against his chest. Her blood streaked his white shirt. Edison cuddled up to her back, probably sensing she needed his warmth.

Dirk was back with a tablecloth. He wrapped it around Maeve's legs. "Ambulance will be here in three minutes."

Tesla twitched, and the dog whimpered.

She looked down at Maeve's anguished face.

It was going to be a long three minutes.

18

Avi had been one of the first out of the Hall of Ocean Life. He turned left and ducked into the Discovery Room. During museum hours, it brimmed with noisy children, but after hours, it was deserted. More important, the cameras had been placed such that there was a blind spot by the door.

Careful to stay in that spot, he shed his glasses, wig, and gloves. He dumped them into a specimen drawer, also in the blind spot, and added a label to it that said "Dress Up." The items would probably be found anyway, but they couldn't be tied to him and with any luck they'd be contaminated by other DNA before they were. He ran both hands through his natural hair and stepped back into the cameras' view.

The crowd had thinned somewhat, but enough people still milled about to offer him cover. The crowd pushed through the 81st Street exit. There hadn't been time to set up a police cordon, and he slipped into the crowd, shedding the bulky watch he'd been given to watch the drone's antics.

A few meters later, he was inside Central Park and heading south. As he walked, he rolled up his sleeves, took off his jacket and tie, and unbuttoned the top few buttons of his shirt. He didn't look like a partygoer anymore, just a guy in black pants and a white shirt, maybe a waiter.

He walked through the park like a man who knew where he was going, but wasn't in any hurry to get there. Nothing remarkable.

Remarkable was Tesla's survival. Avi had lined up the shot perfectly, but the man had turned at the last instant, warned by the tall woman with her arm in a sling who had knocked out the drone. She was either very lucky or very good. He hoped it was just luck. Luck ran out.

Now he was in the position of having to make a second attempt on a skittish target. Tesla was always going to be a difficult target. He lived underground, and the subway tunnels leading to his home were under surveillance. There were many tunnels, of course, which meant there would be more hours of surveillance tapes than the police could ever look through, but Avi didn't like taking chances. It would take a great deal of stealth and time to find Tesla's underground house, and it was probably well fortified.

It would be best to get him when he came out, but Tesla rarely left Grand Central Terminal—a building full of people, surveillance cameras, police, military, and reporters. He ate in the terminal, but switched up the restaurants. He had a dog that would make it difficult to get close to him undetected.

Tesla was a challenge.

Avi didn't like challenges. He liked straightforward jobs, easy jobs, quiet jobs. He tried to mitigate risk and surprise. He'd already broken one rule by trying again after the first shot had missed today. A weakness.

He would go to his hotel room and soak his shoulder. He would eat a healthful dinner. He would pray. And then he would kill Tesla. Soon.

19

Lenox Hill Hospital
March 11, very early in the morning

Joe sat next to Maeve's bedside, grateful the ambulance had delivered her to Lenox Hill Hospital—they had steam tunnels in the basement, and he'd been able to sprint across the city through the underground tunnels and get inside. The police had come and asked questions, the surgery to fix her gunshot damage had gone well, and Maeve slept in her hospital bed next to his chair.

He could do nothing for her except wait.

And find out who had done this to her.

He opened up his laptop and prepared to solve the police's case for them. They had stopped accusing him of manslaughter, either because of the attack or because they had finally examined the crash site properly. Either way, they were now convinced the submarine and the drone attack were both directed at him, but they had no idea who might want to kill him. He had no enemies, no heirs, and hadn't stuck his nose where it didn't belong for months. For the first time in a long time, he couldn't think of anyone who wanted to kill him. The prince might want to kill him now, but he hadn't had a real reason to do so before the accident, and certainly not in a way that had put his bodyguard and submarine at risk. Joe thought both attacks were connected to the prince.

Maeve lay as still as if the shot had killed her. Her doctor had assured him she would recover. Dr. Stauss, Joe's own physician, had stopped by and told him the same. But it would take time and pain. She didn't deserve this.

But this was what she'd gotten. Because of him.

Back to work. He'd sent Dirk to get a copy of the drone footage from the gala the night before. The footage had been streamed to their watches and backed up on a Blue Dreams server. They probably shouldn't have released it, but Dirk was persuasive, and he'd handed him a couple of jump drives when he delivered a change of clothes and his laptop.

He loaded the drives up. Seven (slate) files total. Six (orange) were twenty (blue, black) minutes long, the last fourteen (cyan, green). With any luck, the drone had captured footage of the shooter loading the gun onto it.

"Everything all right in here, Mr. Tesla?" A uniformed cop stuck his head through the door, as he'd done every half hour since he and Maeve had arrived.

"Yes." He kept his voice low and glanced at Maeve. She hadn't stirred. "Thank you."

The policeman closed the door.

He returned to his footage. The shooter had been careful. He or she pointed the camera down every time the drone flew back for a battery change. After more than an hour and another check-in from Officer Friendly, all he knew was that the shooter wore a nice pair of black shoes, well-polished and new-looking, and black dress pants, like practically every other guy at the event. Maybe the police could come up with a shoe size from the video, but the guy's feet didn't seem particularly large or small.

One interesting fact was that the drone had concentrated on Joe from the moment he arrived. Before his arrival, the drone had democratically circled the crowd, zooming in on talking groups, shooting background footage of the exhibits, the empty stage, and the whale. Pretty much what he'd expect.

But after he and Maeve walked in, the drone had turned into an airborne stalker. Within seconds of their arrival, it had zoomed right up to him, probably to confirm his identity. After that, the drone had circled back to check on him every few minutes. It hadn't, he was relieved to see, cared about Maeve or Vivian. If they were near him, the drone captured video of them, but it didn't follow them when they went off on their own. It stuck with Joe. The drone had been interested in him and had aimed at him. Maeve taking the bullet was an accident. Not her fault, his.

He sighed. The shadows of the police officers in front of the door moved. Someone had brought them coffee.

He returned to his footage. For over an hour, the drone had dogged him. It had stayed up high enough he hadn't noticed it particularly, although it had captured him glancing up in annoyance a couple times. His hair looked weird from an aerial view.

An hour later, he'd found his clue. The drone pilot had clipped the gun onto the back during its last battery change. The drone had flown more slowly after that, weighted down by the gun.

The drone hadn't handled the way the pilot had expected, and he'd made a mistake. Not enough to leave a clear picture of his face, but he'd loosed the drone as a waiter walked by in front of him, tucking his empty silver tray under his arm.

Joe slowed the footage of the moving tray. As it traveled to the waiter's arm, it reflected the shooter's face. Not for long, barely a frame, but that was enough.

He went to work on the image. His first company, Pellucid, specialized in facial-recognition software. The software needed certain points of familiarity, and the man's face was badly lit, distorted by a dent on the tray, and not quite in focus. But Joe could adjust for it. Or he could try.

Eventually, he had a usable face. It wouldn't be enough to convict the man, but it might be enough to find him.

He fed the enhanced image into his test databases. Nominally, he still worked for Pellucid, fixing the most difficult problems and sitting through board meetings via videoconferencing. But he'd kept it up to have access to the test databases, including a copy of the FBI's Next Generation Identification system. Another trolled Facebook and downloaded images. He didn't know how legal that was, but since he hadn't created it, that wasn't his current problem.

While the software compared the face he'd captured from the tray with the existing images, he watched Maeve sleep. Deep and even breathing. The monitors showed her heart was beating regularly, oxygen saturation at ninety-seven (scarlet, slate) percent. All indicators green. She was doing well. For someone who had been shot in his place.

He set his laptop on the edge of the bed, took her cool hand, and brushed strands of silver hair off her brow. A few hours ago, she'd been active and warm, laughing and kissing him in the steam tunnel. If she hadn't been near him, she would be home, safe and sound.

When they first got to the hospital, Vivian had lectured him. She'd told him this wasn't his fault. Crazy people did crazy things. He wasn't responsible for Maeve's shooting.

Logically, her words made sense, but in his heart he knew a woman he cared for had been shot, that she suffered, that she had months of recovery ahead, because of him. And that he would do whatever it took to find out why.

Images flashed across the laptop. Partial matches. Nothing to get excited about. The picture had been far from perfect, and the drone pilot might not be in any databases. Most people weren't, after all. He needed a solid match for the police to care. They'd have to reconstruct the work he'd done on their own, of course, but he could give them a place to start.

A quiet ping. Gently, he set Maeve's hand atop the thin blanket and picked up the laptop. A match.

After a few minutes of reading, he left the room. He waved to the uniformed policemen outside of the hospital room door as he left. It had to be boring duty, but he was grateful they were there to watch over Maeve.

Once he was out of earshot, he called Mr. Rossi. His bodyguards, Dirk and Parker, stayed close. Vivian had gone home a few hours before to rest up before going out with Wright in his sub at the crack of dawn. Mr. Rossi answered on the first ring.

"Sorry to wake you," Joe said.

"I haven't been to bed yet. Is Maeve all right?"

"The doctors say she's going to be fine. She's out of surgery and sleeping."

"Where are you?"

"I'm at Lenox Hill Hospital."

"Is it safe there?" Mr. Rossi asked.

"Two cops at her door, two bodyguards at the end of the hall. But that's not why I'm calling." Joe heard rustling sounds.

"Go ahead," Mr. Rossi said.

"I procured footage from the gala—"

"Procured how?" Mr. Rossi asked.

"Blue Dreams was live-streaming the drone, and there's a backup."

"That sounds legal enough."

"I was able to get an ID from the footage. Long process. Mostly legal, although technically I'm not allowed to run names through the FBI database for private use."

"That's more than a technicality. You—"

"The man who put that gun on the drone, presumably also the man who fired it, is called the Avenger of Blood."

Parker looked up and down the hall as if expecting the Avenger of Blood to be there. Which he might.

"I can't imagine that's on his birth certificate," Mr. Rossi said dryly.

"His real name isn't in the database. What's known is he is a hired killer. To date, he's killed thirty-four people, two in the United States."

"That sounds unfortunate." Ever unflappable, Mr. Rossi.

"Either the royal family thinks I tried to kill Prince Timgad, and they're going to keep trying to avenge that insult by killing me, or someone else has targeted me."

"I recommend you change your security arrangements," Mr. Rossi said. "Return to your house and stay there until further notice."

His world had just gotten smaller for the foreseeable future. He understood the logic of it, but he still needed to be able to search for the man who had shot Maeve. No matter what, Maeve was safest if he stayed away from her. "Agreed."

"I can arrange for your bodyguards to follow you, and request additional protection from the NYPD."

"Will they take the guards from Maeve's hospital room?"

"If they do, I'll send additional guards myself," Mr. Rossi said. "Put Parker on the line."

"Before I go, can I ask you to send this information along via secure channels?"

"Consider it done."

Joe handed the phone to Parker.

"It wasn't your fault, Mr. Tesla," Parker said before lifting the phone to his ear. "I hope that's clear."

"Sure," he said.

But it was his fault. And they all knew it.

20

Former sewage pipe
March 11, morning

It was still early when Vivian walked from one end of the
floating dock to the other. The dock was in a giant cave
hollowed out of Manhattan schist. A long time ago,
hopefully a really long time ago, sewage had flowed into this
cave from various pipes. Once enough was gathered
together, the sewage was pumped out into the ocean via a
single giant pipe. Now seawater filled that pipe and one end
was open to the ocean. It was possible to drive a personal
submarine through it.

Tesla swore he'd had the stone cleaned and the long-
unused sewage pipes behind her closed up, but she gave
them a suspicious look anyway. Just her luck something
would break and she would drown in a river of sewage. No
glory there.

Still, she had to admit it was pretty nice in here. Golden
LEDs placed strategically throughout the room illuminated a
rounded ceiling, like a huge egg, with a metal hatch that
looked like it belonged on a ship. The egg was half full of
brackish water and smelled like a hot day at the seashore.
Tesla had told her something about how it circulated so it
didn't stagnate, but she hadn't paid attention.

A round bubble surfaced in the middle of the room.
Wright's sub, bright and early and only an hour later than

he'd scheduled. For someone like Wright, that was practically on time.

His sub was identical to Tesla's—same bubble cockpit, same science skids—except this one was green instead of yellow. Even the sight of it spiked her blood pressure. And she'd thought she'd hated submarines before the crash.

Wright's sub had its name stenciled across one side. It was called, appropriately, *The Green Meanie*. Wright wasn't her first choice as a submarine pilot. She'd never trusted him. But she'd come to accompany him because Tesla was confined to his house until they figured out who had hired an assassin to kill him. If he'd been the original target of the submarine ramming, he couldn't go out in the ocean.

Wright had made it clear it was a one-time offer. Since she and Tesla worried something, or someone, would disturb crucial evidence that supported their version of events before they documented it, someone had to go now. And that someone was her.

Wright waved. "Ahoy, traveler!"

Nautical nonsense. She waved back and walked out onto the floating dock Tesla had installed in this large brick room. The dock had fat yellow fenders tied to it. No chance of scratching *The Green Meanie*. Too bad.

Her phone rang. Mr. Rossi.

"I have to take this," she said. "It'll just take a second."

Unless it was terrible news and she needed to go. Not that she wanted terrible news, but she wouldn't mind not getting on that sub. Maybe Mr. Rossi would send a replacement.

"Vivian?" Mr. Rossi asked. "Is this a bad time?"

"I'm about to climb aboard *The Green Meanie*," she said.

"Someone posted the video online of you getting Tesla out of the line of fire last night."

Hopefully, they hadn't captured her conking that old guy on the head with the tray. "Am I in trouble?"

"Trouble? No."

Wright looked ostentatiously at his wrist. He wasn't even wearing a wristwatch.

She held up one finger.

"It's gone viral. A hundred thousand views already."

Lucy would be furious her big sister had become an Internet sensation, and in that stupid suit, too. "Oh."

"I've been receiving calls requesting your services all morning. I'm quoting twice your usual rate."

"Sweet," she said. "I'll check in when I get back."

Mr. Rossi wished her a pleasant voyage and ended the connection. She hurried back to the sub.

"Is your employer, the brave Mr. Tesla, joining us?" Wright asked.

"Just me," she said. "And my camera."

"I can understand how the sub ride might be stressful for him."

Everything was about points with this guy. She wanted to stick up for Tesla, but couldn't come up with anything that didn't give Wright more information than he should have, so she settled for, "He's busy."

"Did his hot girlfriend make it?"

"Yes." This had *long day* written all over it.

Wright changed the subject. "Loved coming up that tunnel. Shameful to think it was once full of sewage being dumped straight into the ocean. Some amazing organisms are growing on the inside. Has your boss ever had a marine biologist down there?"

"I don't know."

"Tell him those are the kinds of things he needs to make a priority. It's too easy to ignore the natural world."

Wright might care about the natural world, but he was always quite happy to let the human world go, having abandoned his own wife and child. Vivian didn't say anything. Wright taking her out was a favor to Tesla, and Tesla needed all the favors he could get.

Instead, she climbed in through the open bubble and buckled in. Her body remembered what had happened the last time she got into a submarine. Her legs trembled, and she hoped Wright didn't notice. Tesla had suggested Parker get on the sub with Wright instead of Vivian, but she'd insisted. She wanted to get right back up on the horse, not give in to her anxiety and let it grow. That had seemed like a good idea when she was on dry land. Now she wasn't so sure.

Wright closed the bubble and dove. Green water closed over the cockpit. She shut her eyes and took a couple of deep breaths, trying to get her heart rate down. She wiped clammy palms against her pants and tried to think calming thoughts. She had no calming thoughts.

"Are you sure you can do this?" Wright sounded more curious than concerned.

"The last one flooded and almost killed me. Give me a minute." And also, shut up.

"Better to freak out now, before we're a hundred feet deep and you can't get out."

The perfect way to calm someone down, go straight to the worst-case scenario. Wright's wife was probably better off without him.

She took a third deep breath, blew it out, and opened her eyes. Outside, all was black, so they must be in the tunnel. Two navigation lights lit the way forward, but not as well as she'd like. This must be how Tesla felt whenever he tried to go outside. Panicked. It sucked. She had to get it under control, because she wasn't going down Tesla's path.

"You doin' OK, sport?" Wright asked.

"Fine, thanks," she said. "Sport."

He made a snorting sound she thought might be a laugh.

She ignored him and got to work. Keeping busy with things inside the sub might distract her from the crushing weight of millions of gallons of water outside. She unzipped the camera case. Tesla had given it to her this morning, along with detailed instructions on how to use it.

Waterproof, he'd told her, down to sixty meters. Which made it a lot more durable than she was.

She shook that off. Tesla wanted unbroken footage from the time they left the dock to when they returned. If she turned up any evidence, he wanted to make sure it was well documented, especially if the Harbor Patrol didn't ever bother to do a more thorough investigation.

She set the camera up and aimed it through the cockpit window, turned it on and checked the picture on the little box. Recording perfectly—clear picture and a time-and-date stamp along the bottom. That was it, her whole job. She could have done it without leaving the dock.

Not really. She had to watch it to make sure nothing glitched and Wright didn't mess with it. He wasn't the most trustworthy character.

Also boring. Wright was a lot less fun to travel with than Tesla. After his initial jibes, he fell silent. He didn't dawdle or swing the lights around to see things either. Wright drove single-mindedly forward, eyes flicking to the GPS to make sure they were taking the most direct route to the scene of the crash.

Today, she liked that. She wanted this to be over with.

She recognized the sunken sailboat she and Tesla had passed before they got hit, the *Aronnax*. Next up, the transatlantic cable on the muddy ocean floor. No shark this time. Finally, they reached the cracked-up submarine where she'd almost died.

Water filled the cockpit where she'd sat, and a brown fish with big lips swam inside. The back of the sub was flattened. A few feet closer to the cockpit, and they would have had to take her remains out with a teaspoon.

"Damn expensive fishbowl," muttered Wright.

He held the sub steady while she panned the camera across the wreckage. A black scrape straight down the side showed where the larger sub had hit Tesla's sub, and a trench marked where the sub had been dragged before coming to rest against a rocky outcropping. Her heart skipped all over the place, but she held it together, trying not to think about the sub's final journey.

"Looks like you got stomped by Satan's boot," Wright said.

"Exactly. Do you see the scoring on the metal? The sub was hit with tremendous force—way more than the prince's sub could have generated. And those black streaks? They're wider than the prince's sub."

"Let's go look for the prince's sub," Wright said.

"First, can we circle this one?" she asked. "I want to document everything."

Obligingly, Wright turned the sub in a slow spiral. She aimed the camera downward. She didn't want even the slightest movement to make anyone question the validity of her footage.

After the circle, Wright headed over to the prince's sub. Its cockpit had cracked into pieces, like an egg, and the pieces were scattered along the mud in the direction the black sub had traveled—a long arrow pointing toward Tesla's submarine. She swallowed.

"Looks to me like Prince Timgad's sub was hit first and dragged, and then whatever it was hit you," said Wright.

"That's exactly how it happened." It surprised her Baxter hadn't done more investigation, but maybe he had and had been lying to provoke a reaction at the party. Or maybe someone was trying to cover up what had happened.

"Open and shut." Wright dove toward the wreck.

Her stomach lurched. "Be careful! That's evidence."

"You filmed the evidence," Wright said. "Which is kind of a bonus for you. It's not why I'm here."

She considered bonking him on the head and taking command of *The Green Meanie*, but she didn't want that on tape. "I'm not comfortable with this course of action."

"Noted," he said. "And I'll take responsibility."

Like that had helped her out during the Tesla crash.

Clearly searching for something, he pivoted his navigation lights in a straight line, moved them a few inches, and did it again.

"What're you looking for?" she asked.

"The batteries." His spotlight stopped on a black box. "Gotcha."

"If you pick that up, you're disturbing a crime scene," she said.

"I don't see any yellow tape."

"The scene needs to stay intact," she said.

"Not as much as the ocean needs to not have toxins leaking all over the place."

She couldn't argue. "What do you need me to do?"

"Take the controls. I'll use the grappling arm to bring the battery on board."

She followed his instructions. Her hands shook for a few seconds, but then she was all right. Her jaw ached from clenching it, but she'd get through this.

Wright had the first battery inside when she spotted something that looked like a black pipe.

"That's not part of the sub." She maneuvered closer. The camera was still rolling, and Wright was distracted bringing the battery into his collection box.

"I'll take the controls back." Wright snatched them away. He was the snatching type.

"We need to pick that up, too." She pointed to it.

He squinted through the cockpit window. "Why?"

"Because it's an assault rifle."

21

Grand Central Terminal
March 12

Avi had new pets. He held out his palm, and something that
looked like a housefly landed there. Close observation
revealed it wasn't a natural creature, but rather a tiny robot
with six tiny metal legs, a pair of wings made of a tough
plastic film, a miniature camera where its eyes should be, and
a stinger at the end of its abdomen, like a bee. Such a
cunning little creature.

He'd managed to procure only three, and he shuddered
to think of the cost. This purchase would eat up most of his
profit on the job, but it was a necessary expense. Unlike
most targets he'd been assigned, Tesla was difficult to track
by regular means. So far, he'd stayed holed up in his
underground bunker.

Avi had tried to send a fly down the tunnels, but they
were too ill-lit for the creature to see, and the wakes of the
passing trains had knocked the fly around so much he'd
almost lost it. He'd thought of exploring the tunnels himself,
but the police presence had increased since his unsuccessful
attempt on Tesla's life at the museum.

So, he and his little flies had to try something else.

He slipped one creature into his pocket and left his
room. He made it to the elevator without any trouble, then

cut across the lobby to enter Grand Central Terminal without going outside. Tesla must have followed this route from the hotel many times when he first arrived in New York and developed agoraphobia.

Avi wished Tesla would follow it now.

But he hadn't expected this to be easy. He pushed through a heavy glass door and entered the bustling station. He'd waited for rush hour, for the safety in crowds.

The green ceiling soared above his head, the cold marble felt smooth under his feet, and a kaleidoscope of people moved and turned around him. Such beauty to be found in this place. Resisting the urge to look around to see if he was being observed, he dropped a fly behind the paper train schedules displayed outside the information booth and picked up a schedule. A round black woman inside the booth looked at him for a split second, but her eyes moved on. Nothing unusual about picking up a schedule.

He called up the control app on his phone. With everyone always playing games on their phones, his movements were expected. The little fly climbed out from behind a blue and white pamphlet and stepped off the edge. It dipped toward the floor, then caught itself and tipped up toward the vast ceiling. He flew it in a large circle well above the heads of the crowd, monitoring their actions on his tiny camera.

In his peripheral vision, he kept an eye out for the two pigeons who lived in the station. A pigeon might eat a fly, and he wasn't convinced they'd be able to distinguish between a real fly and a robot one, or at least not until it was too late.

The fly landed atop the opal-faced clock on the information booth. This was sometimes called New York's favorite meeting place, and it had a perfect view of Joe

Tesla's front door. It might be a while before he went through it, but Avi would have a clear view of him when he did.

He closed the control app on his phone and wandered downstairs to the food court, releasing another fly. Like everyone else, he was sure he could walk while controlling the tiny drone. Like everyone else, he bumped into someone, said "Excuse me," and leaned against the wall to finish his phone nonsense.

The second fly found a perch on the roundabout that announced Irving Farm. Avi bought a cup of coffee and wandered around to see exactly where to position his drone. He'd have to keep turning the fly in a circle to keep an eye on everything. Still, that was better than having it fly around. That used up too much energy. The coffee was excellent, and he took a long sip while he thought. No point in denying himself the pleasures in life just because he was working.

Now he had two screens open on his phone. One showed the concourse, the other the food court. With any luck, Tesla would visit one or the other. If not, perhaps a fly could hitch a ride on the back of someone who could carry it down to Tesla. The key was remaining patient and undetected.

The third fly slept in his pocket, and he didn't take it out until he was back upstairs. His last little friend flew to Pellucid, Tesla's offices, and landed across the hall on a bin full of umbrellas. Avi turned the corner and went into an eyeglass shop with his coffee to wait.

He didn't have to wait long. A blond woman in a sleek blue suit approached Pellucid's front door, and Avi ambled out of the glasses store and leaned against the wall. The woman fumbled in an expensive purse and produced a key card.

Avi's little fly took off. Yellow and black umbrellas were quickly left behind. It aimed straight for the bag and alit on the back handle. The woman was too busy swiping her card to notice.

The fly rode into the office, past a giant glass brain, and dropped off onto the gray carpet when she set down her purse. It scuttled into the darkest recesses under her desk. After she left, he'd bring it out and hide it somewhere the cleaning crew wouldn't find it, but for now it was safe.

He finished his coffee and threw away the cup. He had his little creatures guarding the portals to Tesla's world—his home, his restaurants, and even inside his office. It would be only a matter of time before Tesla appeared.

Then, Tesla would feel his sting.

22

Russian Tea Room
March 12, lunch time

Vivian slid into a red booth at the Russian Tea Room. On the forest green wall, in a beveled gold frame, a yellow cat looked back at her menacingly.

The woman Vivian had come to meet, Marina, smoothed her metallic blue dress. She reminded Vivian of a wasp—thin, shiny, and dangerous. "That picture is *Tiger* by Franz Marc. Early Cubism."

At least it didn't have fish in it.

"Nice," Vivian said.

Marina poured them both tea into glasses set into silver holders, her movements so fluid and graceful Vivian felt like a lumbering bear. "It is delightful to see you, Miss Torres."

Vivian searched for the right response. She was weak at small talk, whereas Marina was superb. "And you."

"I guess by your demeanor you're not here to take me up on my offer?" Marina added a lump of sugar and a dash of milk to her tea and stirred.

"Not exactly." Marina ran a bodyguarding service, like Mr. Rossi, but she focused on protecting high-priced escorts, particularly those who catered to rich men with unusual tastes. Vivian's mother would kill her if she started working for prostitutes.

Marina crossed her beautiful legs and leaned forward. "Is it intrigue?"

"I guess you could call it that." Vivian took a long sip of a Darjeeling tea strong enough to compete with coffee for her affections.

"I'm a vault, as you must know. I can't divulge client secrets."

"I'm not asking for information about a client." Vivian had worked out her approach on the subway ride here. "I'm looking for information about his enemies."

"You mean the drowned bodyguard who should have been a drowned prince, I presume?"

"Who'd want to kill him?"

"The press believes it was your employer."

A well-dressed server set a plate in front of each of them. Vivian admired the blintzes, artfully stacked with a streak of cherry jelly arcing out from the side and a small bowl of vanilla ice cream on the end.

"I hope you don't mind that I ordered blintzes with our tea," Marina said. "Russian Tea Room blintzes are an indulgence of mine."

Vivian bet she had a lot of indulgences. "I love the blintzes here."

Not true, strictly speaking, because she couldn't afford to eat here, but since this was going on the Tesla expense account, she was liking them already.

Marina took a delicate bite of her blintz, and Vivian went back to their conversation. "No one believes that Joe Tesla wanted to kill Prince Timgad or his bodyguard. And there's since been another attack on Tesla's life."

"If we assume the attack was directed at Prince Timgad." Marina cut off another corner of her blintz. "How do you know the prince's enemies aren't clients as well?"

"Are they?"

Marina sipped her tea. "Perhaps."

"Perhaps they are and you know who they are, or perhaps they are because you have so many clients?"

"Perhaps."

"If no one knows his enemies, then justice can never be done," Vivian persisted.

"Serving justice isn't my purview."

She hadn't expected that tactic to work, but she'd felt obligated to try it. "Are we at a standoff?"

"Never." Marina smiled. "I would say one can always reach a mutually beneficial agreement."

"Knowing my finances, I doubt it." Marina believed in the power of money, and Vivian lived under the shadow of broke.

"I always accept barter." Marina's eyes traveled up and down her body, lingering on her chest.

Vivian set down her metal tea glass holder so hard it thunked. "I won't work for you."

"Not," Marina lifted her eyes to Vivian's face, "in any capacity but your current one."

She hated to ask the next question. "What does that mean?"

"I'm hosting a private party."

She lifted her cast. "I'm in no condition to work a security detail."

"A broken arm takes six to eight weeks to heal, does it not? And I believe your arm is only cracked, so you could be healed in as little as four weeks."

Unsettling that she knew that off the top of her head. "So you moonlight as an orthopedic surgeon?"

"My party is in nine weeks, so your arm doesn't present a problem." Marina smiled. She even had perfect teeth.

"What kind of party?"

"Black tie. Nothing indiscreet. I need someone who can handle drunks without making a fuss, someone who blends in with the scenery."

"A woman in a skimpy dress who can put a joint lock on an offensive businessman and ease him out the door quietly?"

Marina chuckled. "Exactly. I'd be happy to pay your going rate, through Mr. Rossi or directly. It's hard to find women bodyguards who are also attractive."

Vivian ignored the flattery. "I'll pencil you in. Set it up with Mr. Rossi."

"Excellent." Marina finished her tea and set the cup in the saucer with a genteel clink. "Now, as to Prince Timgad."

"Yes?" Vivian tried a piece of blintz with a dollop of ice cream. This was the best lunch Tesla had ever bought her.

"He is a difficult client. He likes to hurt women, and he pays extra for the privilege."

"And you let him?" She wished she hadn't committed to working for her. She didn't want to be part of that kind of business.

"Sometimes, letting men do things to women is my job. For Prince Timgad, I take all precautions—hidden cameras that are constantly monitored, a safe word for the woman, a team ready to intervene, a legal agreement he signed to prevent him from raising a fuss should he be injured during the intervention. That kind of thing."

"Sounds expensive."

Vivian waved her hand. "He can pay for that and more."

She bet he could.

"All his partners know his preferences and are happy to work for the extra compensation. No one is forced to do something she doesn't want to do."

"Do you think any of the...escorts or security team might have wanted to kill him?"

"They were well paid for their work, and they understand the nature of such clients. It wasn't any of my people, I assure you," Marina said. "But you wouldn't be amiss in thinking a woman could have wanted to kill him, although I assume a woman would use something harder to trace, like poison."

"Do you have any names?" That information wasn't worth an evening of kicking out gropers.

"He is a member of the House of Dakkar. A distant member, but he was engaged to one of the king's nieces. A niece from a well-connected brother, as you may know."

She hadn't known, but she said, "I see."

"Prince Timgad is greatly favored by the king and the princes, but he is too distant a relation to consider imbuing with power until he's more closely aligned with the royal family. After his marriage, there was talk, discreetly and at the highest levels, that he would be under consideration for succession as king."

"Doesn't the king's son become the next king?"

"Traditionally, yes, but the king of the House of Dakkar passed a royal decree a few years ago stating the next king would be chosen by a committee of princes instead of through straight inheritance. It's not, I believe, widely known, but Prince Timgad is thought to be the leading choice of the members of that committee."

Vivian had trouble believing she'd nearly been killed because of a squabble for the kingship of a country thousands of miles away, but it wasn't the weirdest thing that had ever happened to her. "You think the next choice for the throne tried to kill him?"

Marina's bright blue eyes went out of focus for a moment as she thought. "Perhaps. But things are more complicated, because the marriage that would have given him the legitimacy he needed could never have taken place."

"Why not?"

"He married the first niece, and it looked as if his path to succession was clear when the king died or stepped down, but then his royal wife died under mysterious circumstances."

"What does that mean?"

"She was found, beaten beyond recognition, in his bedroom."

"What did the police say? She was a princess, after all, so they must have looked into it."

"No one knows." Marina shrugged. "But it's known no investigation followed. The prince wouldn't countenance one, and in his home country, that means there will be no investigation."

"So he murdered her?" Poor princess.

"It's believed so."

Vivian wondered if the royal family had the connections to divert a submarine for a revenge killing. Probably, but it seemed an odd and expensive way to kill someone. "Was his attempted murder about the princess's family taking revenge?"

"The princess's value to them wasn't so high as you might think from your Disney movies. After her death, the family betrothed the second sister, a twin, to the prince, and he had a second chance to become king."

Vivian's stomach did a slow roll. "After he killed their first daughter, they offered him the second?"

"They wanted the alliance and the path to kingship as much as Prince Timgad, I would imagine. They had sons, but none found favor with the king, so their daughters provided the only way."

Vivian was going to go home and give her mother a giant hug for not selling her to the highest bidder. "If the second daughter solved his problem and he was on track to become king, why wouldn't the next guy in succession be a prime suspect?"

Marina lifted her shoulders in a graceful movement that looked practiced. "He might have been, but the second sister also died."

"How?"

"Right before the wedding, she and her wedding party were in a plane that crashed into the Sea of Japan."

"The women in that family seem pretty unlucky." Vivian had another bite of blintz. It was amazing.

"Perhaps the second sister was luckier than the first."

"Because she died quickly?"

"Because she escaped from the prince."

Vivian thought about that. "But she had to die to do it."

Marina shrugged. "She had to appear to die at least."

"Do you think she faked her own death?"

"I think nothing. It is not my place to speculate." Marina took a tiny sip of tea. "Do you have any other questions?"

"If the princess died before the wedding, could the attack on the prince have been from an enemy of the royal family in general? Maybe it's bigger than Prince Timgad?"

"A submarine accident isn't a usual assassination tool, nor is downing a plane in the middle of the sea." Marina refilled their teacups. "Perhaps the deaths were simply accidents."

Somehow, Vivian didn't think so.

"So, he's a sidelined prince?"

"It is said Prince Timgad is in negotiations for a quick marriage to another niece. She's twelve years old, but they're hoping to rush the marriage so that it can take place before the next king is chosen. So, he may yet have a chance to become king."

Poor twelve-year-old. "When will that be?"

"That, my dear, even I don't know."

Or wouldn't tell.

23

**House under Grand Central Terminal
March 13**

Joe locked himself in his bedroom, the only place where he could get any privacy. Two (blue) cops in his front yard, two (blue) bodyguards in his house. He appreciated them being there, but he needed to be alone. He wasn't a social person at the best of times, and this was not the best of times.

He lay flat on the antique quilt and called Maeve. So far, she hadn't spoken to him since she was shot. She'd spoken to Vivian, who'd stopped by with flowers, and to Dirk who had been assigned to her guard detail, but not to Joe.

"Hello?" Her voice sounded sleepy.

"Joe here," he said. "How are you feeling?"

"Drifty," she said. "They have me on some powerful drugs."

"I'm so sorry about what happened."

"Me, too." She sighed into the phone. "Thank you for the flowers."

"Of course."

"Your life is a crazy place," she said. "Did you know that?"

"I'm sorry." He didn't know what else to say.

"I understand that it's not your fault you can't go outside. I was willing to work around it."

That didn't sound good. "Was?"

"At first I thought it was always one-off incidents." She coughed. "Excuse me."

He waited.

"But it isn't. It's like you need extra excitement. Every few months, you get caught up in something bigger than you, something dangerous."

"I don't know what the sub accident was about. Or the shooting. I didn't do anything to cause them."

"You never do."

"In the past, I have investigated stuff that got me into trouble after, but this got me into trouble out of nowhere." He felt defensive, and he tried to push that down. She had every right to be upset.

"Got me into trouble, you mean."

"I didn't mean for that to happen."

"I know." She was silent for so long he thought she might have hung up.

"Maeve?"

"And I think it's best if we don't see each other anymore."

She was dumping him, and he couldn't even argue. She was doped up, in pain, and in the hospital because of him. She'd be insane not to dump him. Still, it hurt. "Why don't we wait until you're feeling better—"

"No," she said. "I want a normal life. A guy I can walk with under the stars. A guy I could marry at any church. A guy who could take our kids to school. A guy who doesn't ever get shot at."

Joe was not that guy. He thought about the ECT therapy, about shocking his brain into submission. "Maybe I could be that guy."

She hung up.

Edison barked from the other side of the door.

Joe got up and let him in. Things had been going so well with Maeve. She was smart and sexy and funny, and he loved spending time with her. She'd seemed happy. He'd worked hard to find places they could meet, finding buildings connected to his house via steam tunnels, making agreements with building managers. A thousand details, but not enough. She was right—he couldn't walk under the stars. He might never be that guy. She deserved better.

Edison bumped Joe's hand, and he automatically petted him. "Just you and me again, buddy."

Edison looked back at the door.

"And our security entourage."

Edison walked halfway to the door and looked over his shoulder. He wanted Joe to follow him somewhere, not to stay in his room and listen to breakup music and make himself miserable.

Joe followed him down to the kitchen and gave him a bone. Andres Peterson, the dog walker, had picked up a few from a butcher shop the day before. Edison dropped onto his stomach and went to work on it. At least someone in the house was happy.

Not sure what else to do, he went into his study and stared at the printouts he'd arranged on the green felt on his billiards table. Earlier that day, he'd printed out his data about Maeve's shooting and the submarine crash, hoping that bringing the data off the screen and into the world would help him to see it in a new way.

One pile represented the royal dead—the princess beaten to death, the prince killed in a training accident during a naval exercise, the plane that had crashed into the sea, and the submarine that had been run down. He rolled a cue ball across the piles on the table, banking it off the sides so it ran over each pile before coming back to him. Maybe the ball would reveal something he hadn't seen, and it helped to have something to do with his hands.

"When did you last eat?" Vivian stepped into the billiard room.

"Breakfast," he said. "A muffin, or something like that. Something bready."

"It's almost six at night," she said. "Maybe time for a late lunch?"

He lined up a shot and hit the ball, rolling it across the piles in a different order. He didn't feel hungry. He chalked his cue stick.

She handed him a roast beef sandwich. "I got two for Edison, but he would only eat one."

The dog looked between him and the sandwich, his meaning clear—if Edison was giving up roast beef for him, the human had better eat it. He patted Edison on the back before taking his first bite. That's when he realized how ravenous he was. The sandwich was perfect—thin-sliced beef, horseradish sauce, a freshly baked bun.

"Thank you. I know I've been a bear since Maeve was shot."

"You shouldn't blame yourself, even though you do. You can't control what people do." She handed him a Bundaberg root beer and pointed to a stack of papers. "Tell me about these."

"That's the pile for the dead. Marine-related."

She leaned over to read the papers without picking them up. Then she looked at the door. She must be going off shift soon, so he tried to keep her talking. He never knew what to say to the other bodyguards or the policemen guarding him. Vivian and Andres were the only people he had to talk to. His small world was starting to feel like a prison.

"From what I can tell," he swallowed a hunk of sandwich, "there's only one suspect."

She looked at him expectantly, because he'd solved mysteries before. Too bad he was going to disappoint her now. "Who?"

"Aquaman."

Apparently not a big believer in superheroes, she grimaced. "And this pile?"

"Those whose fortunes changed because of each death—heirs to wealth, heirs to position or title, creditors who got paid or didn't, people with vendettas. Mourners."

"Don't forget those who want to become the next king."

"They do have an odd line of succession," he said. "And getting Prince Timgad out of the way might help some royal candidates. All those who seem to want to be king are in that pile, too."

"Good. What else do you have?"

He pointed to the smallest pile with his sandwich. "That pile is about the giant sub."

"Hmm," she said without looking at it.

He suspected she was just humoring him, but it helped. "The sub is of Swedish design, but all three known subs of that design are accounted for. It took time to track them down, but I managed. I've checked and checked. The *Halland* is in a submarine yard in Sweden being serviced, which I could confirm with surveillance cameras from the dock. The *Gotland* is on a war-games exercise in San Diego. The *Uppland* is patrolling in the Baltic Sea. They weren't anywhere near New York at the time of the accident. But what if another sub of the same design was built, maybe by a different foreign power and in secrecy?"

"Why would they want to do that?" she asked.

"The builders? Money." He took another sip of root beer. It had a nice gingery snap to it. "The buyers? So they could have a powerful weapon nobody knows about."

"Would the Swedes build something like that?"

"I don't think it was the Swedes." He stared down at the white pages on the green felt. "I think it was—"

"The Chinese?" she interrupted.

He was so surprised he almost choked. She couldn't have heard of the hacking. "Why do you say that?"

"Squares with the assault rifle I found next to the wreckage."

"You never told me the gun was Chinese!"

"Just found out," she said. "I turned it over to the police. Had to get Dirk to look up their findings because they won't tell me anything."

"Do the Chinese allow women to crew their subs?"

"I don't know. Why?"

He talked around a mouthful of sandwich. "We do. Some European countries do. Canada."

"You're saying Aquaman's got a girlfriend?"

"Everyone knows Aquaman is married." He gulped down a mouthful of root beer. "To Mera, Queen of Atlantis."

"Maybe a mermaid on the side?"

"Maybe." He felt like he was close to something. "I did gait analysis of the swimmer who was near our sub, and it's definitely a woman."

She stopped looking at the door and picked up the suspicious-deaths file. "For some of these deaths, nobody ever found the bodies."

"The plane-crash victims? Not surprising."

"Maybe." She skimmed the mind map he'd created linking the women to each other and to the rest of the royal family. Lots of bubbles and lines. It hadn't really helped his analysis any. He knew he was reaching.

"Their plane went down over the Sea of Japan." He took a slower sip of root beer. "No survivors. Black box not recovered. Small jets like that are—"

"Not interested in the crash details." She kept reading.

He gave her space. Maybe she'd see something he didn't. He hoped she did, since he didn't see anything.

When she was done, she looked back up at him, as if she expected him to say something. "I've checked the men who stood to gain from these deaths, and—"

"What about the women?" she asked. "Did you check the women?"

"The women?" He stared at her. "The women don't have a lot of specific motives, and they're also dead."

"The bride on that plane had a strong motive to kill the prince—he beat her sister to death, and she was going to have to marry him." She sounded angry.

"That's not in the files. Her sister's death was listed as a burglary gone wrong. See right there?" He pointed to the cause-of-death line on the mind map, but she didn't even look at it. "Why would you think the prince killed her?"

"I've heard rumors from a source here in New York," she said. "Did you collect the same level of data on the women who died in the plane crash as you did on the men?"

"I collected some." He felt defensive, because he hadn't done much research on the women. He'd viewed them as collateral damage and incidental to the killer, like he and Vivian had almost been, not as the targets of the murder. "They're about her age. Relatives, friends, people who you'd expect in the wedding party. Nothing stood out."

"Educated women. All college graduates. One was even a doctor. Those are motives."

"How so? Laila Dakkar was highly educated. Went to schools in Switzerland and London. Makes sense her friends would be like her."

"Maybe a woman like that didn't want to marry a cruel and powerful man. Maybe these women didn't want to subjugate themselves to a system that views them as expendable brood mares." Her words were tight and clipped.

So obvious. He was ashamed he'd never thought of that. Because he was a man, and he'd never had to think of it. No wonder Maeve dumped him. "Go on."

"I don't know what was going through these women's heads when they were alive," she said. "But these dead women have the strongest motive of anyone on your lists. They suffered under their social system, Laila Dakkar most of all."

He wasn't going to argue with her. She could kick his ass, and she was probably right. "But."

"But what?"

"Those women are dead, remember?" He didn't want to set her off.

"Your data says they're dead, but your data could be wrong, just like they were about the first sister's death," she said. "Since your swimming analysis says you're looking for women who have a motive to kill this guy, why don't you look close to home?"

"Their plane really did crash. I checked the flight plans, the insurance claims, the statements of Japanese investigators. Surveillance shows the women boarded the plane, and the plane never came back. Records show it crashed into the ocean."

"Just because it crashed doesn't mean those women were still on it."

"It's the mostly likely explanation," he said. "There's no record the plane landed."

"It's the most likely explanation, but none of the most likely explanations are leading anywhere, right?"

"True," Joe said. "Go on."

"Let's go a little nuts here. Make some illogical leaps. What if the plane crash was a fake? What if the women are still alive?"

"OK, what if they are?"

"They disappeared at around the same time as the submarine, right?"

"Yes."

"So, what if those facts are related? What if the women got hold of that submarine?" Her dark eyes glowed with excitement.

"Farfetched," he said promptly. "That theory has a lot of what-ifs without a lot of data."

"The existing data aren't leading anywhere else either. Why not give it a second look? You don't have anything else to do."

"Ouch," he said. But it was true.

"You know what I mean. Why not go for it?"

"I can look for more about the women, see what turns up." He felt energized. He had a new lead. "If they're alive, I bet I can find some trace of them, maybe on surveillance cameras, maybe online or on social media. It's hard to disappear. If I find them, we can nail them to the wall."

"Like they haven't been through enough already." She touched the printout of Laila Dakkar's biography. "What if we just let them fight their fight?"

"And I live in this house forever, waiting to be killed by an assassin because someone thinks I tried to murder Prince Timgad?"

"You don't know what these women have been through. Solve your problem yourself. Work diplomatic channels. Get the royal family to call off their assassin, if he even works for them."

"And let the women get away with murder?" He couldn't believe law-and-order Vivian would propose such a thing. "What if they try to kill Prince Timgad again?"

Her jaw jutted forward like it always did when she was angry. "Maybe they should."

24

**Somewhere in the North Atlantic
March 16, 0800 hours**

Laila looked around her once-Spartan bedroom. Aunt Bibi
had given them small carpets to hang on the walls or tack to
the floors, a tea service for the mess hall with ornate metal
cups that wouldn't break if they were knocked off in a strong
sea, packets of fine tea, expensive chocolate, sheer scarves,
pots of paint and brushes, and so much more. The women
had set about brightening up their austere living quarters. If
the Chinese builders could see the ship now, they would
shudder.

But the *Siren* looked wonderful and homey. They would
hate to leave her after they took care of Prince Timgad.
Maybe they wouldn't. Maybe they would sail the seas
forever, resupplying at Aunt Bibi's, living on fine tea and
fresh fish. They didn't have to abandon their vessel when
she'd completed her task.

Aunt Bibi had included backgammon and chess and
other travel-sized board games. Most pieces had magnetic
bottoms, and she remembered playing with similar versions
as a child. Aunt Bibi had also burned DVDs full of music
and movies and television shows. The television in the mess
hall was scheduled for many shifts to come.

They had one more training exercise, and then they had only to wait for their target to come to them, and hope they didn't miss. If they hit their target, a thousand lives would be lost. If they missed, it would be a hundred times that, and Nahal would never let her forget it. They had to practice.

She took a sip of black tea sweetened with so much sugar it made her teeth hurt and ate the last fresh fig. She wondered if the new indulgences were weakening the crew's resolve.

Today would show otherwise.

She walked leisurely to the bridge. Someone had painted the once-gray floor a bright orange with paisley patterns. It brightened the corridor and gave the crew something to do, but she missed the simple gray. It had been restful.

She entered the bridge. No one had changed anything in here, per her orders. This place permitted no distractions. The women sat tense at their posts.

"Captain on the bridge," said Ambra, again with the emphasis on captain. "Coming up on the *Narwhal*."

The *Narwhal* was an oil tanker that had visited New York a few days before to deliver her oil. She was returning to her home base in the country of Laila's birth. A banged-up old tub, she'd been in service for a long time and didn't have the latest in electronics and sonar. She thought she was alone in the middle of the Atlantic.

But she wasn't.

Ambra used her yellow pencil to trace their course relative to the *Narwhal*'s on the paper maps. Laila was thinking about the men aboard the *Narwhal*. She must encourage the crew to think of those men as collateral damage, not as men with wives and children and mothers. Men who would be mourned. Men whose only crime was being in the wrong place at the wrong time. Although, not all the men were innocent. One had beaten Rasha so hard she'd lost her child. And it was a small crew, just over twenty men. They had to practice.

Laila and the crew had discussed this for hours. Some had suggested shooting at ghost ships, others at empty oil rigs. In the end, they had agreed that targeting a moving boat in the middle of the ocean was the only real test they had time for. They had to intercept the *Roc* in six days, so their options were limited.

They had chosen a civilian boat that seemed unlikely to be monitored by sonar. Rasha's husband's presence was merely a bonus. The time for the test had come.

Ambra ran a polished red nail across their course, stopping at the point of intercept. "Right there. They might as well be on Ceti Alpha V."

"Where's that?"

"It's the planet where Captain Kirk marooned Khan in the *Space Seed* episode," Ambra said.

"You know the episode name?"

"You wanted a mathematician. We know this stuff."

"The episode name?" Laila asked.

"They also made two movies about Khan. As a film major, you ought to have seen them."

"I bet they were classics."

Ambra smiled. "In the genre, yes."

"Is Ceti Alpha V a good place to intercept?"

"So long as we don't beam down to the planet's surface."

"Duly noted. Proceed to Ceti Alpha V."

"Aye aye, Captain." Ambra marched back to her duty station.

It seemed like a movie, or a game, but it wasn't. The lives they would end were real.

"Close to firing distance," said Ambra without even turning to look. "No other vessels in range. No other vessels for miles."

So, no one would see their attack, or come in time to rescue the survivors. The ship was helpless. Rasha would get revenge, and they would be able to practice for their more important mission. An ideal scenario, but Laila knew they all felt conflicted about it.

"How long until we're in torpedo range?" Laila asked.

"A little over a minute," Ambra said. "Sixty-seven seconds."

"Load torpedoes."

Ambra relayed the order to the torpedo room.

"Breech door open," said Rasha's curiously deep voice through the intercom. "Loading torpedo."

They waited. She imagined the scene in the torpedo room—they'd opened the inner door, also called the breech door, to the torpedo tube. Right now, they were watching the giant explosive device slide into the firing tube.

"Torpedo loaded. Breech door closed," said Rasha. She sounded uncertain. Laila had thought it would be best to have her man the torpedoes, but maybe she should have used someone else, someone who didn't know one of the men to be killed.

"Roger that," said Laila. "Stand by."

They continued on their course through the deep blue. If she didn't do anything to stop it, twenty-five men would die.

"In range, Captain." Ambra's voice trembled.

This was the first time they would take innocent lives, but Laila had practiced. She'd killed her brother and the prince's bodyguard. "Flood the tube."

"Flooding," crackled from the intercom.

It would take a few seconds to fill the torpedo tube with water. The pressure within the tube had to equal the water pressure outside before they could move to the next step. She'd lain in the escape trunk long enough to know the process took time.

Sooner than she'd expected, the torpedo room spoke. "Ready to open the muzzle door."

The muzzle door was on the outside hull. The torpedo would fire through that opening. Ambra's teeth worried her lower lip.

"Open muzzle door," Laila said.

"Open," the torpedo room confirmed.

"We're in range," Ambra said.

"The torpedo is aimed and ready to fire," announced Rasha.

Laila took a deep breath. She pictured the blood of the innocent crew splashing into the sea, and she looked over at Ambra.

"Ready," Ambra said.

The die was cast. "Fire torpedo."

The submarine rocked slightly, but that was the only indication the torpedo had left the ship. Another rock might have meant the torpedo had hit its mark and exploded.

"Surface to periscope height." She had to make sure.

The periscope was eighteen meters long, so they didn't have to come too close to the surface to use it. If anyone on the *Narwhal* was looking, the *Siren* wouldn't be spotted, even if the torpedo had missed the ship entirely.

"Periscope height," said Ambra.

Laila pulled down the handles and looked through the eyepieces. The *Narwhal* looked unharmed. She moved forward as before.

"We missed," she said. "Acquire the target and try again."

She returned to the periscope and watched the hapless *Narwhal*. It sailed along, completely unaware. That was how she would want to die—happy, unaware, and then gone. "We have to learn before it's important."

"Second torpedo in place," said Rasha. "Target is acquired."

"Fire second torpedo," Laila said.

The *Siren* dipped, and she looked through the periscope. A tremendous explosion of white water blossomed into the air, and the submarine rocked. The outline of *Narwhal* was barely visible through the white screen.

The water settled back to the sea.

"Target is hit," she called.

Ragged cheering broke out on the bridge and sounded over the intercom from the torpedo room.

She watched their unfortunate target. Tall flames licked up from the sea. Black smoke billowed into the sky like a cloud from hell. The water roiled white around the ship. The torpedo had struck the *Narwhal* amidships, and she rode low in the water.

"Nothing on the radio," Ambra said. "They haven't sent out a Mayday yet."

Those left behind might not ever know where their loved ones had died, might wait weeks for the overdue ship, as their mothers and family had waited for news of the women who now crewed the *Siren*.

The *Narwhal*'s deck listed, and figures small as ants spilled off the side.

A hand touched her shoulder.

"You don't have to watch it," Meri said.

"You should be at your battle station," Laila said. "In the medical bay."

Meri squeezed her shoulder and let go.

The tanker burned in earnest now. Flames engulfed the deck. To minimize environmental damage, Laila had waited until the ship had off-loaded the oil, even though she would have liked to have forced her country to take that financial loss. Was the tanker burning up because she carried extra oil, or was this normal? She had no idea, because she'd never seen a ship take a torpedo strike before, not even in the movies.

She swept the periscope back and forth, looking for survivors. Tiny black heads bobbed among pieces of wreckage.

"Mayday message sent out," Ambra said. "They reported an explosion and are requesting help."

No one was close enough to help them.

"Admirable performance," Laila said.

"Thank you, ma'am," said Rasha on the intercom from the torpedo room. She sounded ready to cry.

"We must discover why the first one missed," Laila said. "But not today."

Ambra looked at the periscope, and Laila stepped back to let her use it. Maybe she would be able to see Rasha's brutal husband die. Laila understood the need for that kind of closure.

During the next new moon, they would rendezvous with Aunt Bibi. She would have new oxygen generators.

They would be able to dive and maneuver and fire like a true combat submarine, instead of limping along near the surface. The target would have no chance.

Unless they shot back.

25

**House under Grand Central Terminal
March 16, 8:41 a.m.**

Joe woke to the sound of a sonar ping. It sounded so much like the device in his yellow submarine that it took him a second to realize where he was—in his bed, with Edison nearby, and his laptop on his nightstand. Exactly where he'd been for hours.

The laptop pinged again, and he rolled over to pick it up. Edison stirred in his doggie bed.

"Shh," Joe whispered. "Back to sleep, buddy."

Edison snorted and lay still. Andres had taken him out for most of the day, and the dog was tired out.

Joe checked out his laptop. He was monitoring acoustic buoys around the world's oceans. They tracked sounds in a range lower than normal human hearing. At that frequency, sound could travel for miles. Whales used it to communicate, and governments used it to monitor nuclear explosions anywhere in the world.

It had taken a bit of doing, but he'd been given access. Nobody thought he could actually figure the sounds out. Once he had access, he'd been assigned an acoustic intelligence officer named Fred Mulcahy. When Joe had invited him over from the submarine base in Groton, Connecticut, Mulcahy had given him a crash course in interpreting underwater sounds. So far, there had been a lot of false alarms. Many things made noise in the oceans— whales, dolphins, boat engines, volcanoes, earthquakes.

For the past few days, he'd been tuning the data to filter out natural and expected sounds so he got alarms only when something manmade and unusual occurred. Pattern recognition was his specialty, and he could see the system improving. Fred Mulcahy had gotten excited about it, and Joe had given Fred the source code in return for his help interpreting sounds. He probably could have built another company off this work, but he wasn't interested. It was just a tool to help him find the submarine that had nearly killed him.

This was a new sound.

He studied the data that had triggered the alarm. A second loud sound registered, followed by a series of quieter noises with no pattern he could see. The loud sounds looked like explosions—something blew up—and the quieter ones might be something else breaking apart.

The event had happened in the North Atlantic about six hundred (orange, black, black) nautical miles from New York City. While some parts of the ocean had been seeded with naval mines to damage or destroy ships, that part of the ocean certainly wasn't. The sound couldn't have been a ship that ran into a mine. It could have been a ship that had had a primary then a secondary explosion—a boiler went, and then some kind of explosive cargo went after.

Or it could have been a ship that just got torpedoed. Twice.

He'd had Fred on alert since he'd discovered the pilot of the princess's downed plane lurking in the background of a photo on Facebook. The man probably hadn't noticed he was being photographed by a party at another table, but Joe's software had tracked him down and matched his facial features beyond a reasonable doubt. He hadn't been able to track the man further, but it was enough to know that, no matter what the official investigation said, the pilot had survived the crash. If he had, the women very likely had as well.

He sent the data off to Fred. Fred didn't seem to sleep any more than he did. He was astonishingly adept at focusing for long periods of time and didn't seem to experience fatigue. Joe pegged him as pretty far along the autism spectrum and was grateful he didn't have to make small talk. Fred was about the sounds and nothing else.

He worked on the data for the explosions. They had to mean something.

His phone rang.

"Fred here. I got your data."

No pleasantries from Fred. "What's your take?"

"Torpedoes," he said. "Beyond a doubt. The first didn't do much damage, but you can hear the ship breaking apart after the second one. My guess is the first shot missed, or it went off too early."

"Can you tell what kind of torpedo?"

"It's consistent with the Swedish Gotland you've been hypothesizing, but it could be another kind, too. No known Swedish subs in that area. Doesn't mean anything. Gotlands are quiet, hard to detect."

"Have you reported it up the chain?"

"I have, but I'll never hear back. Above my paygrade. You know that."

Fred was very regimented in what he would and wouldn't do. Joe suspected Fred's higher-ups rarely listened. If he was really viewed as a valuable intelligence asset, they never would have sent him to work with Joe. "Thanks, Fred."

"One new thing. A Mayday message came in from a tanker called the *Narwhal* since I called you. The radio operator said there was an explosion, and they were abandoning ship. He asked for rescuers to come to help him and his crewmates."

"Are we sending someone?"

"Above my paygrade, but we don't usually do long-range rescues like that for non-US-flagged commercial vessels. If we have someone close, though, we'll send them."

"What's the flag?"

"Liberia."

"Liberia?" That wasn't on his radar.

"Flag of convenience. Five hundred and twenty tankers are flagged as Liberian. Doesn't mean they're from Liberia. Tax reasons. Liability reasons."

"Can you see who owns it?"

"Above my—"

"Paygrade," he finished for him. That always meant Fred wasn't going to help.

"Yes." Fred hung up without saying good-bye.

He found Fred's lack of social graces a relief and had often considered hiring him when his tour of duty ended, but he suspected Fred would continue reenlisting as long as he could. The routine suited him.

Joe started to research the *Narwhal*. It didn't take long to track down, regardless of his paygrade. The ship was owned by a shell company owned by the Dakkar family. Another marine tragedy for the Dakkars. That couldn't be a coincidence.

He saved the sounds of both explosions and set them up as another alert on his system. If someone fired that kind of torpedo again anywhere in buoy range, he'd know without having to check with Fred. But the sub was getting away. He looked at the clock on his computer: three (red) a.m. He called Mr. Rossi anyway.

"I'm sorry to be calling so early."

"I assume it's something time critical." Mr. Rossi sounded awake and alert. Joe wondered if he ever slept.

"I think I found the submarine that hit us. It torpedoed a tanker called the *Narwhal* a few minutes ago." He read off the *Narwhal*'s last GPS coordinates and gave Mr. Rossi a brief rundown of what he'd discovered. "The crew needs assistance."

"I'll pass this along to my contacts."

"The sub must be nearby. If they wait too long, they'll never find it."

"I'm certain they'll look into it," Mr. Rossi said. "But I'm also certain we'll never hear about what they find."

Joe thanked him and got off the phone. Not much else he could do to track the sub in the ocean. The Gotland was rumored to be one of the quietest diesel electric subs ever built, and the buoys couldn't hear it.

He'd already tried to find out anything about the women who had died in the plane crash, but as near as he could tell, they really were dead. No social media contacts, no appearance on any surveillance databases he could track. Maybe the pilot had killed them, although Joe couldn't think why.

He sat in the dark for a long moment, listening to Edison's quiet breathing and smelling the lilac scent of his bedspread. The policemen and a bodyguard were downstairs.

If he didn't prove he hadn't tried to kill Prince Timgad and get the royal family to call off the hit man, this would be his life—sitting in his house with guards.

He had to find a way to prove this submarine existed, and that it had been responsible for the prince's bodyguard's death. He had to make sure the killers were brought to justice, despite Vivian's misgivings.

But how?

If the submarine had torpedoed the *Narwhal*, it was moving farther from detection with each passing second. The ocean was a big place, and the sub could hide anywhere.

But it would need fuel, supplies, parts. It'd be tough to track fuel and food, but submarine parts were another thing entirely. He knew where they'd be found.

The dark web.

He'd spent time lurking there, of course. It was amazingly organized, and the illegal vendors had rankings and reviews, just like on Amazon. The anonymity was welcome, but he'd soon grown horrified by the things offered on their criminal marketplace: drugs of all kinds, counterfeit documents, counterfeit money, uranium, explosives, guns, other weapons, and children.

If he wanted to buy replacement submarine parts, that's where he would go.

It took him the rest of the day of hacking and tracking, but he managed to find a supplier for the oxygen generators of the same type as those on the Gotland. The supplier lived in a town near the Swedish and Finnish border with just 435 (green, red, brown) inhabitants. They had a port, although they barely shipped anything out of it.

Then he caught a break. The owner of the bait shop at the harbor had a surveillance camera aimed at the port. Even better, he didn't use a password, and his video was archived for a month. Joe set up a pattern matcher to sort out the movement of anything the size of the oxygen generators or larger. It led to a lot of false positives of boats on trailers and cars, but in the end, it netted him exactly what he needed: footage of two (blue) large and clearly heavy boxes being loaded onto a fishing boat.

Once the boxes left Sweden, he lost track of them. They could be literally anywhere on Earth. Still, he dropped the information into a file and sent it to Mr. Rossi to pass along to his intelligence contacts. Lots of smart people with better tools than he had were working on these issues. Maybe they could find the submarine.

But only if they thought it was important.

26

**Secret elevator to the house under Grand Central
Terminal
March 17, noon**

Vivian went up the elevator with Edison. She'd decided to
go out with him on his walk with Andres Peterson. She
wasn't doing anyone any good down at Tesla's house. He'd
been on the computer the entire day yesterday, and today
looked like it would be more of the same.

Andres stood outside the information booth in a pair of
paint-spattered leather pants and a bright white T-shirt. He
definitely looked like the artist he was.

"Hello, Mr. Edison!" He crouched down, and Edison
launched himself at the man, tail wagging furiously. Edison
was a bouncy and exuberant dog without his service vest.

"I'll be coming along," Vivian said. "If that's OK."

"I was thinking of Central Park," Andres said. "First, we
walk to the park, and then we run around inside looking for
squirrels to chase."

"Sounds like a great afternoon."

"Every afternoon is great if you have a dog." Andres
took the leash, and they walked across the polished marble
to the 42nd and Park exit.

After they crossed the street, she looked back at Grand Central's lovely entrance topped by the winged statue of Hermes. Tesla might never see this view again. She and Andres had stepped out through the door like it was nothing, but Tesla hadn't been able to do that for a long time. Now he wasn't even able to haunt the tunnels.

Dirk was right that she didn't want to trade places with Tesla, even if she could have. Maybe he was right about other things. Maybe she ought to step back, accept the new jobs Mr. Rossi had lined up, and get back outside.

"How is Mr. Tesla?" Andres asked.

"Fine." He'd awoken at the crack of dawn and been glued to his computer ever since. He hadn't showered or eaten. She wasn't even sure he'd noticed when she left with the dog.

"Not so fine, I'm thinking."

She shrugged. She wasn't going to divulge any information about a client, even to his other employees.

"I heard that Miss Maeve and he have parted company."

Vivian had heard that, too, from Dirk. "Maybe."

Andres dropped the subject, and they enjoyed a long romp in the park. Edison chased his tennis ball, sniffed for squirrels, and made friends with a giant Schnauzer named Jake. He and Jake wrestled on the ground, play-growling, until Jake had to go home.

"You're quiet." Andres flopped down on the grass next to her. A strand of blond hair fell across his forehead.

"Edison has a second life with you."

"I try to give him things to sniff, dogs to meet, and a long run." Andres lay flat on his back and looked up at the sky. His eyes were an extraordinary shade of blue. "Dogs need such things."

She wished Tesla could see Edison now. "So do people."

"Is Mr. Tesla happy down there?" Andres asked. "I know he can't come out to play like Edison, but these past days seem worse. I haven't even seen him."

She wasn't sure how to answer.

"See that cloud?" He pointed south. "It looks like a hen with little chicks."

She looked where he was pointing, but didn't see the cloud.

"Put your head where mine is." He rolled to the side.

She positioned herself where he'd been. A cloud hen with a raised comb and sharp beak came into focus. Smaller clouds around the hen's feet looked like chicks. How long had it been since she'd lain in the grass and watched the clouds?

"You pick a cloud. Tell me what you see," Andres said.

Edison dropped the wet tennis ball on Andres's chest and collapsed between them as if he wanted to look at the clouds, too. She felt like the dog was somehow cheating on Tesla. That she was cheating on him, too.

"I need to be getting back." She sat up and dusted grass off her shirt.

"Just a few clouds," Andres said. "Then maybe a coffee after?"

Was he flirting with her? If so, he was doing an admirable job. He looked adorable with the dog next to him, grass in his wind-blown hair, and a smile with dimples.

She leaned back and pointed at the sky. "That looks like a sailing ship."

"I see the sails and even some rigging." Andres had moved his head next to hers.

"And that's a giant kraken underneath trying to sink it." She wanted to keep him there, talking.

"Or a wave buoying the ship up, moving it along to its destination."

It did look more like a wave than a kraken. "The optimistic version."

"What harm is there in that?" He laughed. "Gloominess is not to be courted lightly. The sun, the sky, they are bigger than that."

She wasn't sure exactly what he meant, but it sounded good.

"That cloud will turn a delicious shade of pink soon, when the sun decides to rest for the day. Shall we wait for it?"

"Yes," she said. "Let's wait."

It was dark by the time they got back to Grand Central. Even though she'd offered to take Edison back on her own, Andres had insisted on coming, and she hadn't put up much of a fight.

"My art opening, you will come?" Andres asked. "In a fancy dress to entice buyers in off the street to look at the art?"

"I'll come." She walked down the corridor toward Vanderbilt Hall and loosened the strap on her cast. "Can't guarantee any enticing."

"If you come," he said, "the enticing will take care of itself."

From anyone else that would have sounded corny, but for Andres it worked. Maybe it was the accent.

Edison tugged at the leash, practically dragging them back into the main concourse with its starry ceiling.

"He wants to see his master, don't you, boy?" Andres crooned.

He sounded good when he crooned.

They had almost reached the round information booth that led to the elevator to Tesla's home when something brushed her casted arm.

Edison jumped into the air and hit her hard in the chest. She fell right onto her ass. Her casted arm hurt when she landed. An open-mouthed Andres looked down at her.

She rolled to the side, reaching for her gun. Edison didn't knock people around for no reason. She scanned the huge room. A few people looking at her in surprise, a few more walking by like nothing had happened, and a man leaning against the wall playing with his phone. Nothing suspicious.

"Are you injured?" Andres helped her up by her good arm.

"I'm fine."

A crunching sound came from Edison's mouth as if he had a spring in there. He spat something out onto the marble.

"You naughty dog." Andres shook his finger at Edison and bent over the pile of dog spit. His face changed, and he scooped the wet object up with a handkerchief and pushed her toward the information booth so fast she almost fell over.

"Inside," he said. "We must get inside."

Evaline saw them coming and had the door open before they even got there. Andres closed the door when they were barely through.

"Are you OK, Miss Torres?" Evaline asked.

"Fine." Vivian watched Andres.

He was looking out through the glass like he expected to see an army. She looked, too. Nothing unusual.

"What's going on?" Vivian asked.

"Into the elevator," he said. "We talk there."

Evaline looked like she wanted to know what was going on, too, but she only said, "Give my best to Mr. Tesla."

"Will do." Vivian barely had time to answer. Andres rushed her down the hatch and the spiral stairs to the elevator.

Once they were inside the elevator's cage and moving down, he took the handkerchief out of his pocket. "This thing. I have seen something like it before."

She studied the wet object laid out on the white cotton: a collection of tiny gears, microchips, and something that looked like plastic wrap. "What is it?"

"First, we go to Mr. Tesla's Faraday cage."

"OK." How did he even know what a Faraday cage was? He was supposed to be a simple artist and dog walker.

He gave Edison a treat out of his pocket. "You're a good boy. A smart boy."

Edison wagged his tail.

She examined her cast where the object had touched her. The cast didn't look any different.

Officer Chan and Officer Fitzgerald met them at the elevator door. Chan had experience—a few white hairs threaded through his black hair, and he was careful about his job. Fitzgerald was his opposite—young and ready to jump. Parker was the only one unaccounted for. He was another bodyguard from Mr. Rossi's office. He was probably inside with Tesla.

"Hello, Miss Torres," said Fitzgerald. "And Mr. Peterson. Did you have a good walk?"

Chan stepped inside to wedge the elevator lever in its down position so no one could call it back up to the concourse.

"Fine," Vivian said.

"Let's go see your master." Andres unclipped Edison's leash.

The dog trotted off toward Tesla's crazy underground house. She'd initially liked the Victorian house and had loved its new garden, but she'd gotten heartily sick of it in the past few days. She didn't know how Tesla could stand it cooped up down here. Because he had to, her mother's voice said. People do what they have to do.

She and Andres followed the dog. Once they got to the red front door, they knocked, as per protocol. Parker let them in. He must have sensed something was up, because he tensed.

"Weird but no immediate danger," she told Parker.

"Another ordinary day," Parker said.

Andres went into the house, marched down the hall, and entered Tesla's billiard room. Soon after he moved in, Tesla had built a Faraday cage in there. The cage was made of a fine mesh and covered the walls, floor, and ceiling, designed to keep out electronic signals, not that there were many down here in the middle of nowhere. She'd always thought it a paranoid indulgence, but maybe she'd been too hasty.

"Mr. Tesla!" Andres called.

Tesla came down the stairs with Edison. At least he'd showered since she'd left. Hopefully, he'd even eaten. He looked distracted.

Andres set the handkerchief in the middle of the table. "Your fine dog snatched this off Miss Torres's arm and broke it."

Tesla was already bent over the collection of parts.

The officers had crowded into the room, but they didn't say anything.

"What is it?" Vivian couldn't take it anymore.

"A spy robot, I think," Andres said. "But I've never seen one this small before."

Tesla pointed at the mishmash of metal and dog slobber. "It has a stinger that leads to a small compartment. It doesn't look like it was broken open. Was anyone stung?"

Andres went pale. He'd picked it up and carried it like it was nothing.

"Poison?" Vivian asked. "It might have poison in it?"

"Might." Tesla reached down and petted Edison. He checked the dog's eyes and mouth and put his head against the dog's chest as if to listen to his breathing or heartbeat. "Edison seems fine."

Tesla took pictures from several angles, then lifted the object and put it in a mini-Faraday bag he sometimes used for his phone. He must be worried the object was still transmitting, but hard to imagine that after the dog had smashed it.

"So, was anyone stung?" Tesla repeated.

"It landed on my cast. But not my skin. Edison got it pretty quickly."

"How did the dog know it was dangerous?" asked Parker.

Tesla examined the dog. Edison looked healthy as ever, but Vivian worried. "Maybe he smelled the poison. After my poisoning a few months ago, he and I have worked on training him to respond when something smells off."

Tesla and Andres examined her cast. Tesla even retrieved an antique magnifying glass with a silver handle from one of his bookshelves, and they passed the lens back and forth.

"There's no hole. It didn't sting you," Andres finally said, sounding as relieved as she felt.

Tesla wiped her cast off thoroughly with a wet washcloth, bagged the cloth, and added it to the Faraday bag.

She ran her fingers over her cast. Nothing there.

"I'll need an analysis of this." Tesla handed the Faraday bag to Fitzgerald. The guy took it in one freckled hand, but he looked thoroughly confused. "Have them check the stinger for poison, and be very careful with it."

When no one was looking, she touched her cast where the creature had landed. Maybe Maeve was right. Maybe Tesla was a danger magnet.

Fitzgerald broke into her musings. "I'll take the bag up. We've called for a new officer to replace me. Officer Khan."

"I'll come up with you," Vivian said. "I want to check something."

Back into the old elevator they went. Fitzgerald looked nervously at the chandelier suspended from the ceiling. "I always wonder if this thing is going to stop working and I'll be trapped here until someone digs down to retrieve my desiccated corpse."

A bucket of joy, this guy. "It might be better than whatever poison is in that bug in your hand."

He started and looked down at the bag. It really wasn't nice to tease him. Her mother wouldn't have approved.

"Do you think there are more of these little buggers?" he asked.

"I do." She wasn't really sure, but the prudent thing to do was to act like there were, which was why she was in the elevator.

They reached the top, climbed the stairs, and came out into the information booth.

Evaline blocked their way out with her round form. "A minute, if you please, Miss Torres."

"Just the woman I want to see," Vivian said.

Fitzgerald's light blue eyes stared into the concourse like it was full of killer bugs. Maybe.

"I don't know exactly what happened out there with you and the dog." Someone came up to Evaline's counter, and she held up one finger to tell them to wait.

Vivian had never seen her do something like that. Evaline never let anyone wait a second longer than necessary. This was going to be good.

"Don't look," Evaline said. "But at my three o'clock is a man really focused on his phone."

She saw the guy out of the corner of her eye. Officer Fitzgerald looked down at the bag in his hand.

"He's been in the concourse off and on for the past few days, always just staring at his phone, but he never goes down to take a train," Evaline continued. "I notice things like that. It keeps my job interesting."

"And?" Officer Fitzgerald said.

"Just before Edison knocked you over, Miss Torres, he looked right at you. Then, during the confusion when you looked like you were going to shoot someone, he was the only person who didn't seem surprised."

"Maybe he just likes his phone games," Officer Fitzgerald said.

"Maybe," Evaline said. "But he's still there, and you've been down there awhile. And every so often, he takes a look around above everyone's heads, like he's looking for someone really tall."

Or something that flew.

"Thank you," Vivian said. "We'll look into it."

Fitzgerald dropped the Faraday bag into his inside jacket pocket. "You're a civilian."

"Right. So you can't tell me what to do."

"I'll handle it," he said. "No need for you to get involved."

"This guy might be staking out Tesla, and he might have tried to kill me. I'm involved."

"OK," Fitzgerald said. "The important thing is we get him."

"We split up when we leave the booth. I'll break left, you go right."

"Keep your firearm holstered," he said. "Grant me that much."

In answer, she gave Evaline a quick smile and headed for the door.

"Good-bye!" she called over her shoulder to make onlookers assume she and Fitzgerald were just splitting up to go their different ways. Then she shut the door quickly in case a bug robot was trying to get in. She wasn't going to put Evaline in danger.

She hadn't looked directly at Evaline's guy yet. Oblique glances told her he looked like the Avenger of Blood. Tesla had said, in describing him, *He's what we in facial recognition call an exceedingly ordinary-looking man—medium height, straight black hair, brown eyes, no distinguishing characteristics. He has the kind of face people forget.*

He slouched against a tan wall with his eyes glued on his phone. Nothing out of the ordinary. Was that camouflage, or was he using the phone to control the flying robots? That seemed like his MO—first the flying drone at the party, and then the bug that tried to sting her.

Take out the phone first.

Or at least that was the plan. A group of girls in silver and black cheerleading uniforms burst through the door and ran right in front of her. She was enveloped in a sea of perfume and ponytails and gray makeup. They weren't just cheerleaders—they were zombie cheerleaders.

Fitzgerald was coming up on Phone Guy, and she wasn't in a position to back him up. That was probably Fitzgerald's plan all along.

Fitzgerald didn't even reach the guy before he stumbled and hit the floor. Had he been stung?

The nearest exit was behind her, and Phone Guy sprinted toward it. He hadn't noticed her with her hot teen camouflage. She elbowed through the zombie pack, stuck out her foot, and tripped Phone Guy as he sailed past. All those hours looking for this criminal mastermind, and she'd tripped him like a bully in the schoolyard. Sometimes better to be lucky than smart.

He went down hard, and she landed with her knee in his back. She smashed his hand against the marble. She couldn't let him hold on to that phone. He twisted sideways and tried to keep ahold of it, which made her even more determined. She whacked his hand against the floor harder, and the phone slid across the polished marble. She hoped nobody stole it, but didn't have time to think about that.

The guy bucked around, but she kept him pinned. She had to get him subdued before he remembered she had only one strong arm. She went for one arm and yanked it back. That was a start.

As soon as she pulled his arm across his back, he gasped in pain and went limp. A shoulder injury. She eased off a fraction, but not much. He was a dangerous guy, and she wasn't taking any chances.

"Do you want to cuff him?" Fitzgerald dangled handcuffs in her face.

"Can't," she said. "I only have one arm."

"Right." Fitzgerald dropped down next to her and cuffed the guy's hands behind his back. Then he started patting him down.

"What happened to you?" she asked.

"I thought I saw a bug." Fitzgerald hadn't come up with anything, even a wallet. "And when I slapped at it, I went ass over teakettle."

"It's a slippery floor," she said.

"Excuse me," said a voice behind her ear.

She turned. A zombie cheerleader with plastic brains stuck to the front of her sweater held out a gray hand.

"Everything's OK." Vivian hoped the girl wasn't going to panic. She didn't want to deal with a hysterical teenager.

"I know." The cheerleader handed her a cell phone. "I think your suspect there dropped this."

Not the panicking type, this zombie.

"Thank you." Vivian took the phone gingerly, not wanting to add any more fingerprints to the surface.

The cheerleader shook a raggedy black pompon.

"Go, team!" she said before turning and rejoining her pack. They waved to Vivian and Fitzgerald and the guy on the ground before heading down toward the food court, presumably in search of brains.

Fitzgerald hauled the guy to his feet. Phone Guy had no expression on his face, like this kind of thing happened to him all the time. Maybe it did, although she suspected he didn't often get caught.

"I want a lawyer," he said in unaccented English. "I know my rights."

Fitzgerald shrugged.

She looked at the phone. Its screen displayed a bug's-eye view of the concourse. Four white arrows were on the bottom of the screen. It couldn't be as easy as that. Could it?

Clumsily, she worked the arrows. The view changed and started moving closer, careening around like the drone was drunk. Her sister, Lucy, would have been horrified at her remote-control incompetence. Even so, within a few minutes she'd guided the little fly to a shaky landing on the floor next to her.

Fitzgerald plucked the fly up and dropped it into his Faraday bag next to its smashed-up companion.

She went over to thank Evaline.

27

**Main concourse of Grand Central Terminal
March 17, 3:41 p.m.**

Avi's shoulder ached. Tesla's bodyguard, Vivian Torres, had
wrenched it as if she knew he was injured. He rolled both
shoulders as well as he could and sent a calming breath to his
aching joint. He couldn't afford to be paranoid or angry.
He'd been in custody enough times to know staying calm
and acting just submissive enough would keep him alive.

The beefy American policeman seemed almost kind as
he shepherded Avi through the busy concourse. He stayed
close, but he didn't need to. Avi couldn't outrun him, not
with his hands cuffed behind his back. He'd trip, and
without his hands to catch him, it would be an ugly fall. He
might even lose teeth. Better to bide his time.

With extra care, he walked forward, weaving away from
a crowd of men in suits. Their dark suits were identical,
except for a rainbow pattern of ties—reds, blues, pinks, and
yellows. He wouldn't see such refined clothing for a while,
and he saved up the memories of such fine things.

The men in suits didn't spare him a second glance. The
story of his life. No one noticed him, even when he was
trussed up like a string of lizards meant for the table. The gift
and curse of looking ordinary.

The policeman caught him when he stumbled, and pain knifed through his shoulder. He kept the pain from showing on his face or in his body. He wouldn't display weakness in front of his enemies. His training in torture would prove a useful gift. Although he didn't expect the Americans to torture him. His lawyer would negotiate his release or extradition back to his home country, and his compatriots there would set him free. Only a matter of waiting out the time and preserving his silence. The wheels of justice turned slowly, and the wheels of international justice more slowly still. He needed to marshal his strength to outlast the machine.

They reached the street. A police car waited in front of the grand doors like a valeted limousine. A man so tall he could have played basketball instead of working with criminals opened the back door, and Avi was pushed into the backseat.

It didn't smell like a limousine. It smelled of vomit and piss and the sharp bite of ineffectual disinfectant. He sat as straight as he could. He would have to shut down his finely honed senses to survive the next months, and he felt too old to do that one more time.

"—guy give you any trouble?" the tall one asked.

"Miss Torres subdued him." The redhead chuckled. "Kicked his ass one-handed."

Not entirely accurate, but Avi wouldn't allow himself to be baited into a response. The car lurched forward, then stopped in traffic. This action was repeated again and again. Every stop pained his shoulder.

As Avi headed to jail, Joe Tesla was being set free. The man could go back to work, wander around Grand Central and his beloved tunnels, wear fine suits, and date gorgeous women. He would do these things while Avi waited behind bars. But not for long.

He was angry at Tesla, but he was mostly angry at himself. After the dog caught the first fly, he should have left. But he'd been anxious to finish the contract and leave New York. He'd grown weary of the long wait, and he'd let himself become careless. Maybe he was too old.

As old as he was, he'd known to install fail-safes for this exact situation. If he didn't check in soon, his employer would be notified he was unable to complete the contract at this time, and they would probably hire another man to mete out justice to Tesla.

But if they failed, Avi would come back. He wouldn't give up until the man was dead. And as the man's life was slipping away, Avi would turn his attentions to the tall woman who had thwarted his plans and wounded his arm and his pride.

She would not escape either.

28

Joe dropped clothing into a duffel bag, checking everything off against the list in his head. He couldn't afford to forget anything. Edison followed every movement, probably wondering what this packing was all about. Andres had brought the dog back later than usual, but the dog seemed so relaxed and happy he was glad he had.

He glanced back at the bookcase covering the secret exit from his bedroom. No one knew about it but him and Leandro Gallo. Leandro wouldn't exactly be a problem. Joe would disappear, and no one would know how.

As if she'd heard his thought, Vivian slammed open his bedroom door and marched in. He could have sworn he'd locked that door, but he couldn't point that out since his bodyguards had insisted he not lock it.

"You're supposed to knock." He tried to move between her and the duffel bag.

"I just wanted to tell you we apprehended the man controlling the bug robots. He looks like the guy who shot Maeve."

"Good." He just wanted her to leave.

"Evaline tipped us off." Her eyes danced with adrenaline. "We took him out in the concourse. Fitzgerald has him at the station. It looks like you're free to get out and about."

"Good," he said again.

"What are you doing?" She looked over his shoulder at the duffel. "Sir."

Busted. That changed things.

"Cleaning up," he lied.

"Looks like you're getting packed." She pointed at the duffel.

"Putting stuff in storage."

"Looks to me like you're getting ready to sneak out the back door."

"What back door?" he asked.

"You know I can't let you do that." She moved her feet apart and dropped into a low stance. He wondered if she even knew she was doing that.

"You've only got one good arm," he said. "I think I could take you."

"I have one arm and one cast." She touched it. "And you're welcome to try."

It would be embarrassing if she pinned him, but just as bad if he got past her. If she yelled for help, there'd be three (red) guys in his bedroom inside of a minute. They'd practiced it in a security drill.

"You don't have to put yourself in danger and leave," she said.

"Maybe I want a quiet walk."

"With a duffel bag full of clothes and weird electronic gear?"

"You never know when you'll need a change of clothes."

"I can't let you leave," she said.

"You work for me," he pointed out.

"You can always fire me."

"Would you leave me alone if I fired you?"

"I'd be free to do whatever I wanted." She sat next to him. "Including not leave you alone."

Edison licked her hand. Even the dog wasn't on his side.

"Tell me what you're up to," she said. "Then we'll see."

"I've hired a ship to go look for that submarine." It sounded crazier when he said it aloud. "It's too dangerous for me here, and for anyone around me."

"I like ships." She flashed a completely insincere smile and didn't budge.

"You hate ships."

"Sounds like you'd have to pay me extra."

"What if I paid you extra to sit quietly outside my door for an hour and then start an ineffectual search?"

"That job doesn't interest me. Not like the ship."

He sighed. "I don't want you to come."

"Thanks," she said. "I'm touched."

He felt himself flushing. "I didn't mean it like that. It's just—"

"Dangerous?" she asked.

"Not if I do it right." He'd made a checklist for his bag, and he looked at it to avoid looking at her.

"I know you're my boss," she said. "But you're not my commanding officer, and I don't have to watch you do stupid crap and say nothing."

"You're saying plenty," he said. "Over and over."

"I know you're stir crazy," she said. "But you just got a get-out-of-jail-free card."

"I find your faith in the process astounding," he said. "Even if they caught the right guy, the Dakkars will send another. So long as they still think I tried to kill the prince."

"If they do, we'll deal with it," she said. "No reason to cut and run."

He added a pea coat to the pile. New, purchased by Andres Peterson. He and Andres had set up a system to get things past the cops and bodyguards. Edison had gone outside with Andres every day—up the elevator, through Grand Central, and right out the front door with a list taped to the inside of his collar. Every day before Andres brought the dog back, he'd turn in a backpack containing the items on the list to the Lost & Found Office at Grand Central marked with Joe's name. All Joe had to do was sneak out his back door and retrieve the backpack without getting caught. Perry, the clerk at the Lost & Found, had been in on the plan.

"It's a new moon tonight," he said. "We won't get another for a month. That's how moon cycles work. And I'm not cutting and running. I've been planning this for a while."

She went into his bathroom and tossed stuff around. She came out carrying a little canvas bag. "I took your toothpaste, an unopened toothbrush, and your comb."

"It's not really a good idea."

"Right." She crossed to his closet and took out a couple of pairs of socks, a pair of jeans, and a couple T-shirts. She even grabbed a pair of clean underwear Maeve had left and tossed everything into a pillowcase.

He shouldered the duffel bag and whistled for Edison. The dog leaped to his side. He must have known they were leaving the house, but he'd no idea how far they were going.

Joe straightened the antique quilt on his bed, tidying up and inhaling the comfortable smell of lilac that had probably permeated this room for a century. He wondered if he'd ever come back.

"I'm going out the back door," he said. "Don't try to stop me."

"I won't," she said. "I always wondered where the back door was."

"Vivian," he said. "I'm about to do a crazy thing."

"Just another day at the office."

"On the water," he said. "For a long time. And you won't have many extra clothes."

"Extra pay," she said. "That'll make it up to me."

"Any way I could go out that door without you?" he asked. "Pay raise? Kitchen appliances?"

She folded her arms, good arm on top of the broken one.

"It might be dangerous."

"I'm more worried about what my mother is going to think when your bodyguards realize you're gone and the press discovers we've both disappeared."

"That's its own kind of danger," he said. "You want to avoid that."

She pointed to the antique bookcase near his bed. "It's behind that, isn't it?"

29

Vivian whistled when he slid open the bookshelf. "Did you press something?"

"Maybe," he said. "Maybe not."

Even watching him she hadn't been able to see how he opened it. When they got back, she intended to figure it out, but for now she just added it to her to-do list.

He patted the edge of the tunnel, and Edison jumped in. Joe pushed the duffel into the hole and climbed in after it.

She hurried to follow. His last chance of leaving her behind would be to lose her in the tunnels, and she expected him to try. Her mother called it her suspicious nature.

He reached to pull the bookcase closed. That'd give the bodyguards a nasty shock. "Aren't they going to freak out when they can't find you? Maybe go to the press and make a fuss?"

"An email will be delivered to Mr. Rossi in a half hour, telling him I've left of my own free will. The police and bodyguards will be withdrawn from my house and taken out of danger."

He turned around and crawled forward.

She got a quick glimpse before his flashlight pointed forward, and he started retreating at a good clip. The tunnel was of rough-hewn rock, with a ceiling so low she had to crawl on her hands and knees. Or rather, her hand, cast, and knees while dragging the pillowcase. This must be Tesla's first test to see if he could ditch her.

As hard as she tried, the lead between them grew. If she'd had two good hands, she'd have been able to keep up. Did he plan to leave her trapped?

A puff of cool air crossed her face. He'd reached the other end and opened the door. She upped her crawl to double time and had almost made it to the opening that must be the end of the tunnel when a shadow moved across it.

Tesla was closing the door.

"Hey!" she hollered and pressed on.

Before the door closed completely, a light-colored form jumped in the way. A bark echoed down the tunnel. When she reached the door, Edison was half in and half out. Tesla whispered something, but the dog ignored him.

She climbed out and stood next to Tesla.

"Problem with the door?" she asked.

"I slipped," he said. "Sorry."

She bent and patted Edison on the head. "Good boy!"

The dog wagged his tail. With the dog on her side, she was basically unstoppable. Tesla had to know that.

Tesla closed the door. It looked as old as the one that led to the submarine dock—thick metal with a rubber seal on the inside. If the subway ever flooded this far up, water wouldn't get into Tesla's bedroom.

He locked the door with an old-fashioned key.

They walked down the dark tunnel for a few moments before he stopped and touched his fingers to his lips to warn her to be quiet. They must be close to the bodyguards stationed outside his official tunnel exit. Edison tucked in tight against Tesla's heels, and they set off at a brisk trot.

Tunnels converged on tunnels, dark tracks gave way to well-lit ones and dark ones again. She had a good sense of direction, but she still lost track of the way back.

After a half hour of this, she spoke. "Is this really the most direct way to your submarine dock?"

Tesla looked sheepish. "I'm avoiding the trains."

"You're not going to shake me off," she said. "And we had a deal."

"I'm not trying to shake you off."

But after that, he started heading in one direction, and it wasn't long before her surroundings began to look familiar.

They had to flatten against the side of the tunnels four times to avoid oncoming trains. Every time, Edison's head swiveled between the two of them, as if he was afraid to let either one out of his sight in case they did something stupid. Smart dog.

"We're here." Tesla unlocked the door to the dock and gestured for her to go in first.

She threaded her arm through his. "Let's go in together."

But it hadn't been a trap. Wright's green submarine was parked where it had been before. Wright stood on the dock. She wasn't looking forward to another submarine ride with him.

"Is this going to be a tearful farewell?" Wright asked. "Because you're running late."

"She's coming along," Tesla answered.

Wright looked back at his sub. She knew it was a three-seater, so he couldn't trot that out. "Going to be a tight fit with the dog and your luggage."

Not that she had any luggage except for the pillowcase of stuff. She started to wonder about what was at the other end of the submarine ride. While Tesla loaded stuff, she fired off a quick text to her mother.

Don't worry. Ask Mr. Rossi in an hour. Might be gone awhile.

She hoped she wouldn't be too long. Andres had invited her to his art opening in two weeks, and she didn't want to disappoint him. He was an intriguing guy. Cute, too.

30

Joe's heart started hammering as soon as he saw the sub. Edison knew it and brushed his nose against the back of his hand. *Together,* the dog seemed to say, *we can do this together.*

Joe dropped his duffel inside the cockpit. Alan didn't try to catch or help, but he was doing plenty already. He wondered why Alan had agreed to take them out to the ship. Alan always had an angle, and Joe couldn't see it. That bothered him.

He climbed into the cockpit with Edison. Vivian came in right after. She'd been close since they left the house. She'd known he would try to ditch her, but the time for that was past, and he was grateful to have her along. She always had his back.

Once they were settled, Alan closed the cockpit, and down they went.

The water went from green to black almost immediately. Blue navigation lights showed the way forward. Before the accident, he'd loved this moment, but now it filled him with dread. He practiced his breathing techniques. He'd made a lot of progress in his virtual therapy sessions, but he wasn't sure he was ready for this.

Edison licked his fingers, and he ruffled the dog's ears. Vivian sat quietly behind him, and it sounded like she was doing breathing exercises of her own. He felt guilty for asking her to go down with Alan so soon after the accident.

He hadn't realized how difficult it must have been until this moment. He was a self-absorbed jerk.

As if she knew what he was thinking, Vivian leaned forward and squeezed his shoulder, making him feel guiltier. But at least the guilt distracted him.

"Keep your shit together," Alan muttered. "No panicking on my boat."

"You're a font of empathy," Vivian said.

Alan snorted. "Not my job, being Mr. Feelgood."

Joe had taken a Xanax before he left the house, but it didn't seem to be doing anything. He ought to write the drug manufacturer and demand his money back. *To whom it may concern: Despite taking your medication, I still felt anxious taking a submarine soon after I was almost killed in one.* He chuckled at the thought of that letter being read, and Edison wagged his tail. That meant he was doing better.

Alan pushed the submarine hard, making much better time than Joe ever did. He clearly wasn't interested in a scenic tour.

"How are you doing in the contest?" Joe asked.

"First," Alan said. "Since the guys ahead of me died and dropped out like pussies."

"Wow," said Vivian. "Just. Wow."

They pressed on in awkward silence.

Too soon for his liking, Alan slowed down. "Almost there. Should I surface?"

"Yes. Please," Joe said.

The sub tilted up sharply. Joe's heart hammered against his ribs, and he started to sweat like he'd just finished a marathon. Edison licked his fingers and nuzzled his leg.

"Vivian, your job is to get Edison on board." His voice cracked halfway through, but he kept going. "Safely."

"Got it."

They broke the surface. Rain pelted the cockpit, and black waves roiled around them. Alan swore.

Joe looked at his hands twisting in his lap. How had he thought he could do this?

Alan pressed the cockpit-release button, and the protective bubble started to lift. The smell of salt air flooded the cockpit. The first real outside air Joe had breathed in a long time, and he wished he could savor it, but instead, he shivered and tried not to lose control of his bowels. His hands clamped tightly to the sides of his seat.

A rope splashed on the sub's skids. Alan grabbed it and started pulling them closer to a dark shape that rose out of the black water. Water droplets stung Joe's face. He didn't know if they were rain or seawater, and he didn't care.

He closed his eyes. If he ignored the pitching underneath him, the smell of the sea, and the water lashing his face, he could pretend he was home, sitting in his shower with a plate of fish. That image was so ridiculous he almost laughed, and the terror receded.

Edison huddled against him. The dog's warm form, his tongue on Joe's cheek, even the smell of wet dog—all helped to drive away the fear. Edison was there. He heard the clank of a safety harness unfastening, and Edison moved from his side.

"Come on, Edison," Vivian said. "You're with me."

The dog growled.

"Go with her," Joe whispered. "Good boy."

Edison whined like he wasn't sure. His place was with Joe. Always.

"Go. I'm right behind you." Joe ordered, and the warmth of the dog against his leg disappeared. He counted, numbers blooming behind his eyes. He shivered, and his teeth chattered. Fear swamped him.

A warm hand touched his shoulder. Vivian. She'd come back for him. "Edison's aboard. It's just a little jump onto the swim platform and then up onto the back deck. There's an enclosed tent there."

"A hop, skip, and a jump," Joe said. Farnsworth, the vet from the circus, always said that.

"I have a syringe," Vivian said quietly, probably hoping Alan wouldn't hear. He'd be an ass about it if he did.

"Not yet," Joe answered. "Not yet."

He focused on his right hand, willing each finger to uncurl. She stood next to him, her breath warm on his neck, her hand squeezing his shoulder.

"Take your time," she said. "I'm paid by the hour."

"I don't have all night." Alan's abrasive voice cut through the rain and the wind and the fear.

Anger flared in Joe's chest. Without opening his eyes, he stood. He was standing outside, for the first time in months.

"Just a step here." Vivian guided him forward.

The sub pitched up and down, and he wondered if he would fall and be crushed between the sub and the boat he knew waited next to it in the darkness. That thought wasn't so frightening. At least then he wouldn't be so damn scared.

Vivian lifted his hand and placed it against cold metal. Rough rope scraped his palm. He grabbed with both hands.

"One big step!" She yelled through the sound of the rain. "Hurry! Don't leave me trapped back here with this asshole."

He made a mental note to laugh about that later, but for now he focused only on the platform with his feet and pulling himself aboard. Nearby, Edison barked. Not far to go.

A wave drenched his legs, rain pounded his face, but he didn't care. The only thing that mattered was getting back inside.

Hands grabbed him and dumped him facedown in a pile of rope. It smelled like tar. Edison licked his ears, his neck, his cold hands.

He'd done it.

31

Vivian hauled herself one-armed onto the deck and glanced over the side at the pitching black waves. Wright had already submerged. No going back now.

She headed across the dark deck to a bank of windows and a closed door. She couldn't really tell the size from the sub, but it had looked like a pretty big powerboat—maybe eighty feet long. Hopefully, they'd turn on the lights soon.

A man in black cargo pants and a black sweater stepped out of the doorway in the side of the cabin. He was tall, probably about six-foot-four, and barrel-chested. He looked like he could throw her off the boat one-handed. "I'm Captain Glascoe."

"Vivian Torres." She held out a hand, and he shook it.

"We weren't informed you would be boarding as well. I thought you were here to deliver the dog and Mr. Tesla."

"It was last-minute." Very last-minute.

"We'll have to bring you inside to verify with Mr. Tesla before we leave."

"Of course."

Glascoe gestured for her to enter the darkened door ahead of him. She didn't like turning her back on a stranger in the dark, and she held her wounded arm straight by her side so he couldn't see the cast and tried to walk like a civilian, and a woman, instead of a retired Army sergeant with her arm in a cast carrying a pillowcase.

"What do you do for Mr. Tesla?" Glascoe asked.

"Personal assistant." She shrugged her shoulders in what she hoped was a helpless-looking gesture. "A little of this. A little of that. And I help take care of the dog."

The door to the main cabin opened from the inside. Someone flicked the light on when she entered like it was some kind of surprise party. She squinted. Tesla sat on a bench seat with the dog pressed up against his legs and a wooden table in front of him. Stairs behind him and a set of closed wooden doors. Lots of places for people to pop out of.

Tesla looked like death warmed over—pale and shaking. Next to him, a hairy redhead was leering at her. There had to be at least one more guy driving the boat, maybe two. Based on the boat's size, she was guessing there were at least six crew on board.

"How are you doing, Mr. Tesla?" she asked.

"Fine," Tesla said. "Seasick."

"I met Captain Glascoe on my way in," she said. "I explained I'm your personal assistant and it was decided last-minute I would come with you."

"Will you be needing your own cabin?" The hairy guy smirked. Apparently, he thought she was that kind of assistant. As angry as it made her, she couldn't really blame him. She'd shown up at the last minute with the clothes on her back and a sack. Her position was odd.

"She'll need her own cabin," Tesla said quickly. "And clothing and supplies."

"Marshall, show Miss Torres her bunk," barked Glascoe.

"Where is it?" the hairy guy asked.

"Next to Mr. Tesla's cabin."

"That's my bunk." Marshall's eyes narrowed.

"And clear your crap out." Glascoe smiled. "I hope you enjoy the voyage, Miss Torres. Welcome aboard the *Voyager*."

"Thank you."

Marshall stood. He was a good six inches shorter than Vivian, but muscular and he looked as if he'd be good in a fight. "Let's go."

She followed him down a set of stairs toward the stern. He was bowlegged, but his straight posture indicated a stint in the military, or maybe a back disorder.

It had been an expensive boat once, but even a landlubber like her could tell it hadn't been well maintained. The floor in the initial cabin had looked like teak, but it was gray with age, and the metal fixtures were corroded green. She hoped they took better care of the engines and the radio. Tesla could afford a much nicer boat, so there must be another reason besides comfort to explain why he'd rented this tub.

Behind the doors was a dimly lit galley with a curved island, a table with bench seats, a stove, microwave, refrigerator, a stocked bar, and barstools upholstered in what looked like orange velvet. Everything was clean, but it looked dilapidated.

They went down a spiral staircase like the one that led to Tesla's elevator. Marshall headed toward the bow, opened a door, and slammed it, leaving her alone in the corridor. She tried the door handle. Locked.

"Marshall?" she called.

"Just a sec."

She looked around the corridor. Next to Marshall's door was another one, probably to a second cabin. On the other side of the stairs was another door, probably a third cabin. Based on the hum she'd been hearing, the engines were aft of that.

Marshall came out carrying a duffel bag, a paperback, a towel that smelled like it hadn't been washed since Edison was born, and a lamp with a half-naked hula girl on the base.

"All yours," he said.

She opened the door and went in. The smell of mint chewing tobacco was overpowering, and a puddle of wet brown liquid told her his opinion of giving up his room. The bottom bunk smelled like Marshall, and she stripped the sheets and blanket and tossed them on the floor. She sniffed the bottom mattress.

Top bunk.

She found a set of fresh sheets in the locker. They smelled like mildew, but that was way better than Marshall, and luckily, she'd brought her own pillowcase from Tesla's. Even after being dragged around all night, it was still probably cleaner than what they had here. Next to the top bunk were two tiny windows that didn't open. A quick look through the lockers turned up a set of rubber boots and a wool pea coat that looked older than she was. Both were too big for Marshall and might actually fit her. A copy of a magazine called *Big Asses* was under the bottom mattress. She left it there because she didn't want to touch it. The bathroom was a fetid mess, but she found a bottle of bleach under the sink, a set of towels that looked and smelled fairly fresh in the locker, and a wet towel on the floor. Marshall probably hadn't noticed the fresh towels.

The cabin could be made livable if the smell of chewing tobacco ever went away. All in all, it wasn't the worst place she'd ever stayed. No point in whining instead of working. She was, after all, on the clock.

She used the wet towel to mop up the chewing tobacco puddle, moving it around on the floor with her foot. Then she kicked the dirty towel into the corner, sacrificed a washcloth, and wiped everything down with diluted bleach. By the time she was done, the room wasn't half bad.

Someone rapped on the door while she was washing the slimy feeling of bleach off her hands. She recognized Tesla's knock and let him in. Edison came in after his master and wrinkled his nose.

"You should have smelled it before," she told him, and the dog trotted off to inspect her tiny bathroom. He wasn't going to like that much either.

"I'm sorry your quarters are so..." Tesla looked around. "Spartan."

"Spartans made good warriors," she said.

He closed the door, glanced at the towel she'd kicked into the corner, and gestured to the bottom bunk. "Mind if I have a seat?"

She sat next to him.

"I know you might be wondering why I picked this ship."

She waited him out.

"The engines have a particular sound signature," he said.

If he hadn't said weird things like this all the time, she would have been more surprised. "Uh-huh."

"It's outside the range that the particular Swedish-designed sub we're tracking listens for."

That sounded like Fred. She'd met him only once, but he seemed like an even weirder version of Tesla. Super smart, but odd. "Did Fred Mulcahy recommend this ship?"

"He did," Tesla said. "Only a few ships have this particular sound profile, so my choices were pretty limited. But on this ship, we're as close to invisible as we can get while chasing the sub."

Made sense, as far as it went. "That's half of the equation."

"The other?" Tesla hated to forget things.

"How do we find them?" Edison came back out of her bathroom and licked her knee, probably out of sympathy.

"I know where they were a few days ago. I have an idea where they might be now—"

"Like, you drew a giant circle on a map?" She wished she'd had the chance to pack more clothes. This might take a while.

Tesla laughed. "Better than that. I was able to track oxygen generators I think they ordered online."

Of course he had. Everything led through the Internet for Tesla. "Where are they?"

"They're being delivered to a yacht called *Shining Pearl* in Halifax tomorrow. We ought to be able to intercept the yacht, then follow it at an undetectable distance until it meets up with our sub."

"Then what? This ship doesn't look like a destroyer. A submarine could kick our ass. Hell, a luxury yacht could probably sink us."

"I'll stay in touch with my naval contacts, and hopefully, they'll step in."

"Like they have in the past?" All they'd done was give him Fred Mulcahy, and she suspected that was because nobody else wanted him. Either way, she was going to locate the life rafts and make sure they were well stocked.

"I'm going to take pictures and slap a transponder onto the side of the sub. It transmits on a specific band Fred can track. Once they see this ghost ship, they'll step in then, or I hope so. Once I've done that, I'll have done all I can."

"First off, I'm sure you'll think of something more to do." He always thought of more. "'Done all I can' doesn't ever really stop, not with you."

He shrugged.

"Second, how are you going to stick a transponder on a submarine in the middle of the ocean?"

"Rest up," he said. "Because I have a plan."

He always had a plan.

32

Laila sat alone in her cabin. Her short hair was wet from the shower. She'd used up more than her share of hot water, but she still didn't feel clean. Perhaps she didn't need to. Her crew was ready for their final mission. She'd had doubts—doubts they would be able to take the sub, doubts they would be able to pilot it in combat conditions, and doubts they would be able to take lives. Now her doubts were settled. Once they picked up the replacement oxygen generators from Aunt Bibi's yacht, they would be ready to go.

An eye for an eye, a life for a life. Her crew understood, but she dreamed often of the man's body crushed under her submarine. In her dreams, he woke up and begged for his life. He always told her his death was meaningless, that he was innocent, and even if she killed the prince, it couldn't bring back her sister. But the people they had killed had to die in order to save many others. Difficult choices had to be made. If she didn't make those choices, others would.

She leaned against the hard wall and let the now familiar hum of the engines thrum through her body. The narrow bed usually felt comforting, but today it felt claustrophobic. She wanted to pace around outside, or even inside, but she couldn't let the crew see her agitation. She was the captain, and she needed to stay in control.

A soft knock sounded at her door.

"Come." She longed for a distraction. Nothing serious. Maybe a minor mechanical problem.

"Meri," said a soft voice.

Meri had been at the top of her class in medical school, had dreamed of being a surgeon, and had instead been ordered to marry and give up her career. Meri's fury at that fate had led Nahal to her. Meri had been one of their first recruits, and she was the one most loyal to the cause.

Meri entered and stood next to the swivel chair in front of the captain's desk. It, like all the furniture, was bolted to the floor, a stable object in an unstable world.

"The crew is happy they downed the *Narwhal*, Captain." Meri closed the door, the sound loud in the once quiet space.

"Any regrets?" The crew wouldn't tell her their feelings. As the captain, she needed to stand above them and show no doubts.

"Rasha," Meri said. "Of all the women, only Rasha seems affected."

Laila sat up in surprise. "But we killed the man who injured her. She should rejoice!"

"Collateral damage happens in wartime. It has to." Meri sighed. Laila wasn't sure if it indicated sadness at this tragic truth, or exasperation that Rasha didn't accept it.

"It's my duty to fulfill our original mission and to keep the crew as safe as I can. I cannot be responsible for those who get in the way." Laila noticed how shrill her voice had become, as if she needed to convince herself and Meri.

"Innocents will die," Meri said. "This submarine is a blunt instrument. It's not like a scalpel that cuts with precision."

"Does Rasha think the cost is too great?"

"Are *you* doubting our mission?" Meri asked. "You must be the most committed of all. Many more innocents will die if we are successful. We've always known that."

"I am committed." She couldn't appear weak, or Meri might try to take over the ship. "We took this vessel for a reason, and I will not waver in the execution of that. Nor will I let those under my command fail in their duties. The cost is too great."

Laila stood then, straight as the princess she was, and Meri stepped back. Laila was the highest-ranking royal on the ship, and they had deferred to her since childhood. Laila must not let them forget.

Another knock on the door, and Rasha entered without permission. A slight woman with giant eyes, she reminded Laila of a Chihuahua.

Meri was pushed back against the desk. There wasn't room for three in her cabin, but Laila didn't sit. She needed to be in a position of power, not sitting on her bed like a teenager.

"I wish to leave the ship," Rasha said. "Put me ashore anywhere. I won't tell anyone anything that's happened."

She hadn't expected Rasha to be the first with doubts. "You signed an oath to this ship, to your sisters, and to me."

"I didn't understand it then. I didn't know how it would feel to be made a murderer."

"We killed the men on the *Narwhal* for you. For your unborn daughters. And the woman who would have followed after you."

"He only did what his father did before him."

Meri touched her arm. "It's difficult to watch men die. As a doctor—"

"As a doctor, you're sworn to save lives, yet you're helping this one take them." Rasha gestured toward Laila. "We just killed twenty-six men, and we will kill more than a thousand if we stay on this path. That's too many."

"You signed an oath upon your honor," Laila said.

"As did you. And where is your honor now?" Rasha's voice was too loud in the small space. "Didn't your honor die with the men on that ship?"

Meri reached past her and closed the door. As if it would be so easy to contain Rasha's anger and guilt now that they were trapped on a giant tin can together.

"The deaths of the men on the *Narwhal* were necessary," Laila said. "We have only one more target. We must fulfill our purpose, or they have died in vain."

"All the deaths were in vain," Rasha said. "I want to leave."

"We must complete our task. After that, we can go our separate ways, and we can grieve for those we have lost," said Meri. "We must be strong, all of us, like doctors. We are treating a sick society, and the only way to make it well is to lance the evil boils who keep the society ill. Only then can it heal for all of us."

Laila nodded in what she hoped was a regal manner. "As Meri says. We must endure for four more days."

"Those aren't boils you're lancing. They are flesh-and-blood men," Rasha said. "Some are hard and cruel, but what right do we have to murder them for those sins?"

"We took that right." Laila was close enough to slap her. "Just as they have taken the right to murder us for generations. It is only by the merest chance that you didn't die at the hands of your brutal husband. My sister did. I would have, too."

"And in the end, when the sea teems with the bodies of the slain, will the world be better off?" Rasha advanced on her, hands clenched in fists at her sides.

"With whom have you spoken about this?" asked Meri. Bizarrely, Laila noticed her grammar, correct but archaic, rather like Meri herself.

Rasha whirled to face her. "With no one. I wanted to talk to our captain first. To beg her to release us from our oaths. Let us keep what innocence we have left."

"We only have one more task to perform," said Laila. "Then everyone can go their own way."

"Don't kill the people on that boat," Rasha said. "Don't make your sisters and cousins and friends into killers."

"They've already killed." Meri stuck one hand in her pocket and put the other on Rasha's shoulder in a gesture that might have been meant to be reassuring, but looked somehow menacing.

"They want this," Laila said firmly. "They've wanted this from the beginning. I'm sorry you've changed, but everyone else has stayed the same."

"Do you know that?" Rasha asked. "Have you talked to them? I'll talk to them. I'll make them see."

"We can't afford doubt," Laila said. "It will be over soon. You know what will happen to the people of New York if we fail. Then the people of our own country. War. We are stopping a war."

Rasha was so close Laila smelled her delicate floral perfume, a gift sent by Aunt Bibi. "We don't know that. Not for certain."

"Step away!" Meri said in a loud and unnatural voice. "Don't hurt her!"

Shocked by her tone, Rasha and Laila turned to look at Meri.

Meri took her hand out of her pocket and, quick as a snake, she struck Rasha on the throat. Bright red blood shot out in a single glittering strand. Droplets freckled Laila's face and stung her eyes.

Almost in slow motion, Rasha lifted her hand to cover the wound.

Laila reached for Rasha, but before she could touch her, Meri's silver knife rose and slashed Laila across the forearms. Wetness soaked her uniform.

Rasha crumpled to the floor, blood leaking around her long fingers.

"She attacked you." Meri pressed her hand hard against Laila's wounds. "You got the knife away and slashed out. You didn't think you would kill her. I saw."

"I didn't kill her." Laila tried to pull her wounded arms away.

"Rasha had to die for us to finish our work. You know this." Meri's words whispered against Laila's blood-damp face.

Laila looked at her friend, the doctor. Meri's brown eyes met hers without flinching.

"It was necessary," Meri said. "We've come too far together to falter now. We must stop this madness of the prince's before it leads to war. Rasha's life is a small debt to pay."

She pushed Laila back until the bed pressed against her knees and she sat. Before Laila could answer, Meri released her arms and spun toward the corridor.

"Help us!" Meri screamed. "Please come!"

She threw the knife into the corridor. When it landed, Laila recognized it as a scalpel. A tool of healing used to bring death.

Chattering voices grew closer.

Laila held one wounded arm with the other. Blood dripped off her elbows and flecked her blue fleece blanket. On her clean floor, her cousin's eyes had already gone glassy. Her hand had fallen away from her neck and rested on the floor, her upturned palm full of the blood of the house of Dakkar.

33

Vivian hated wetsuits. She hated stuffing herself inside one, like a sausage into a tight casing. Probably how the sharks viewed it. Gift-wrapped lunch.

She'd met the crew—six guys with varying degrees of facial hair and hygiene. Captain Glascoe, Marshall, two guys who disappeared every time they spotted her, and two burly blond guys named Billy and Bob, who had turned up to watch her suit up and train. Lots of testosterone on deck.

Captain Glascoe slipped easily into his suit. Had he coated the inside with Vaseline? There had to be a trick to it.

"Do you need a hand with that?" asked Marshall.

"I got it." She tried not to fall off the swim platform and yanked the wetsuit up to her waist one-handed. Now for the top.

"You won't get the sleeve over your cast." Marshall stepped forward and took the arm of her wetsuit. He drew a folding knife out of his pocket, unfolded it, and slit the wetsuit to the elbow. She was glad that Tesla had paid for the suit, as it was basically ruined. Still, it was the only way she'd get it on.

"Thanks." She put her casted arm through and then put on the other arm. "How will we keep this arm from leaking?"

Marshall picked up a roll of gray tape. "Duct tape solves all problems."

She held still while he taped her arm in. He was quick at it.

Once that was done, she reached back for the long zipper pull and zipped herself in, then donned the dive hood. The suit was originally intended for Tesla, but it fit her just fine. Tesla was supposed to join her for training, but he was puking in his cabin with his dog.

"You and I will go off the back with our DPVs. You can learn how they work, and then we'll get back on course," Glascoe said.

"Sounds good." Vivian wasn't sure it did.

Glascoe put on his BCD and tank, and she followed suit. She'd told him the extent of her scuba training before they started. He'd stifled a wince. At least Tesla had diving experience.

She took a deep breath and approached her DPV. DPV stood for diver propulsion vehicle. They looked like propane tanks cut in half and painted black. With their tiny engines, divers could cover a lot of ground without a lot of effort. Tesla's plan involved using them to get close to the sub. Originally, he'd been intending to go on his own, but Vivian had insisted on going with him, so she had to be trained. She suspected that, despite what Tesla had told Glascoe, he'd never used one of these.

Glascoe grabbed his device and slipped off the swim platform like an otter. She followed clumsily, slipping her regulator in her mouth and falling into the water like a log, her good hand holding the DPV.

Glascoe had talked her through the controls on the boat, and it took only a couple of tries to get her buoyancy under control, then she grabbed on with both hands, and opened up the throttle on the surface to see what the DPV could do.

Awesome.

She'd be in the ocean all the time if she had one of these.

Her DPV reminded her of an underwater motorcycle. She curved a wide circle around the boat, passing Glascoe. He increased his speed, but she was lighter. So long as she stayed in a hydrodynamic position, he'd never catch her. She let him get close, then opened up the throttle and left him behind.

After she'd had time to think it over more, she slowed. No point in antagonizing Glascoe. He caught up and held up one hand in a fist to tell her to stop and they surfaced together.

"Nice work," he said. "I want us to do a side-to-side run about a hundred meters from the ship, exactly two meters under the surface. That's what you'll be doing on your mission."

She removed her regulator. "Roger that."

"Do you need a refresher on your controls?"

"Nope." She'd been paying attention on deck. A lot of attention.

"Then off we go."

They put the regulators back in their mouths. She reset the DPV's buoyancy and started to sink. Cold water closed over her head, and she gritted her teeth against the rubber mouthpiece of her regulator. It reminded her of leaving the sub.

But in a couple of minutes, she was fine. Light green water above, dark green below, and nothing ahead.

She kept an eye on her navigational equipment, turning right when she hit the hundred-meter mark. Glascoe stayed in position throughout the turn. They headed straight back to the ship, and Glascoe climbed up first. She levered herself up and out with one arm. With the broken arm and the tank and the DPV to haul around, she was glad she'd put in her time at the gym.

"Ahead full!" Glascoe called, and the ship started to move.

Billy and Bob started down toward them, but the captain waved them off.

She took off her BCD and closed her tank valve.

"You're one hell of a diver," he said. "If I didn't know better, I'd say you have some experience."

"Nope." She sat on the deck for a second to catch her breath. "Pretty straightforward."

"Do you think your boss can do it?"

Vivian was torn. Truthfully, she had no idea. "He has a lot more scuba experience than I do."

"He's a civilian," Glascoe said. "And a computer nerd."

"I'm a civilian," she pointed out.

"Not hardly," he said. "I'm guessing Army, because you don't seem to like the water that much."

"Former Army." No point in lying about it.

"But your Mr. Tesla wasn't in any kind of service."

"No, he was not." She removed her hood.

"I'm not exactly sure what you guys are going to do once we intercept whatever it is you're looking for, but I'm guessing it's not entirely legal, and I know it's risky."

"I imagine you were paid enough to take whatever risk you think you'll be taking." She pulled off her fins and laid them next to her BCD. "Tesla might not look like much, but he's got a cool head in stressful situations. He's the smartest guy I've ever met, and he doesn't have a death wish. If he has a plan for getting in, he has a plan for getting back out, and he believes he has a good chance of executing it."

Which didn't exactly guarantee success.

"For your sake, I hope so." Glascoe stood, lifted up his tank and DPV, and walked off.

Vivian leaned her head back and drank in the sunshine. The Atlantic was cold. And when she went in next time, it would be dark and dangerous. Tesla worried her, but he did dream up some exciting adventures she'd never get to do otherwise. She'd crossed some items off her bucket list on this job.

"You beat Glascoe in a race." Marshall stood between her and the sun. "Nobody else can do that."

Because you guys are too heavy. "Beginner's luck."

Marshall flopped next to her. "Doubt it."

She shrugged and inched away from him so she was back in the sun.

"Lots of cool equipment came on the ship before you and your boss arrived."

"What do we have here?" She pointed to a cable running off the ship and disappearing into the sky.

"That's a towed airborne lift system. The cable attaches to the winch on this end. There's a parachute on the other end. The parachute is holding up a bunch of surveillance gear. So we can spot other vessels before they can spot us."

Then they could follow the yacht from a far enough distance that they'd remain undetected. Very Tesla. "Do we have any drones?"

"Yup," he said. "Top of the line. A couple black ones for night flying. All the lights blacked out. Illegal, but good for taking pictures of things that don't want to be photographed. A couple blue ones for flying during the day. We even have a submarine drone, but I don't know what that's for."

Putting the transponder on the giant submarine.

She pointed to a bow leaning against the side of the boat. It looked like the bow Tesla used to shoot at the little flags underwater, but on steroids with a grip on one side, a cable and pulleys on the other. "What's that for?"

"That's ours." Marshall picked it up and handed it to her. "It's a compound bow. We use it for bowfishing. I've even shot sharks with this baby."

Vivian studied it. It looked like a regular compound bow, but the arrows next to it had fishing line attached to the back. The line was coiled up on a reel. "So you shoot the fish and reel it in?"

"Yup. Range is about forty yards, long for bowfishing. But you want to aim for fish that are close to the surface. It loses power fast once it goes underwater."

"Too bad Tesla's under the weather. I think he'd like to play with this one."

"He chartered the boat and everything on it." Marshall took the bow back. "He can play with it if he wants. I like to shoot it down here or from the bridge. You can see everything from up there."

Tesla would panic on the bridge. All that glass.

"Maybe he will." She stood and unzipped her wetsuit.

Marshall cut the tape off her suit so she could take her arm out.

"Ex-Navy?" he asked.

She might as well get her unit number tattooed on her forehead. "Army. You?"

"Ex-Marine," he said.

"Once a Marine, always a Marine," she quoted.

"Semper fi," he answered back. Always faithful.

"Is there coffee somewhere?"

"I'll show you where to hose off your gear and store it, then I'll make you a pot myself."

Marshall wasn't so bad.

34

North Atlantic aboard the *Voyager*
March 19, afternoon

Joe thought he was ready for anything—he'd chosen the
right boat, he'd equipped it with long-range sonar so they
would be able to detect the *Shining Pearl* before she detected
them, he had long-range cameras, he had drones, he had the
Pearl's schedule, he had the schedule for the boat delivering
the oxygen generators. He had the gear.

But he hadn't planned on getting seasick.

Instead of manning his equipment, he was crouched
down in the head, wishing he'd never left dry land, both
hands on the toilet seat, waiting to hurl.

"I got ginger ale from the captain," Vivian called from
his cabin. She sounded horrifyingly chipper. She was fine.
He'd heard from the captain that she'd been out testing the
equipment. The captain seemed to be eating out of her hand,
and even that Marshall guy was treating her with a lot of
deference. He wondered what she'd done to impress them.
Probably kicked somebody's butt. She was a tour de force.

He let out a moan and contemplated death. Death
didn't seem so bad.

She came in through the open bathroom door. As soon
as he could stand up, he intended to lock that.

"And air-sickness bands for your wrists. Marshall swears by them."

She pressed a cold glass into his hand, and he took a swallow. It stayed down, which was a miracle. She handed him small gray bands, and he slipped them on. They had a plastic ball in the middle that dug into his wrists. He didn't see how they could possibly help.

She reached over and positioned the ball in the exact center of the inside of his wrist. "They use pressure points."

"Go watch the monitors," he croaked.

"That's another thing. I'm thinking you probably shouldn't be looking at those monitors so much," she chattered away. "Looking at a close-up point of focus might be making you sick."

"The ocean is making me sick. Let's not talk about it."

"Right." She backed out and gently closed the door. Edison went with her.

He thought about locking the door, but didn't want to stand up. Instead, he sipped the ginger ale. It'd give him something to throw up. When it stayed down, he hauled himself to his feet and tottered out to his cabin.

"I've been watching the *Pearl* on sonar. She's been traveling at a pretty fair clip due east, but she started to slow." She tapped the screen. "See? Her engines have changed pitch."

The yacht rolled, and he barely made it back to the bathroom. The ginger ale tasted worse coming up than it had going down. Like everything.

"I'm going to alert Captain Glascoe," she called. "We need to maintain our course if we can, but we can't run over them either."

"Yeah." Joe didn't have the strength to say anything more.

Vivian's footsteps receded, and he closed his eyes. Maybe he could get a little nap in. He couldn't be seasick if he was sleeping.

"It'll be dark soon." She was back and talking through the door. "I figure if the *Pearl* and the sub are going to meet up, it makes sense they meet at night. Sure, we can track them, but if there are any satellites taking pictures of random ocean, they're not going to set off any red flags."

He staggered back out and lay down in his bunk.

"Do you want another Dramamine?" she asked.

"It gave me all the bad dwarf attributes."

She looked over at him. "What?"

"It made me sleepy and dopey." He closed his eyes.

"And grumpy," she said under her breath.

"Heard that."

She looked back at the monitors.

"I bet they're slowing to a preset position so they can rendezvous with a helicopter," he said.

"Helicopter?"

"The *Pearl* has a helipad, and I'm guessing that's how the oxygen generators will be delivered. They haven't gone into a harbor since the generators were ordered."

"Are you sure the oxygen generators are for our sub?"

"Not positive, no, but all the data seem to support it. It's the right kind and make, and I don't know why anyone else would order them through a third-party vendor. Most militaries have their own sources, and it's not the dark web. Once they're aboard, the sub will come right to us." He hoped.

"We have a drone up. It's pretty high up, not visible to the naked eye," she said. "Should I bring it back if a helicopter's coming? They might spot it."

"Maybe." He'd hate to mess everything up if the helicopter pilot saw the drone.

The images on one of the monitors pitched sickeningly, and he closed his eyes.

"I see a helicopter!" Vivian said. "It looks like a Bell 204."

"Can that carry a ton?"

"They're rated up to three thousand pounds, including passengers." She'd considered becoming a helicopter pilot once upon a time.

"Get as far back as you can," he said. "We don't want them to see us."

"On it." The screen monitoring the drone showed them winging away from the *Shining Pearl* at full speed.

The helicopter had arrived. The submarine couldn't be too far behind. He hoped.

.

35

**North Atlantic aboard the *Siren*
March 20**

The biggest room in the submarine was the mess hall. Most
of the crew packed in, with a few left at their posts. Laila
looked around at the familiar faces. The women's hair was
still short, and they wore blue overalls, but they didn't look
like generic crewmen anymore. Some wore bright
headscarves, others had hair ribbons, bright colors decorated
their once-identical overalls. They were a collection of
individuals, not a crew. But she needed them all.

A pale and drawn Nahal stumbled in from sick bay. Her
gunshot wound was not healing very quickly, and Laila
wondered if Meri was doing her best. Ambra helped her
through the crowd to a seat. Soon, this would be over and
she could go to a real hospital.

Laila climbed on a table and cleared her throat. "I have
a couple of announcements."

The women grew quiet and looked at her. They had
been quiet since Rasha's death the day before. Laila worried
that they would not believe Meri's story, that they would
mutiny and throw her out the trunk escape and into the
pitch-dark water. But they hadn't.

"First, we will be meeting with *Pearl* soon to load the new oxygen generators. I'm sure Aunt Bibi will have prepared a feast for us."

Uncertain smiles. And this was the easy part.

Laila took a deep breath. "And now to the second announcement. We have located Prince Timgad's yacht, the *Roc*, and we are ready to go after it. We have only two days to intercept it and destroy it."

A whisper swept through the audience. The smiles disappeared.

Ambra stood to speak. "When you approached us, we each signed up to take this submarine."

Nods from a few women.

"And we took this submarine because we knew the prince intended to load a weapon onto it, a weapon that could trigger the next world war. We hoped that taking the submarine and killing the prince would be enough to stop that," Laila said.

"But we didn't manage to kill him." Meri climbed on the table next to Laila and smiled at her. "Yet."

Laila wasn't sure she wanted Meri as an ally. Laila continued speaking. "As we suspected, the prince has loaded the weapon onto his yacht, and he intends to aim it at New York City."

Instead of trusting her, the women turned to looked at Nahal.

"It's true," Nahal said. "I can show anyone the proof on my laptop. To save lives, we must send his yacht, the prince, and his weapon to the bottom of the sea. If he reaches New York and triggers it, it will do millions of dollars of damage, and thousands of people will likely die. After that, it could lead to international war with untold casualties."

"Or it might not," Ambra said. "The weapon might not work. No one might die. Even if they do, it might not lead to war. We don't know any of that. What we do know is that if we torpedo the *Roc*, we will kill most of the royal family and their retainers. Our uncles and cousins and brothers are on that ship."

A murmur of approval at Ambra's words ran through the crowd.

Nahal struggled to her feet. "We can't do this without you. We need every woman in this crew to man her station."

"Some of us just want to disappear and set up our new lives," said Cara, a willowy cousin of Nahal's. "We thought we would take the submarine and kill the prince and that would put an end to it."

"Well, it didn't." Nahal had gone paler, but she didn't sit back down. "We had our hopes, but it didn't work out that way. If we stop now, everyone we have killed will have died in vain, and the blood of everyone who will die after the weapon is activated will be on our hands. An ocean of it."

"This will spread beyond New York to the shores of our country, to the deserts of Israel and beyond once the device is activated and Israel is blamed." Laila watched the women's faces. "We can stop that. We have the tools. We have the knowledge. All we need is the will."

The women looked between Laila, Nahal, and Ambra.

"I will continue," Meri said. "I gave my oath."

"I gave my oath." Nahal's legs trembled, but she stood straight and proud.

"I gave my oath," Laila echoed.

Slowly, the words spread around the room. Woman after woman reaffirmed her oath. Even Ambra. Laila hoped that they remembered their oaths. If more than two of them decided to jump ship and stay with Aunt Bibi, or faltered during the engagement, they would all die for nothing.

36

"They've stopped, sir." Vivian sounded excited and energetic and all the other things Joe ought to be. "And an object is approaching them from underwater."

Joe opened his eyes and tried to sit up. His stomach told him that was a bad idea. This entire plan was a bad idea. He should never have left his cozy house underground. He should have sent the Navy. But they hadn't been interested, and he couldn't leave the mystery alone. His stomach berated him for his stubbornness and his curiosity.

"I'm bringing the mini-drone in," she said. "The captain blacked out the lights, and it's high up, so they shouldn't notice it this time of night. We'll change out the battery. Smart of you to order so many extra batteries."

"Yeah," he said.

The view on the monitors swayed sickeningly. A roiling black sea. He almost lost the meager contents of his stomach.

"I'm filming," she said. "It's streaming live to Mulcahy, as you requested. I'm also sending him the sonar feeds. He has all the data we can give him."

Joe struggled into a standing position, his hand on the wall. "We need to affix the transponder. I'm going for the DPV."

"With respect, sir, I don't think you're in any shape to do that."

"Noted." She was right, but he wasn't going to admit it. "I'm going to suit up."

She stood in an easy, relaxed movement. Like people move who aren't seasick. "I've set the drone to hover. I'll get Marshall to take over the feeds and keep the drone on track."

He started for the door. Edison walked next to his leg, a calm presence in a rolling world. She slipped by him and jogged down the corridor like a superhero.

He kept going forward. He could make it to the end of the corridor without throwing up. He could. He did.

When he opened the door that led outside, his heart jackhammered, even though he wasn't really outside. The captain had set up a long canvas tube across the deck to the swim platform. Like walking inside a hamster tube, but enough to keep his panic at bay. It just needed railings, barf bags, and lights.

The air smelled fresher out here, and his stomach calmed down. Wind rattled the canvas around him. Because it was night, he could barely see a few steps ahead, but that didn't bother him. Edison strode along in front of him, showing him the way. Dogs saw better in the dark than humans, and Edison saw better in the dark than most dogs.

Too soon, the tube opened into a tent pitched on the swim platform. A dim red light illuminated what looked like tiny bombs—bullet-shaped cylinders with a round propeller on the end. As ridiculous as they looked, they were key for the next part of his plan. They were diver propulsion vehicles, called DPVs, bought by Captain Glascoe as military salvage.

In theory, a diver could hold on to the handles, and the vehicle would propel him forward at about ten miles an hour. They were quiet and small. The only trick was supposed to be controlling the buoyancy control. Or so he'd read.

He'd planned to practice driving his vehicle around the boat as they traveled after the *Shining Pearl*. Instead, he'd spent all that time throwing up in his cabin, monitoring the feeds. Vivian had used them and given him detailed descriptions of how they worked. If using them to drive around underwater bothered her, she hadn't said anything. Not that she ever complained.

She popped into view with an armful of gear. "I sent Marshall down to keep an eye on the screens and to watch our six. I'll leave Billy piloting the drones. He's got an eye for it."

"Thanks."

"I know you originally planned to take the captain with you on this expedition, but he and I've agreed it's better if he and I go and you stay."

A lot less danger for Joe. "You don't have experience with the equipment."

"I trained on the DPV while you were indisposed." She'd already stepped into her wetsuit. "You're about my height, so everything fits, and he said I check out fine."

Even with the fresh air, he still felt terrible, but he argued. "I set this up. I've studied this equipment a lot."

She zipped up her suit. "Agreed. You're strong on theory. But you're short on practice."

Captain Glascoe appeared next to her. He wore a pair of black pants and a dark turtleneck. The guy always dressed like death on the high seas. "Sergeant Torres is more than capable of completing this mission. As am I."

Joe swayed on the deck and swallowed hard. This wasn't the moment to puke.

"More capable than you." Vivian wasn't ever one to soften the blow.

"I paid for this trip. I'm going. No arguments."

She and the captain exchanged glances, and the captain reluctantly stepped back.

Joe put on his wetsuit, and the captain helped him into his buoyancy compensator and air tank. Edison barked and wagged his tail.

"Not this time, buddy." Joe patted the dog. "Too dangerous."

The propulsion vehicle required both hands when moving. He could probably strap the dog to his body somehow, but he wouldn't be able to help him if things went wrong, and he couldn't take that risk with Edison's life. Edison nudged his knee and looked up with pleading eyes. The dog didn't pull out the big eyes very often, and they almost always worked.

"Nope." Joe fastened his weight belt, adjusted his mask, and checked his regulator. Everything worked. He added the underwater night vision goggles, but didn't turn them on. Too bright here. "Go back to the cabin to wait for me, Edison."

The dog looked between him and Vivian, then headed back down the tube. His tail drooped as he walked away. He didn't want to go back alone, and Joe didn't want him to leave either, but he couldn't come along safely. Not that Edison could understand.

"When we get closer, I expect their boat to be lit up. Anything else would be suspicious, as they've had it lit all the way," Joe said.

"Yup," Vivian said.

Captain Glascoe wrapped duct tape around her arm, and it took Joe a second to figure out why. Her cast must not fit into the suit. She was doing everything he was, but with a broken arm. She was tougher than he was.

He decided to review the plan. "The plan is to stay undetected. I've set this up in circles—the first circle was the extra distance we got from towing the surveillance gear. Because it's so high up in the air, we can detect them because we have a longer range, but they can't detect us. Or at least the yacht can't. The sub hopefully can't hear our engines, but they can find us on sonar if they want to use active sonar. I'm betting they want to stay undetected and won't."

"I got that far." Vivian looked at the water. She clearly wanted to get going.

"The second circle is this one. We'll use the DPVs to get close. If we keep the DPVs within three feet of the surface, we'll get lost in the froth or look like marine mammals even if they do use active sonar."

"That's Mulcahy's theory?" Vivian asked.

"Not just him." Joe's stomach was starting to settle. Giving the briefing was taking his mind off his seasickness. "We'll stop about a hundred yards from the submarine and send in the remote-control submarine to affix the transponder. It has a camera on its nose, so we should be able to see what it's doing, and we're far enough away to be undetected."

"We went over this," Vivian said.

"Humor me," he said. "Are you checked out on the scuba gear?"

He'd originally wanted to use rebreathers, but he'd been too sick to practice on one, so they were going with standard scuba gear.

"Mostly," she said. "I practiced being towed behind the ship."

Her face said it hadn't been a pleasant experience.

She tapped her DPV's control panel. "I've programmed the GPS coordinates for both vessels in here. Just follow the equipment and you'll get there and back."

"Thanks." He should have been doing that, instead of spending his time curled up around his toilet. "I know you've done a lot."

"That's what you pay me for. Plus a combat bonus." She lifted her DPV and slipped it over the side without even a splash. It bobbed to the surface, and she went into the water beside it, gave him an OK sign, and waited. He could barely see her against the black water.

He patted the pocket of his BCD. He had a couple of transponders in there and the tiny remote-control sub strapped to his side. The sub was about as big two cell phones strapped together, and he'd already made sure it was working. Nothing more to do but jump out into the open air, then dive beneath the water. The first part was the worst.

He bent and grabbed the DPV with both hands. He had to cross only a foot of open air. His heart rate jacked up at the thought, and he felt shaky. On the bright side, his nausea was better.

"It'll just be a minute." He tried to explain it to the captain. "I need to get ready."

He started his first breathing exercise. Control the breath, control the heart, control the mind. In that order.

Before he could even exhale, Captain Glascoe picked him up by the suit and threw him into the ocean.

Cold water splashed his face, chasing away the last vestiges of nausea and leaving only panic. Before he had time to give in to fear, he set the propulsion device to negative buoyancy and sank.

Underwater was pitch black, and his heart rate slowed. He wasn't outside. He was underwater and, paradoxically, his brain had decided that was safe. He was only three (red) feet down, but it was enough.

As crappy as his system was, Captain Glascoe had done him a favor by tossing him in. Not that he was going to tell him.

Vivian moved up alongside. A faint red light shone from the compass attached to her device. It illuminated the outline of her head. Like him, she wore a hood that covered everything but her face, and a scuba mask and regulator covered most of that.

He kept her on his right and tried to control his buoyancy. The device wanted to sink, and he constantly had to aim it toward the surface. He'd read up on how to use it, of course, and listened to Vivian's instructions while throwing up, but that wasn't the same as holding on to an anchor while fumbling with switches in near darkness. Then he remembered his night vision goggles and turned them on. The world got a lot brighter. The glow from his instrument panel was readable, and he could see Vivian, too. He could do this.

He concentrated on following the heading, keeping the device stable, and trying not to throw up. His nausea was better than it had been in hours. Apparently, he'd needed a shot of adrenaline. Nothing like the fear of death to trick the body into not caring about inner-ear messages.

Even with night vision goggles, the water was dark. In the past few years, he'd made his peace with darkness, but at least in the tunnels he had gravity to orient himself—he knew down from up and backward from forward. Here, he rushed through the cold water and could trust only his instruments and Vivian.

His hands gripped the handles so tightly they ached, but he was afraid to loosen his grip. If he lost the vehicle, he'd become practically invisible. His heart pounded, and he took slow breaths, shutting out the sensation of water pressing against his wetsuit, the taste of rubber in his mouth, and the worry they would miss their target and shoot off into the sea until they ran out of fuel and air and died.

37

Vivian loved flying through the sea. The surface glittered green in her night vision monocle. If they hadn't been trying to stay hidden, it would have been amazing to ride at the surface under the moon like a dolphin.

She'd always hated watersports, but the DPV changed everything. The device was incredibly maneuverable, it was easy to navigate, and it could move much faster than she could swim. But she wasn't trusting her safety to just the DPV.

Unlike Tesla, she was armed. She'd borrowed a Heckler & Koch P11 underwater pistol from Captain Glascoe. It looked like a flare gun and had only five shots, but it was supposed to be fairly accurate underwater. She hadn't been able to test-fire it, because it had to be sent back to the manufacturer for reloading after five shots. She hated going into a dangerous situation with a weapon that looked like a toy that she'd never actually seen work before, but better than nothing. Maybe.

Hopefully, they'd complete their mission and head back to the ship without being detected, and she'd never need to worry about using a gun. That was the plan. But she'd done enough missions to know that nothing ever went according to plan.

She glanced over at Tesla. He was hanging on to his propulsion device, shoulders tense and arms pulling it too close. She wished she could tell him to ease up and save his strength for later. But she had no way to talk to him underwater, and he couldn't surface. He'd just have to tough it out.

If only he'd had time to practice instead of puking. If only she'd had time to review the plan. This kind of mission took weeks to set up in the service, preferably with a dry run, or ten. But instead, she was executing an untested strategy designed by a civilian with only a few days' practice and deadly stakes.

Not that different from any other day, really.

Relax and go with it, she told herself. *Control your breath. Be ready when you get to the submarine. Conserve your strength and your air.*

Clearly having trouble with his buoyancy control, Tesla dipped up and down like a drunken dolphin. That couldn't be good for his seasickness. She knew she should feel sorry for him, but he should have stayed on the boat. Captain Glascoe would have been an asset at her side, not a liability. But instead, Tesla had insisted on coming along.

The range finder showed they were close, and she crossed in front of Tesla so he could see her. Then she slowed down and was relieved when he followed suit. He was a smart guy, but he wasn't used to military ops or even working in teams.

A few minutes later, the hull of the submarine came into view. Backlit by lights from the yacht, it looked smaller than she remembered, but everything always seemed bigger when it was trying to kill you.

She cut her engine and decided to risk surfacing. She'd be a tiny black dot in a black sea with the light source in front of her. Not invisible, maybe, but practically.

A quick tug of Tesla's sleeve. She pointed up, then at herself. He gave her the traditional thumb-and-forefinger-together OK sign.

A few kicks of her flippers later and her head broke the surface. Stars above, wind on her face. Better than being surrounded by water and blackness. She popped out her regulator and took a long breath of salt-scented fresh air, then stuck it back in and turned her attention to the yacht and the sub.

Even though the boats were sitting with most of the lights off, it was still too bright. She adjusted the gain on her night vision. Everything came into focus.

The submarine was about fifty yards away and right next to the yacht. Probably tied off, but she couldn't tell for sure. Tiny figures carried boxes from the boat onto the deck of the submarine and down the sail. They were moving at double time.

A crane attached to the yacht was lowering a box onto the submarine deck. Figures below moved to receive it. That must be the oxygen generators Tesla had tracked online.

The drones were sure to have good pictures of it.

Now for the transponder.

She dove under to a depth of three feet. Tesla was right there waiting for her.

He held his tiny flashlight under his chin like a kid in summer camp. He jerked his thumb in the direction of the submarine. This was the part of the plan she liked the least—get a little closer and use the submarine drone to attach the transponder. Fred Mulcahy had promised the transponder would broadcast on a frequency that was almost never monitored. Unlikely the submarine would ever know the transponder was there. Or at least that's what Fred believed.

Tesla bucked a couple of times. It took her a second to figure out what had happened. He'd puked into his regulator. Nasty. He pressed a button and purged it into the ocean with a rush of air. A swarm of tiny fish came up to eat it.

She swam back a few strokes to put space between herself and the vomit. Not that it should matter, right? The ocean was full of fish pee. Even so.

But how often had he had to purge his regulator? After all, they had limited air. If Tesla was venting his air to blow out his puke, which he had to do to keep from clogging up the system, then there might be a problem. Especially combined with the cold water, his mild panic, and the death grip he had on the DPV. All those things used up air.

She checked his dive computer. He'd used half his air. He didn't have time to mess around with placing the transponder. He needed to go right back to the *Voyager.*

She tapped the dive computer and watched him look at it. His eyes widened. He must have done the math, too. After all, Tesla was good at math. She pointed to her dive computer. She still had two-thirds of her air, a nice margin of error.

She pointed back toward the *Voyager.* He shook his head. She pointed back to his air gauge, then made a throat-slitting gesture. Arguing in charades was a pain.

Again, he looked at the dive computer. She could see him thinking, but there was no other answer. He had to go back. If she'd run out of air, she could swim at the surface, even all the way back, but Tesla couldn't do that.

As if he'd read her mind, he pointed to her tank, then his and flipped his hands from side to side. He was suggesting they swap tanks. Then he pointed back to *Voyager* and at her. As if she would swap tanks and go back, leaving him to do the most dangerous part of the job while puking sick. Even though he was the least-qualified member of this team.

Plus, his regulator had been puked in who knew how many times, and she wasn't going to put it in her mouth. Sure, he had a spare, but he'd probably puked in that one, too.

She shook her head violently and took the transponders and the tiny submarine drone. Tesla had brought three transponders, just in case they lost two. He was usually overprepared. But not for this.

His shoulders slumped. Even with most of his face obscured by the mask and regulator, she could tell how much he hated accepting reality. He had to go back.

She clasped his shoulder and gave him a thumbs-up. She made swimming movements with one hand, then the other, and then brought them together. She hoped he knew that meant she was saying she should go back with him.

He shook his head, pointed to his chest and back to the *Voyager*, then pointed to her chest and forward to the *Shining Pearl*. He wanted her to complete the mission, and he would go back on his own.

She shook her head. She couldn't let him go back on his own. Too dangerous. He couldn't surface if he had an equipment failure or ran out of air. He'd just drown.

He glared at her and took a dive slate out of his pocket. She'd forgotten they had those. He wrote, *I'll go slowly. You can catch up.*

She took the slate and wrote, *NO! Too dangerous for you to go back alone.*

He took the slate out of her hand and wrote, *If transponder isn't attached, they can't track it. I'll never be safe.*

She wondered if that was true. Would the House of Dakkar keep sending assassins after him if he didn't prove it had been a sub that tried to kill their prince and not him? Would the US government let him show the pictures he'd taken? Would they track the transponder? Would any of that be enough to change their mind?

Please, Tesla wrote, *stay and do this for me.*

He didn't have time to stay and argue. She had to make a decision quickly.

She linked the wire-control sub to her BCD. *Straight back?*

He nodded, then set out.

Every protective instinct urged her to follow him, but instead, she turned to the ship and their mission, like she'd told Tesla she would. At the range of a thousand feet, Mulcahy said they needed to keep the DPV's motor off, so she'd have to swim the next leg. They were putting a lot of faith in a guy who spent more of his life listening to nonhuman sounds than to human speech.

The sub drone had a five-hundred-foot cable. Because radio signals don't work underwater across long distances, the sub had to have a tether to send signals across. She had to get within the range of the tether to send the sub on its way. Once she was close enough, she hovered three feet underwater and set up the tiny device. Pretty straightforward—just drive the drone toward the yacht and sub. It had a camera mounted on top, and it would send the image back along the wire. She unwound the cable slowly, making sure there were no knots or kinks.

She turned the underwater drone on and sent it toward the sub. For the first two hundred feet, everything looked fine. Through the camera, she saw dark water flowing around the drone and a subtle brightening ahead that must come from the yacht. *Just keep on going.*

Then the video sent by the drone lurched to the side. The faint glow was replaced by complete darkness. She had no idea what direction the drone was heading in. A malfunction. Or it had hit something.

She'd have to start over.

Slowly, she pulled the cable back, one handful at a time. Nothing to worry about. But then she reached the end of the cable.

The remote-control drone was not attached.

The drone must have fallen off the cable. She'd never be able to recover the tiny sub. Tesla had set the sub to have negative buoyancy so it wouldn't float to the surface if they lost control of it.

It was halfway to the ocean floor by now.

She looked down at her dive computer. She had plenty of air.

Decision time.

She could abandon the mission and follow Tesla back to the *Voyager*. The flying drones had captured plenty of pictures. She and Tesla had proven that the submarine existed. They could let the government take care of the situation.

On the other hand, the people on the submarine were going around killing innocents. They had sunk an oil tanker. They had killed the prince's bodyguard and almost killed her and Tesla. If she put a transponder on the sub, it would be easy to find them and stop them. If she didn't, or didn't even try, wouldn't the lives that they still might take be on her?

Unsure, she hovered in the dark water, the useless cable in her hand.

She remembered her terror in the submarine. Tesla's determined face on the other side. He'd stuck with her. He hadn't let her die down there. She couldn't let him down. They had set out to tag the giant sub, and that's what she was going to do.

But quietly.

She stabilized at three feet under the surface and kicked toward the sub, pushing the silent DPV in front of her with her good hand. She had two transponders left in her pocket. Two chances to attach one to the sub.

When she reached the back of the submarine, she was careful to stay away from the giant propellers. Captain Glascoe had told her they'd "chew her up to chum" if she got too close when they were on. Trying to put that mental image out of her head, she swam on.

She drifted up next to the sub's hull. Almost close enough to touch. She kicked back a stroke and took out a transponder. Painted black and about the size of a coaster, but fatter, it was supposed to be so tiny the people on the sub would never notice it. Step one was to not drop the transponder into the depths of the sea.

Step two was to stick it to the sub. Before she could attach it to the hull, a light from above cut through the water and overwhelmed her night vision.

38

Joe bounced through the ocean behind the DPV, trying to decide if it would be easier to just die. He'd never been so sick. He didn't have any way to rinse out his regulator, so his mouth tasted of seawater and vomit every time he took a breath, and it felt like he was getting stabbed in the side every time he took a breath. He'd long since run out of things to throw up, but that didn't stop the dry heaves.

Worse, he'd left Vivian behind.

But she was efficient. She'd probably already carried out her mission. She was a better navigator and lighter than he was. She'd probably reach the *Voyager* before he did.

He pointed the DPV east. Cold water pressed against the outside of his suit. At a depth of three (red) feet, waves lifted him up and down, and pale starlight shone on the surface. Just enough to trigger a light panic attack.

The compass heading was all that mattered. He used breathing exercises to ignore rising nausea, pain in his ribs, increasing light-headedness and guilt. He had to focus on one (cyan) thing—getting back to the ship. There'd be time to feel everything else later.

Eventually, a bright blue spot beckoned. Captain Glascoe must have dropped a light into the water. Joe made for it. The boat was moving more slowly than he, and he kicked to speed up the DPV. Harder and harder to hold on.

He headed toward the light. Safety. But he hadn't practiced getting onto a moving boat. He'd planned, but he'd been too sick.

The most important thing was to keep clear of the propeller on the stern. He knew that much. Unfortunately, that's where the swim platform was. He had no idea how he'd scale the smooth sides of the boat. He swam around, looking for something.

On the port side, he found it. A fishing net trailing into the ocean. But he knew from pictures he'd seen that once he got to the surface, it was at least a six-(orange)-foot climb until he'd reach the railing and someone could pull him in. Six (orange) feet. Above the water.

He latched on to the net and hung on. The wake banged him against the boat, knocking the wind out of him, and the pain from his side was so bad, he almost passed out. His DPV smacked his other side, but he couldn't do anything to adjust it. He lifted himself up until his head was just below the waterline and started doing breathing exercises. Part of him wanted to let go and drift off into the sea. Quit fighting and rest.

But he had to get on board and make sure Vivian was OK. He hung on.

Then the net started to move. He threaded his feet through the holes and curled his fingers around the rope. Only then did he notice the cold. His fingers were claws. He shivered so hard he worried he'd fall off the net. How long had he been shivering?

Unseen figures lifted the net out of the water. Hands helped him over the side and dragged him until his back settled against the inside of the boat. Someone tugged off his hood and regulator. A warm tongue licked his cold face.

"Vivian's back there," he said. "She stayed behind to attach the transponder."

"I know." Captain Glascoe's deep voice rumbled out.

Joe tried to push himself up into a standing position but collapsed against the wall.

"Sallow complexion." The captain peeled back his wetsuit and put warm fingers on his neck. "Pulse fast but weak. Get him on an IV, saline, and an antiemetic. And warm him up."

Joe's brain was having trouble parsing what the captain had said.

"Vivian. Vivian OK?"

"I don't know." The captain gestured to someone Joe couldn't see. "Get him inside."

"Yes, sir," said Marshall.

The captain turned to someone else. "Increase speed along the submarine's last heading."

"Vivian. She'll never find us if we change course."

Someone heaved Joe over his shoulder. Pain lanced up from his side, and he screamed.

"Broken rib," the captain said. "Shift him to the other side."

"Wait!" he yelled. "Vivian!"

"She isn't coming back to the ship. She's been spotted." The captain gestured to the man carrying him. "I'll be inside soon to explain."

Joe's world got hazy. His head bumped some guy's back. Out of the corner of his eye, he saw Edison trotting along. The dog didn't seem worried. If the dog wasn't worried, then he shouldn't be either. Wasn't that the rule?

But Vivian was still out there.

His arms ached. His stomach ached. His side ached. How could he have broken a rib? His head throbbed, and his mouth tasted foul.

The guy carrying him—Marshall, he could see that now—dropped him down on his own bed.

"Stay," Marshall said, like he was a dog.

Joe tried to sit up, but couldn't. He'd never felt so weak. Edison jumped up on the bed next to him and licked his face, then his hands. He wanted to pet him, but couldn't even move his arm.

Marshall was back with a bag and an IV pole.

"I'm a trained medic," he said. "Don't worry."

"Worry?"

Marshall grabbed his hand, swabbed the back of it with a gauze pad, and inserted an IV. It hurt a lot less than Joe would have expected.

"You're suffering from pretty serious dehydration. Probably had some when you went into the water, and it looks like you've been vomiting a lot since then."

Joe closed his eyes.

"You were vomiting so hard I think you broke a rib." Marshall pressed his fingers down Joe's sides until he got a groan. "Yup."

Joe tried to open his eyes, but they wouldn't listen to him. He felt himself drifting off to sleep. He tried to fight it, but his eyes were too heavy.

Marshall fussed around with his gear, taking it off. Joe wanted to thank him or help him, but he couldn't formulate the words. He had to go back for Vivian.

"Vivian," he said.

But Marshall ignored him.

39

Although Vivian's instincts said to run, she tucked herself next to the submarine and waited for the light to pass. Before the light came back around, she pressed the transponder onto the sub. Hopefully it would stick, because that was as good as she was going to get.

Then she pushed herself and the DPV farther under the curve of the hull. Motionless, the DPV hovered next to her hip. She shouldn't be visible from the surface.

Still, she pulled out her ridiculous toy gun. She slung the strap around her wrist, making it feel even more like an accessory and less like a weapon. She had only five shots, so she'd better make them count. But hopefully it wouldn't come to that.

Should she flip on her propulsion device and head away from there double time? If she took off, whoever was up there with the light might spot the movement. She'd be hard to pick up on sonar, but not impossible. If they spotted her, she couldn't outrun either the yacht or the sub with her little DPV. Running away had to be a last resort.

She could escape the yacht if she dove, but the sub could dive deeper than she could, and they had a huge sonar range. Miles. There would be no escaping them. They could either kill her right away, or follow her back to the ship and kill everyone there, too. More bad options.

That only left stealth. She hung motionless in the darkness, shoulder pressed tight against the hull. They were just shining the light around. Maybe they were trying to spot a fish. There's no point in borrowing trouble, as her mother used to say.

Then a light caught her full on. She fumbled to adjust the buoyancy on her DPV, set it to descend, and hung on. The DPV dropped like a stone, and she swallowed again and again to equalize pressure in her ears.

No good. Six divers entered the water, lights pointing in her direction. She brought up her gun, ready to fire. Then she saw the divers were carrying the same kind of Chinese assault rifle she'd retrieved from the ocean floor in New York. A QBS-06. Its underwater range was nearly a hundred feet. Her little pepperbox, in contrast, had a range of about fifty feet, and the range would shorten the deeper she went.

She was outgunned and outnumbered. Nowhere to run and nowhere to hide. She had no option left but to surrender, lie, and try to protect Tesla and *Voyager*. Assuming the women let her live long enough to question her.

She let go of the DPV. That stopped her descent, and she adjusted the air in her BCD to start a slow rise to the surface. She didn't want to die down deep. The divers and their lights grew closer.

Wishing she didn't have to, she unfastened the pepperbox gun and let it drop. As designed, it sank. Captain Glascoe wouldn't be happy about that. A pang of guilt shot through her at the thought that the she was littering, and she almost smiled. That response felt like hysteria, and she tamped it down. No time for weakness.

She activated the transponder in her pocket and stuck it in her dive bootie. Glascoe and Tesla would be listening, and they could track her, although how they could get her back from the yacht was another issue. She ran through everything else she carried, but there was nothing else to drop. Her suit and scuba gear were commercial, not military. All she needed was a good story to explain why she was over a mile off the coast of Halifax in the middle of the night next to a luxury yacht and a submarine.

As she kicked to ascend, she held up both hands in surrender. If these women were civilians, they might hesitate to shoot if she didn't look like a threat.

Or they might not.

40

Laila had a hundred-fifty-pound problem. That was easily solvable. A bigger problem was the witnesses. Aunt Bibi was standing next to her, looking at the woman dripping on the aft deck. Behind Bibi was a woman Laila knew only as Jin. Jin pointed a gun at the stranger's chest. Next to her was Ambra, biting her lip. Lined up behind them stood four guards from Aunt Bibi's ship. All armed. Seven witnesses.

The woman sat on a bench on the ship's stern. She had short dark hair and wore a black wetsuit and had battered-looking scuba gear with one arm cut open to accommodate a broken arm. She looked frightened. Considering Jin's gun and impassive expression, Laila didn't blame her.

Ambra knelt next to the woman and started stripping off her scuba gear.

"Why were you under my ship?" asked Aunt Bibi in English.

Jin raised her gun a centimeter.

"I come to get away." The woman had a strong Hispanic accent. She held up her arms to make it easier for Ambra, but her eyes never left the gun.

"On the bottom of the boat?" Aunt Bibi trembled with rage. Laila had never seen her so upset.

The Hispanic woman shook her head. "I hide in your boat because I hear it is going to Boston. I work for a bad man in Halifax, and I want to leave there."

"Show me your identification," Aunt Bibi demanded.

The woman hung her head. "The bad man, Mr. McKay, he keeps it so we can't leave. That is why I have to sneak away on a ship like yours."

"You bring trouble to my boat," Aunt Bibi said. "Maybe, if you'd asked honestly, I could have helped you."

"I ask you now." The woman looked Aunt Bibi straight in eye. "Please help me. Take me to Boston. Let me jump off your boat, and I will swim to shore. I can swim far."

Aunt Bibi looked torn.

"What's your name?" Laila wanted to short-circuit any sympathy.

"Elena Torres," the woman said. "I come from Mexico."

"How did you get to Canada?" Laila asked.

"In a truck. I paid a man to get me across the border. For work cleaning. With thirty-five women. He took us to Canada. Not North Dakota. And not house-cleaning work." She spat.

Aunt Bibi winced when the spit hit her clean deck.

"How would a woman like you come upon scuba gear?" Laila asked.

The woman looked down, as if she were thinking up a lie. Which she probably was. "A man who visits with me. For money. He give it to me and say I can use it to swim out to catch a boat to America. I do, and I hide away. When the boat stop, I think we are in Boston, and I climb over the side. I see no city light. I try to get back aboard, but you chase me. I swim away at first. But there is nowhere to go, so I come back."

Unfortunate if true, Laila had to concede. The woman had terrible luck, because Laila would not let her live.

Aunt Bibi looked at Laila and spoke in Arabic. "We cannot let her go in Boston. She has seen the submarine, and she can link it to me. The family lets me be free, but if they knew I was connected to your plans, that would change. All my crew would be at risk."

"Agreed." Laila waited, readying her argument.

"After you leave, Jin will kill her." Aunt Bibi looked sad.

Argument forgotten, Laila gaped. She hadn't expected it to be this easy. "You'd have to strip her naked, throw her overboard, then put her gear in a bag with weights and dump that a few kilometers after so it won't be connected to her."

"I know my business," Jin said.

What was Jin's business? Laila wasn't sure she wanted to find out.

"No," said Ambra, also in Arabic. "She's innocent, and we don't need to kill her. After tomorrow, this is all over. Why can't we release her then? She doesn't know anything—"

"She's seen the *Siren!*" Laila said. "And the *Pearl*. And all of us."

"What can she do with the information? She's a Mexican prostitute. No one will listen to her." Ambra folded her arms.

"Perhaps Ambra is correct." Aunt Bibi looked at the woman uncertainly. "Perhaps there is another way."

Elena Torres couldn't understand what they were saying, but her eyes brimmed with tears. She knew they were determining her fate.

"Please don't take me back to Canada," she said. "Mr. McKay will be very angry."

Going back to Canada was the least of her problems.

"Maybe we should take her back to Canada," Aunt Bibi said in Arabic. "We could dump her in the water about a mile offshore from Halifax and let her take her chances on swimming to land."

Laila had reached a decision. "Or we could do that in the *Siren*."

Ambra's eyes widened. "Really?"

Laila couldn't leave the woman with Aunt Bibi if there was even a small chance Aunt Bibi would let her go. She had to take Elena Torres with them. Tomorrow, after they were finished and Ambra left the sub, she'd kill this Elena Torres herself and dump her body in the sea. "Yes, Ambra. You're right: She's probably an innocent. We can release her after we've completed our mission, when she's no longer a threat to us."

Aunt Bibi studied Laila's face as if deciding whether to trust her. She must have, because she turned to Jin. "Escort this woman to the submarine and make sure she is suitably restrained."

To the woman, she said in English, "They will take you to America, but you must swim ashore yourself."

"Yes, señora," the woman said. "Gracias. Thank you. You are so kind to me."

Ambra gave Laila a long look, then took the prisoner's arm and led her across the deck. Jin followed at a distance, as if she worried Torres might attack her.

A good policy.

41

Vivian stumbled across the yacht's pitching deck. She didn't like her odds. As part of her Army training, she'd taken a class to learn Arabic. Her Arabic wasn't as good as her Pashto, but she didn't need to be a linguistic genius to know they'd been talking about how and when to kill her. The one with the gun, Jin, looked like someone who'd pull the trigger without hesitation. The guards looked pretty serious, too. The three women who'd argued over her she wasn't so sure about.

Jin and the guards seemed to work for the woman who owned the yacht, and Plan A was to get the hell away from Jin. The chubby one, Ambra, had seemed to be arguing for letting her go. She might become an ally. So, going with her was Plan B.

No one had questioned Vivian's scared-prostitute act, but that might be because they didn't really care where she came from because they planned to kill her anyway. Or, she was a fantastic actress, she'd tugged at their heartstrings, and they intended to let her go. That wasn't much to bet her life on.

Glascoe and Tesla would send the Navy for her. She still had a transponder tucked into the top of her dive bootie. They'd find her. She was glad she'd sent Tesla out. He'd do whatever it took to get her back. Plus, he would have made a terrible hostage.

Jin poked her hard in the ribs with a gun barrel. "Walk."

Vivian walked. She assumed they were taking her to a stateroom where they'd lock her in. She'd sit tight and wait for rescue, escape if she got close to shore. Not great options, but she'd work with what she had. At least she had regular air to breathe.

The white cabin of the yacht towered over her head. Everything was immaculate—freshly painted, spotless, and shiny. The captain ran a tight ship. So long as Vivian stayed in her good graces, maybe she'd get out of this alive.

Then she saw the sub.

The rounded hull rode above the waves, blacker than the water, blacker than the sky. Three women stood on the deck holding assault rifles. Their postures weren't as precise as the guards on the yacht, but they still looked like they knew how to use the weapons.

"Go onto the deck." Jin pointed at the submarine.

"No." If she went onto the sub, she'd lose a lot of control. She wouldn't be able to see if she was close to land. If she was able to escape, she'd have no idea if she was stranding herself in the middle of the ocean. She looked at the lit windows of the yacht. "I stay here."

Jin prodded her hard enough to leave a bruise. "Go."

The four women behind Jin glared at Vivian and raised their guns.

"What is that thing? I don't want to go there," Vivian said. "It doesn't look safe."

She did a quick scan of the horizon. No ships. No sign of shore. Not that she'd expected any. The remoteness of the location was why everyone had picked it.

"You go on that ship, or you go in the water with a bullet in your back," said Jin.

Not much of a conversationalist, Jin. But she did get her point across.

"Please. Let me speak to the nice lady." Any of the other ladies were nicer than Jin.

Jin leveled her gun at Vivian's head. "You're speaking to me. I say get on the other ship, or die right here. We can roll your body right into the water. No problem."

The woman wasn't bluffing.

42

Laila and Ambra climbed onto the *Siren* ahead of the prisoner. Laila just wanted to get away from the *Pearl* and complete her mission before something else went wrong.

"You first." Jin gestured to one of her guards. The woman looked like a bodybuilder. She was so huge Laila worried she might get stuck in the tube leading down from the sail.

"No one comes aboard my ship but my own crew," Laila said.

"I do. And so does one of my guards. We will secure the prisoner in your brig, and then she is your responsibility."

"She's my responsibility now," Laila said.

"My orders are clear." Jin looked at one of her hulking Amazons, and the woman trained her gun on Torres. Jin swung her gun until the barrel was pointed straight at Laila. "Personally secure the prisoner on your vessel. Not have you do so in my place."

"Just you, then," Laila said.

"Muhjaa will go first so that she can watch Torres descend. You may either board before Muhjaa or after I do." Jin's gun didn't waver.

Laila didn't want to look weak in front of Ambra, but she also didn't want a confrontation with Jin. She would lose. Jin was armed and ruthless. As children, they had told stories about sea monsters, and the stories had ended with Jin saving them, because she was the only woman they knew who was strong enough to take on any monster.

"I will precede you," Laila said. "Since I am captain."

Unhurriedly, she walked to the sail and climbed inside. The tube was barely wider than her shoulders, and the metal rings felt cold under her palms. In a breach of etiquette, Muhjaa clambered in a few seconds after she did and practically stomped on her hands.

Laila wanted Aunt Bibi's women off the ship as quickly as possible, so she said nothing.

Torres climbed down awkwardly, clearly trying to keep weight off the arm with the cast. Muhjaa's gun was trained on her the entire time.

"Don't fire," Laila said. "A bullet would ricochet around the compartment and do who knows what kind of damage."

"If you don't want me to fire, don't do anything suspicious," said Muhjaa.

Jin came down last, and Muhjaa's gun never wavered from Torres's worried face.

"Lead," Jin barked at Laila.

Laila passed through the bridge and went to her own stateroom. The only place to keep a prisoner. Her submarine didn't have a brig. Her crew squashed themselves against the sides to let her party pass.

"Here." She opened her door.

Muhjaa went in first, then Torres, then Jin. Laila squeezed in last, and Ambra peered in from the corridor.

Nahal was asleep on her bed. Meri had insisted they clear up space in sick bay in case they needed room for casualties during the battle. Laila had volunteered her quarters, as she wouldn't need them until this was all over anyway. Nahal was sound asleep. Meri had picked up additional medical supplies from Aunt Bibi, and she planned to keep Nahal knocked out until they could get her to a real hospital.

Jin put a handcuff on Torres's casted wrist, yanked her forward until she was seated at Laila's fold-down desk, threaded the handcuff through the support, and handcuffed Torres's wrist on the other side. She could barely move.

"Ouch." Torres hunched forward. "This hurts me."

"She can't sit like that for twelve hours!" Ambra said.

"She can. She does." Jin looked at Laila. "She stays here until you are done. Then you do as Miss Bibi says."

"Of course." Aunt Bibi hadn't said she needed to be alive when she was dumped offshore.

Jin and Muhjaa stepped out of the tiny room and into the corridor. Without a word, they marched back the way they'd come. As angry as she was at Jin for the way she'd treated her, she was envious of her quiet, single-minded attention to duty. Ambra could learn from it.

"Why this?" Torres rattled her handcuffs. "I am not a criminal."

"It's just for a few days," Ambra said. "Then we'll let you go."

Torres still looked frightened. "Why not let me go now? I can help. I'm a good cook."

"We have a cook." Laila practically pushed Ambra out the door and closed it.

She and Ambra stood in the corridor, and Ambra looked at the closed door.

"Soon, we'll take out the ship and go our separate ways," Laila said. "We can release this Torres woman then."

"She has nothing to do with any of this," Ambra said.

"And we'll let her go."

"We can still turn back." Ambra gestured down the corridor. "Go undercover. Stop killing."

"We did this for a reason. Those men died for a reason."

"What about Rasha? And the people who will die on the ship?"

"Casualties happen in war. If we sink that ship, we save many more lives than we take. It's why we took the *Siren*. You know this."

"But we have time to take a different path."

"You swore an oath," Laila said. "To me. To our shared mission. We cannot falter. We are almost there. Now get the *Siren* untied from the *Pearl*. As soon as we're clear, we follow the trajectory to Prince Timgad's ship."

Ambra dipped her head and left. Her shoulders brushed both sides of the corridor as she walked. Ambra was practically as big as Muhjaa.

They would encounter their target soon. She just had to keep her crew focused for one more day and this would be over.

43

Vivian kept her head on the desk to which she'd been handcuffed. It had been worth all the language training she'd ever taken to overhear that the women planned a large-scale attack, today. The target was something bigger than the tanker they'd already sunk. Hundreds of people were going to die if they succeeded. After that, Laila wouldn't balk at killing Vivian. Barely noticeable collateral damage.

She leaned forward as far as she could, forehead sliding across the cool surface, then yanked back hard. No give. She had maybe three inches of movement.

Bracing her legs against the wall, she pulled with all her strength. The cuffs slid forward, cutting into her good hand. The table support didn't budge. She kept yanking against the table, but it didn't help. To make matters worse, the cuffs were on too tight, and her left hand was going to sleep. At least the cast protected her right.

She looked around for another way out.

"Who are you?"

Vivian started and looked at the woman in the bed. She'd assumed the woman was unconscious or dead. "Elena Torres."

297

"Nahal. Why are you here?" The small woman struggled into a sitting position. Dark circles smudged her pale skin. She looked fragile.

"I was taken. Why are you here?"

"I am part of the crew. Why were you taken?"

Vivian gave her the same explanation she'd given to the women on deck when she'd been captured. It didn't sound as convincing this time.

"Nonsense," Nahal said. "You are Vivian Torres, bodyguard to Joe Tesla."

Vivian shrugged, but her mind raced. "I am not this person, Miss Nahal."

How had Nahal recognized her? And who would she tell? Vivian yanked on the cuffs again. They didn't budge.

As if reading her thoughts, Nahal said, "I saw your picture online. Your boss is a hero."

Tesla, a hero? "My boss?"

"He's accomplished some incredible feats of hacking, some public and some not."

That sounded like him. Vivian moved the cuffs back again. Maybe if she could remove her cast, she could slide her hand out. But even if she had the tools for it, Nahal could call for help long before she got her arm out.

Nahal gushed like a fangirl. "Lucid's facial-recognition algorithm is amazing! Complex, but so very elegant. After he left the company, their security got weaker and I managed to hack a copy. That never would have happened if he'd stayed, of course."

What were the odds she would end up locked in a room with a Joe Tesla groupie?

"Are you guys sleeping together?" Nahal leaned forward. "What's he like?"

Vivian wouldn't have answered even if she hadn't been pretending not to be herself. Instead, she tried to look puzzled.

"Your face is distinctive, you know. Everyone's is. I'm sure Joe has told you. You probably know more about facial recognition than most experts."

Now she was calling him by his first name.

"Has anyone ever told you that you have amazing symmetry around your eyes?" Nahal went on. "It's rarer than you think, and it's considered very attractive. No one else in the world has eyes like you, of course, or like me. But the tiny scar in your eyebrow would give you away even if your eyes were closed."

Vivian had been nicked by a piece of shrapnel in Afghanistan. Most people didn't even notice it. "My eyebrow piercing? I was a silly teenager."

"Shame on you for trying to fool me." Nahal shook a finger at her. "Your scar came from shrapnel from the IED that killed the man you wanted to marry."

Vivian swallowed. This woman had done her homework, and she seemed a little crazy. Sane people didn't hijack submarines, but Nahal seemed crazier than Ambra or Laila.

"I downloaded your military records. Tesla's woman, how could I not?" Nahal fell back against a bunch of pillows. "You don't approve of how my country treats women."

"I don't know what you mean."

"Your dishonorable discharge, Sergeant Torres."

More denials seemed useless, so she decided to stay quiet and see where this was leading. Her situation couldn't get much worse. Now, that was probably just a lack of imagination. Things could always get worse.

"Only someone as smart as Tesla could have tracked us down. It was Laila's misfortune to run into Tesla's submarine."

Not just Laila's misfortune.

"I voted to deal with Prince Timgad in a more subtle fashion, but Laila's the captain, and I can't do much from sick bay." Nahal fidgeted with her blanket. "I thought I knew her. I thought her different from her family history, kinder, more noble. Do you believe we are more than just our genes?"

"Yes." Although Vivian had to admit she was more similar to her mother than she liked. "We make our own choices, and we can change."

"Nobody expected you to not follow orders, did you know? I read your whole file, things you probably haven't even seen yourself. Your commander fought hard for you. He blamed it on the stress of your beloved's death. But I don't think so. You have a nobility about you. You are strong, and you protect the weak. It's why you had to do what you did. It's why you became a bodyguard. It's why you love Joe Tesla so."

She didn't love Tesla. She cared about him. She liked him. She felt guilty she'd let him down on the first night she was supposed to be guarding him. But none of that was what Nahal was talking about. Vivian knew she had a habit of protecting the weak. She found it more inconvenient than noble. Either way, she wanted Nahal to keep talking. Maybe she could become an ally.

"Laila is not so noble as you. Or as I want to be. At first, she was. She was ready to save the world when we stole this submarine. But now I think she did it to get revenge against the prince. Revenge against her father. Nobility is about grander things than hate."

Nahal looked at Vivian like she expected an answer.

"You stole this submarine?" Vivian kept the accent, just in case.

"Of course we did. And of course you know."

For all she knew, they were on a government-sponsored mission and the submarine was right where it was supposed to be. But she decided not to pick a fight and stayed quiet.

"Laila has developed a taste for killing since we got this sub—the prince, the tanker, Rasha. I didn't expect it from her, even though that streak of madness runs through her family. I thought it would have spared her, since she is a woman and the others are all men."

"Is she going to kill me?"

"I wouldn't. Ambra wouldn't, but Laila will if she gets a chance."

"Why?"

"Because she's changed. And she wants to preserve her secrets—she took this sub, she killed her own brother, she has killed others, and she will do more killing when the time comes. But, if you're here, it's not much of a secret, is it? Your appearance means Tesla has found our sub. He probably filmed it. He probably even knows where we've been and where we're going."

Vivian hoped so, but she thought Nahal might be giving Tesla a little too much credit. "Then why not let me go? If I'm no threat and there's no secret, why keep me here?"

"This is bigger than you. Bigger than us."

"If I'm supposed to die for this, why not tell me why?"

And Nahal did. If Nahal was right, Vivian, once a soldier and always a soldier, understood. It was bigger than her.

44

North Atlantic aboard the *Voyager*
March 21, early morning

Joe woke with a start when someone touched his ribs. "Ouch!"

"Sorry." Captain Glascoe sat on the edge of the bed. "Tell me what happened."

Joe felt better than he had since he got on board the *Voyager*. His stomach was calm and his head was clear. "Water."

Captain Glascoe handed him a glass of apple juice, and Joe drank it in a single long, glorious swallow. His mouth tasted and felt a lot better.

He summarized everything that had happened since he'd left the boat. The captain gave him a glass of water when he was finished.

"Vivian," Joe said. "Tell me what we're doing for her."

"Not a whole hell of a lot we can do."

"Not good enough." Joe struggled into a sitting position. "What happened to her? How did you know she wasn't coming back to the boat?"

"Things would be the same if you'd been with her."

Joe shrugged that off. If he hadn't let her onto the boat in the first place, she'd be safe and sound back in New York. "Tell me what you know."

"She's a brave soldier, your Sergeant Torres."

"She is."

"After you were separated, something must have gone wrong with the little wire-control sub, because it looks like Torres swam out to the sub to attach a transponder by hand."

"That wasn't the plan." She wasn't supposed to get close.

"But it happened."

"How do you know?"

"She activated one and stuck it onto the hull of the submarine."

Of course she did. She got results.

"But it fell off."

"So we can't track the sub?" His head throbbed. They'd lost her. His fault, and they'd lost her. "What about the other transponder?"

"It was activated, too, and it moved to the surface in a controlled ascent, which means she was probably carrying it, and she was probably alive at that time."

Probably. At that time. Not reassuring. "And?"

"We have drone footage of her being taken out of the water, standing on the deck, and then being marched into the submarine. After that, the transponder stopped transmitting, which makes sense since it can't transmit through steel."

They hadn't killed her right away. Vivian might still be alive! Joe still felt weak. His seasickness had retreated, but the long swim and the dehydration had taken it out of him.

It didn't matter—he didn't have time for weakness. He had to find her. Both he and Captain Glascoe knew she might already be dead, but both of them were acting like that couldn't be true.

"I'll call the Navy," Joe said. "Get reinforcements."

"Sure," said Glascoe. "They'll send someone right out."

"Sarcasm doesn't help."

"Nope," Glascoe said. "And neither will the Navy."

He walked out and left Joe alone with Edison. Joe lay there for a long moment, staring at the ceiling. Then he checked his email.

A message from Vivian's mother, asking if she was OK. Apparently, she'd been emailing her mother every night before bed so her mom would know she was fine. How could Joe tell her that she wasn't?

45

North Atlantic aboard the *Voyager*
March 22, morning

Marshall had given him something to help him sleep, and Joe had slept the clock round. He had a pounding headache, but he still felt stronger than the day before. He dragged himself to the bathroom, washed, and changed into clean clothes. He had to get to work. He had to find Vivian.

When Marshall brought him a plate of eggs and toast with a pitcher of orange juice, Joe engulfed them like a starving man. They stayed down. He was ready for anything now.

First things first. Joe called Fred on his satellite phone and filled him in. "What do you think, Fred?"

"The pictures you sent last night helped. I've moved it up the food chain."

Joe wasn't interested in Fred's food chain. "The people on the sub have Vivian. What's the Navy going to do?"

"By your own admission, she was a civilian operating in international waters and trespassed on a yacht flying a foreign flag. It's not viewed as a naval matter."

Joe ground his teeth. He couldn't blow up in front of Fred. Fred was his only ally. "But?"

"But the pictures got their attention. They think she's a Swedish Gotland-class sub."

"I told you that." A while ago.

"With no explicit verification. Now we have verification. I don't know what they're doing up there. They'll never tell me, or you either, but I think they've probably sent a vessel to check her out. A rogue sub with those capabilities is no joke."

"I know."

"But she's a very able vessel. She won't be easy to track."

He wished Fred didn't keep calling the sub *she*. It was hard not to confuse it with Vivian. "You know where the sub was and the exact time. Doesn't that help?"

"She could be a lot of places by now." Fred rustled something next to the phone receiver. It sounded like a candy wrapper. "But I bet they're looking."

"How can I help?" Joe said.

"Seems like you've helped enough."

"What if I can find out the sub's next target?"

"They'd be interested, probably send someone to check that out."

That was what he had to do.

Knuckles slammed his door.

"It's open," he called. He should have brought a first aid kit. He'd chewed through the ship's aspirin already.

Marshall stepped into the stateroom. "Captain Glascoe says you might have a course for us, sir."

"No course correction." Glascoe was following the sub's last heading because it was the only thing they could do. They'd cut their speed, hoping for a ping from Vivian's transponder, but so far it had remained silent.

Marshall left without another word.

Joe closed his eyes and saw pictures of Vivian. Vivian helping him onto the boat. Vivian standing in his bedroom demanding to come along. Vivian knocking out the drone with a tray. Vivian scared inside his sub. Vivian joking with him about showing Prince Timgad that women could participate in submarine races. Vivian standing in his billiard room with a smile and a sandwich. She was his friend, maybe his best friend, and he'd let her down. Her mother wouldn't even get a body to bury.

Edison nudged his knee, then looked at the computer.

"You're right, boy. The answer's in there. The answer is always in there." He would finish what he'd started here. He owed Vivian that. That and so much more.

Edison wagged his tail and jumped up on his bed. He lay with his back touching Joe's leg.

"No dogs on the bed," Joe whispered.

Edison closed his eyes and pretended not to hear. That was good enough for Joe.

He stroked the dog's head once, then picked up his laptop. He had to push down his grief. Vivian would never give in to grief in this situation, and he do what she would have wanted.

He had to get to work.

He'd start with what he knew. At this point, he was pretty certain the sub was under the control of the women who'd been in the plane that supposedly had crashed. The yacht belonged to the aunt of the woman who'd been engaged to Prince Timgad—Laila Dakkar.

She was an unlikely sub commander. She'd majored in film studies at King's College London. Not much else about her on the Internet. A few essays about films, her face in the background of pictures on Facebook, usually next to her now-deceased twin sister. They'd seemed happy and at ease. The loss of a beloved sister and the thought of a lifetime as the wife of her murderer could drive anyone to extreme lengths.

What was her end goal? She'd killed the bodyguard and had probably intended to kill the prince, but there were easier ways to kill him. She could have sent an assassin after him, like someone had after Joe. She'd blown up an oil tanker, but that hadn't been a particularly high-value target, and it hadn't had any oil in it. With the submarine, she could have taken out a military target, or an oil rig, or laid mines to destroy a harbor. Even sinking the sub and walking away would cost her government millions, assuming they had paid for it.

She had to be after a target worth more than all that.

A few hours later, he was no closer to an answer. He'd investigated every woman on the plane. They'd all probably known one other for years. Most were related—cousins or second cousins or some kind of far-flung relatives that Joe couldn't name. They showed up in each other's childhood pictures, usually taken abroad. They'd attended private schools together, received college degrees from Western institutions together. Some had been married, most hadn't. None had living children. As Vivian had said, these were not women who would want to settle down to a life of subservience behind a veil, but that was exactly what they had faced.

They disappeared after the plane crash. They could have gone off into the world and pursued their own destinies. But they hadn't. Instead, they'd boarded a submarine they could barely have known how to control and set off across the sea to sink the prince's sub, to torpedo the tanker, and then?

He used the head and ate a handful of crackers with ginger ale, glad his stomach was finally settled. He had to figure this out soon. Edison wandered off, probably to eat or to use his toilet mat on the back deck (the poop deck, Vivian had called it), and came back. The ship plowed on, maybe getting farther from her with each moment.

He hadn't learned anything from the women's online profiles. They'd been discreet and careful, as if they'd always been preparing to sink into obscurity. That left their men.

Laila's former brother-in-law and fiancé. Laila's brother and father. The retiring king. The potential male heirs.

He'd trawled through tons of websites before he finally caught a break.

The king's son, Mishaal, had just posted a picture of himself on Facebook. He was standing next to a railing with a blonde with seriously augmented breasts. Behind him was a dark ocean and a starry sky. A quick run through translation software elicited a tag line of "Partying with the bitches" which didn't help. The picture wasn't tagged by location, although Mishaal usually tagged his pictures.

Joe opened an app that could determine a location based on the position of the stars in a photograph. It took work to clean up the photo enough to run it through the app. Worth every second.

"Edison!" he yelled.

The dog jumped. He'd been sound asleep.

"Sorry, buddy." He stroked his back. "Fetch Captain Glascoe!"

Edison jumped off the bed and sprinted out the door like his tail was on fire. God, he loved that dog.

Less than a minute later, he came back with Glascoe in tow.

"The dog says you needed me?" Glascoe strode into the room.

"King Dakkar's son posted a picture of himself on Facebook about an hour ago." He turned the laptop around so that Glascoe could see. "I determined the GPS coordinates. It's only fifty miles from here. On the ocean between here and New York."

Glascoe didn't answer.

"Glascoe?" Joe said. "I think the yacht is the target."

"Target?"

"The king is thinking of abdicating."

"So?" Glascoe said.

"He's old and he's stepping down." Joe recited his conversation with Vivian. "According to his current law, he needs to choose his successor."

"Won't his oldest son automatically become king?"

"No," Joe said. "It's complicated. Rumor has it that the man tapped to be his successor is Prince Timgad. And I'm willing to bet that the heirs to the throne are all on that ship, waiting to find out for sure."

Glascoe took a small step back. "The whole royal family?"

"A lot of them anyway. Probably hundreds. It's the perfect revenge target for women who suffered all their lives at the hands of the royal family."

"They're going to take out the entire royal family?" Glascoe was keeping up, but he looked stunned.

"I'll call my contacts, you call yours. Someone needs to warn them."

46

Joe hated waiting. He spent way too much of his life waiting. Today was no different, but it felt different. Vivian was locked up on the submarine, maybe being tortured, maybe already dead. He should have been with her. Or they should both be back on the ship, safe. But he had persuaded her to put the transponder on the submarine in his stead.

Captain Glascoe had headed for the last-known location of the *Roc*, based on the coordinates of the Facebook photo. He'd poured on all possible speed, but even so, they wouldn't meet up with the *Roc* for hours. They tried radioing, but the *Roc*'s radio operator wasn't responding. Of course not, the ship was on a secret mission. They had left the land far behind to make their decision without anyone's knowledge or interference. The last thing they'd do was respond to some random boat.

Joe had talked to everyone he could. He'd warned the US Navy via Mulcahy. He'd sent all the information he had to Mr. Rossi to have him work through his own mysterious channels. He'd persuaded Captain Glascoe to put his own ship and crew in danger. That hadn't been easy. While Marshall seemed serious about finding Vivian, Glascoe didn't. It had taken a lot of money to get him to change course. But Joe had prevailed. He'd done all he could.

Then he remembered his conversation with Vivian right after they boarded *Voyager*. She'd said he always found more things to do.

So he found one. He would backtrack the *Roc*'s voyage. Maybe there would be something there to tell him why that yacht was being targeted by the submarine, something beyond just the royal family. Their electing of a new leader was his guess, but maybe there was more. At the very least, he'd know more. The more he knew, the better.

He determined the *Roc* had left from the Emirates Palace Marina nearly four (green) weeks before, a few weeks after the princess had faked her own death in the plane crash. According to airlines records, some of the *Roc*'s crew would be flying out of New York the day after tomorrow, so the ship was probably due to arrive in New York before that.

He called Captain Glascoe's cell phone and, after brief hellos, told him the *Roc*'s destination and projected course.

"I'll adjust our course to intercept," Glascoe said. "But they don't seem to want our help."

"Not yet," Joe said. "But if they get attacked by a submarine and have people bailing out, I bet they'll want our help."

"It's only your supposition this will even occur."

"That and a check with a lot of zeroes on the end."

Joe listened to static on the line.

"I'll adjust course," Glascoe said.

The pitch of the engine changed, and the ship listed slightly to the right. Glascoe had adjusted course. He glanced out the window. Blue water. Lots of it. It would be hours before that view changed.

He went back to his detective work on the *Roc*. It took some doing, but he eventually found footage of the yacht being loaded. Most items seemed straightforward, but a large box caught his attention.

The box looked heavy and awkward. The prince himself stood on the dock supervising the box's arrival, although he hadn't cared about anything else that went onto the ship. The crane operator seemed nervous, as the crane operated in jerks and stops, unlike the boxes he'd put on board earlier. Was it the content of the box or the presence of the prince that upset him? Or maybe he was just getting tired?

No matter how much Joe enhanced the footage showing the crate, he couldn't read the markings on the outside. Orderly rows of black figures. He could tell they weren't written in Arabic—too blocky. Or English. The symbols looked like Chinese characters, but he couldn't be sure. He isolated each and tried to run them through translation software, but they were too indistinct.

Maybe it was a giant refrigerator or engine parts, but he didn't think so. The Chinese hack of the submarine plans. The Chinese-made assault rifle recovered at the crash scene. They seemed to indicate the Chinese were supplying the royal family with weapons. He suspected whatever was in that box was some kind of weapon as well.

But what could it be?

He researched the yacht herself, from public records to building plans. The *Roc* had a private submarine on board, probably similar to the one the prince's bodyguard had died in, a helicopter, and a missile defense system. It might even have anti-submarine weapons. The *Roc* might not be so easy for a submarine to sink. And the submarine might not escape unscathed. His worry for Vivian kicked up another notch, something he hadn't even thought possible.

Out of ideas in the virtual world, he decided to visit the bridge and check on their progress. He walked down corridors lined with windows. Just the sight of them made his heart race, but if he closed his eyes when he got near, he was able to walk past them. Edison stuck close to his leg, and when his eyes were closed, he guided himself using the motions of the dog. He probably looked exceedingly lame, but to him it felt like progress.

He was exhausted by the time he reached the bridge. Before he boarded, he'd insisted the bridge be connected to the deck via a canvas tube, and he hurried through the tube, trying not to think about how thin the barrier was between him and the outside world. When he got to the bridge, he stood in the doorway. Glascoe and Marshall were the only ones there. Both staring forward. Windows surrounded the bridge, and Joe couldn't step into the room without closing his eyes. That wasn't going to give him any authority.

"Captain Glascoe?" he called from his position on the threshold. "Any news?"

"We've found the *Roc* with sonar." Glascoe called over his shoulder. "We're closing in."

Joe looked at the wooden floor because he didn't dare look at Glascoe with all that open glass behind him. A bow rested on the floor by the door. It seemed utterly out of place, but then he remembered Vivian telling him that Marshall used it to bowfish from up here.

"I suggest we keep a lot of space between us and the yacht," Joe said.

"Why?" Glascoe sounded annoyed. Joe couldn't blame him—first, he'd insisted they approach the yacht, and now, he was saying they should stay away.

"My research indicates she's heavily armed—security forces, antiballistic missile defenses, probably also some kind of ship-to-ship defenses."

"Great." Glascoe's shadow turned to Marshall, who was piloting the boat. "Maintain a distance. We'll see what goes down and be ready to pick up any survivors."

"You got it." Marshall's freckled hands moved easily around the controls. He clearly knew what he was doing.

"I'll get drones in the air." Joe turned and hurried from the tube to a tent pitched in the middle of the deck. He'd set up a backup computer station there where he'd intended to watch the sonar feeds and pilot the drones, although he hadn't spent much time there since his arrival. He'd been too seasick before, but either he'd gotten used to the motion or the antiemetic in the IV was still working. Either way, he felt comfortable up here.

He stood by the drones. Each had a belly-mounted camera to relay information back to Joe's screens, and he wanted them in the air. Maybe he'd be able to get a good aerial view of the *Roc*.

Unfortunately, the drones were under the tent. Ordinarily, he'd ask Vivian to drag them out onto the deck so he could pilot them. But she wasn't there. It would be too embarrassing to ask Marshall or Glascoe or the other men on the ship. But he didn't have to.

"Edison." Joe pointed to a drone, then out to the deck near the railing. "Take the drone out there."

Edison tugged a drone onto the deck where Joe had pointed. It was a day drone, painted blue on the bottom and white on top. On a sunny day like today, it would be hard to spot. Or at least he hoped so.

"Good boy!" He gave Edison a treat from his pocket.

Edison wagged his tail and crunched it down. He looked expectantly at the drone. Edison knew what was supposed to come next.

Joe worked the controls to make the drone take off. He didn't have much practice, but the drone rose jerkily and hovered a few feet above the deck. He checked the camera—teak boards. So far, so good.

Joe aimed the drone toward the faraway yacht and flew it high above the waves, but not so high he didn't feel queasy watching it. Maybe the motion sickness drugs were wearing off. He increased the drone's altitude.

Slowly, the *Roc* came into view. The yacht was huge— white with teak decks and giant windows. At six hundred (orange, black, black) feet long and four hundred and fifty (green, brown, black) feet high, it was bigger than a naval destroyer. An H with a circle around it on the gleaming main deck was mostly obscured by the helicopter parked on it. The helicopter was white with blue stripes that matched the ship. Three (red) windows on the sides, several in front. It made him anxious just thinking about flying in it. He guessed it could hold eight (purple) passengers.

People strolled around on the main deck and on the upper decks. He counted about twenty (blue, black), but wondered how many people were below. Many. If his guess was correct, all at risk.

No one looked up at the drone, so he judged it high enough that they hadn't noticed it.

Studying the yacht, he banked the drone in a large circle. The yacht looked just like its blueprint, which he'd seen online, except for a device mounted on top of the bridge. The device didn't look like a standard antenna. He drifted the drone down for a closer look.

A copper coil glinted in the sunlight. A large conductor. A white tube that looked recently painted to match the ship. On the end, a cable ran out the back and down the side of the roof, presumably to a power source. The device looked like something his erstwhile ancestor Nikola Tesla might have built. A Tesla coil on top of the most expensive yacht in the world. It had to mean something, but he didn't know what.

Joe stared at the image, trying to make the pieces fit into the list of things that might be expected to be on top of such a ship—antenna, wireless transmitters—but this device was different. Maybe it belonged to the missile defense system. Maybe the captain was a tinkerer. Maybe it transmitted porn.

Maybe it was none of these.

The device was approximately the size of the wooden crate he'd seen being loaded before the *Roc* left port.

The thoughts dancing around his head moved into formation.

This device was the weapon. An electronic weapon capable of delivering a large electromagnetic pulse.

An EMP bomb.

Heading straight for New York.

47

The *Roc* was almost to New York. It had taken Laila longer than she'd expected to find the prince's ship. The ship had stayed in regular shipping lanes, and her people had to sift through many false positives. She had worried the giant yacht had slipped through her fingers.

"I'm sure." Ambra pointed her pencil at a bright object on the screen. "That's the prince's ship."

"The *Roc*." The ship was huge, long and thin. The bow tapered to a knife-point edge, the stern rounded. A distinctive profile. No commercial vessels were that size, no military vessels that shape. The prince's vanity had made his ship distinctive.

"The Israeli protest boat is here." Ambra pointed at another ship a few miles away. That ship was aimed straight for New York, several miles ahead of the *Roc*, but the yacht gained on them with every minute. The people on board probably had no idea that the giant ship behind them was a royal superyacht that sought to destroy their lives.

"Are you sure it's the protest boat?" If she had to shoot it from the water, she wanted to be sure.

"It's a former Greenpeace boat. Slow old tub with noisy engines. Easy to see and hear." Ambra pointed her pencil again. "Nothing else like it in this part of the ocean."

Laila pictured the scruffy settlers aboard, come to complain to the United States and demand more support in their plans to steal more land from the Palestinians. They weren't innocents in the conflict. Religious zealots who wanted to take all the lands for themselves. They didn't care about the refugee problem and how its ramifications spread far beyond the borders of their tiny land.

Just as the refugees fled far beyond the lands of their birth, so too would the consequences spread throughout the world if these ragtag settlers were blamed for the crippling EMP discharge the *Roc* would send straight into the heart of New York. She'd thought of simply sinking their boat, but had decided that if this ship were to be sunk so close before the EMP discharge, tensions would rise.

"Once the *Roc* reaches that ship, it can discharge the device at any time," Ambra said. "We can aim for the *Roc*'s engines. We can stop them without sinking them."

Laila thought of the men aboard—the prince, the king, her cousins, her brother, her father, servants, and soldiers. According to Nahal's evidence, few of them understood the true purpose of their voyage. Even fewer knew the prince intended to sink the Israeli ship and then the *Roc* as soon as it delivered its EMP charge. His men were trained to kill everyone but the prince and his allies. No one would be left to challenge him.

She had no love for the current king. She and her sisters and cousins had suffered under his tyrannical rule. He, too, thought of women only as beasts of burden and pleasure. Even so, he was not as vicious and ruthless as the prince. No one was.

Except for her.

She had to be.

"Hit her broadside," Laila said. "We must send the device, and the prince, to the bottom of the sea."

They had to act now, before they were detected. The *Roc* could outrun them if she chose, and the yacht was so close to New York that she didn't have to stay afloat much longer to shoot the EMP weapon into the sky.

"Ready torpedoes," Laila said and heard her words immediately echoed back from the torpedo room.

It had begun. And no one had doubts.

"Another ship is heading toward the *Roc*." Ambra bent lower over the sonar table. "The engines are running on a weird frequency, or I would have picked it up on passive sonar. It looks like an old military boat. Probably just using the shipping lane. Unlikely to be armed."

"Not a threat. Close on the *Roc*." If she perceived a threat, she would sink the new ship later. For now, everything was about the *Roc*.

The helmsman was already changing direction. They were closing in on their target at their top speed of twenty knots. The *Roc* had a top speed of thirty-four knots, but she was still plowing ahead on her regular course at twenty knots, like a horse heading back to the barn.

The *Roc* didn't know they were there. She was helpless before them. As helpless as Laila's sister had been before the prince.

"Surface to periscope depth." Laila wanted to see every bit of destruction. Flames. A hole ripped in the sleek hull. Bodies spilling off the decks. Blood and oil on the water. If the *Roc* launched lifeboats, she would shoot them, too. She would leave no survivors. All leadership would have to be rebuilt.

Ambra paced the tiny bridge. The planesman and the helmsman looked at her as if they expected her to do something besides pilot the submarine. Laila watched the women study Ambra. She hated to think what they expected Ambra to do. Mutiny?

But they had come too far to turn back now. They all knew it.

Ambra tucked her yellow pencil behind her ear and looked up.

Laila waited. Ambra knew her duty. They all did.

If they didn't, she would remind them. Or Meri would.

She looked over to where Meri stood near the periscope. A pistol was tucked into her overalls. As Laila well knew, Meri wouldn't hesitate to use it against any obstacle. Meri met her gaze, her expression resolute.

"Ready to fire," Laila said.

And they were ready.

48

Vivian jerked upright from an uneasy sleep. Pain lanced from her shoulders down to her wrists. The hand not protected by her cast was numb. Hoping to get some blood flowing, she opened and closed both hands.

Nahal had curled up near the head of the bed. Her bright brown eyes studied Vivian. She'd probably been watching her sleep. Creepy.

"Please take off the handcuffs," Vivian said.

"How do I know you won't hurt me?"

"What would be the point?" Vivian tried to massage one hand with the other. Both hands were cold. "Would your boss care if I took you hostage?"

"She would not. She is a Dakkar, and that comes with a certain ruthlessness of spirit. She will spare no one, including me." Slowly, Nahal sat and inched closer to Vivian. With one small hand, she unlocked the cuffs and set them on the desk.

Vivian stood and rolled her shoulders. Her back and neck popped. She bounced from foot to foot. She wanted to do a couple jumping jacks, but worried that might freak out Nahal. Best to keep it slow and steady. Instead, she stood still and massaged her numb hand. A little feeling returned to her wrist. It was going to hurt like hell soon. Good. Pain was just weakness leaving your body. Who had said that?

"Is your hand all right?" Nahal asked.

"I think so. It's warming up a little, so that's a good sign." Vivian opened and closed her hands over and over.

"Aren't you afraid to die in this tin can deep underwater? To never see your family again?" Vivian looked around the tiny room. "I sure don't want to die here."

"I already died when the plane crashed. We all did."

"Not really."

"I can never see my family again. Never go back to the places I consider home. The submarine is my home now, and I'm prepared to die again." Nahal sat back. "If necessary, we will all drown together. So long as the men of the House of Dakkar drown with us, it would have been a sacrifice I'd gladly make."

"They must have really pissed you off." Vivian moved between Nahal and the desk, blocking her view. She scooped up the handcuffs and stuffed them in the top of her cast.

Nahal laughed. "If they hadn't turned to creating a global war, I would have let them go their way and I would have gone mine. Perhaps I would have needled them from afar, damaging their banks or their investments to make them pay. But that would have been all."

It didn't seem like Nahal was so convinced, she kept saying *would have been* instead of *would be*. Something had changed for her, and Vivian hoped it would be enough to keep them both alive. "Will killing them make you feel better? Will it really change things?"

"It will not." Nahal struggled to her feet. Like the other women on the ship, she wore blue coveralls, but hers were so big that the pant legs and sleeves were rolled up. The top was unzipped halfway to her waist, and a white bandage was visible on her chest.

"What happened there?" Vivian pointed to the bandage.

"I was shot when we took the sub."

"How many other people were shot?"

"I don't know."

"How many people died?"

"Some. Soldiers, but still innocents, I concede." Nahal touched her bandage. "As were those on the tanker."

"How high does the body count need to go before it's worse than what you're trying to prevent?" Vivian said. "I've been trained to kill to stop war, too. Is the cost worth what you gain?"

"For this, today, yes."

"Will sinking the prince's ship stop his plans? If it does, will Laila stop? Will she let me go?"

Nahal turned away and closed her eyes. Vivian breathed through the pain in her hand, flexing it and shaking it. She even tossed in a few jumping jacks, her hands nearly touching the walls. Eventually, Nahal opened her eyes.

"Are you ready to sentence me to death?" Vivian felt guilty hammering on a wounded woman, but she was the only leverage around.

"I have been thinking about these things," Nahal sat up again, "since long before you arrived to pester me."

Vivian ignored the dig. "And what's come out of all that thinking?"

"Before your arrival, I gathered what I need to prove to the world the prince is a traitor. That he planned to attack New York, sink his yacht, and blame Israel for the deaths in New York, the deaths of the royal family."

That was a lot right there. "How are you going to get the information out there if the sub sinks with you inside?"

"I worry, of course I do. If I don't explain, no one will know why the *Roc* sank. Or we sank. And if the prince or his conspirators survive, they may try again. It was a high risk, but I had no other choices. But now I do."

"Am I part of these new choices?" Definitely a new risk, but Vivian would rather go down fighting hand to hand than sink to a watery tomb to die in the cold darkness without any air.

"Your Mr. Tesla has the means for me to distribute my information. He wouldn't have ventured into the real world without still being connected to the virtual one. He can help me bring Prince Timgad's villainy to light so no one can use his plan."

"What about saving New York?"

"Laila will save it. If only to thwart the prince in his greatest ambition. She thinks she used me, that she uses all of us. But we use her as well. What she does not see, what she cannot see, is this plan didn't begin with the prince and it won't end even if she kills him. Others will carry it forward. You and I must stop them."

"How?"

"Help me get to the surface. Tesla will find you."

"Will he?" Vivian sure hoped so.

Nahal ignored her. "Once he does, he and I can work from his boat. There are places we can post this information, ways we can frame the story so that the world understands."

"So, I'm supposed to help you, a woman I barely know?" Her new job sounded like her old job—risking her life to help some crazy nerd save the world. Except with a greater chance than usual of drowning. "Aren't we too deep to get out of the sub now?"

Nahal shook her head. "Laila is a Dakkar. She will want to watch the battle. I bet my life the submarine will surface to periscope depth when the torpedoes are fired. About sixty feet. Not so deep at all."

An Olympic-sized swimming pool was only one hundred and sixty-four feet long. Vivian could swim that far holding her breath. Not that she would. She'd be in some damn suit, breathing out and praying. It still seemed like a better option than staying here.

"OK," she said.

"But we will only stay at such a shallow depth until the *Roc* is sunk. After that, the *Siren* will dive and hide."

"If we don't try to escape?"

"Perhaps Laila will let us all go our separate ways. Perhaps not. I think she will not let me go so easily, because I am useful to her. But you must know that she will kill you."

Vivian had to agree with her. Laila would kill her as soon as she got a chance. All that was left was the logistics. "Who will activate the escape trunk to let us out? Can we do that ourselves?"

"We can do it ourselves once we're inside."

The sub dipped.

"Did you feel that?" Nahal asked. "A torpedo has been launched."

Vivian's hand burned. She opened and closed it and promised it a better future.

"There are coveralls in the locker." Nahal pointed. "Put on a pair. It is not much of a disguise, but I think everyone will be too busy to look closely."

Vivian opened the metal door and took out the overalls. Her hands felt like flippers. Nahal helped with the zipper and tied a head scarf over her head, presumably to hide her long hair.

"Ready?" Nahal asked.

Without answering, Vivian opened the door and stepped into the corridor.

49

Joe flew the drone in a wide circle around the *Roc*. The scene played out on various screens—video feed from the drone, sonar feed from the *Voyager*, and the view through the bridge from a camera he'd installed there. The submarine was within striking distance of the yacht. It was at periscope depth and visible from the sky.

Edison crowded up next to his folding chair. Absently, he stroked the dog's back.

"It's OK, boy," he said. "They don't care about a little minnow like us."

He studied the black bulk of the approaching submarine. If she was still alive, Vivian was in there. She should have been back in New York babysitting some spoiled executive at a cocktail party. Bored, but safe.

A flash of white from the submarine, then a quick black line, and a massive bubble of white foam fountained up higher than the *Voyager*. The *Siren* had fired its first torpedo. The *Roc* lurched to the side and then righted herself.

"Detonated too soon," he told Edison. "Close, though."

"Back full!" Captain Glascoe's shout came through the monitor. He wanted to run away. Joe didn't blame him, but he couldn't let that happen.

Joe set the drone's controls on his makeshift desk. When left to its own devices, the drone would hover in position—right over the *Roc*. It continued to film and to send those images back to Joe's computers. Whatever happened, the drone would keep recording until it ran out of battery power.

And he had more important things to do.

Edison on his heels, he sprinted through his makeshift tunnels to the bridge. They couldn't leave.

"What are you doing?" Joe spoke from the doorway.

"Getting out of here until they're done fighting," Glascoe said. "Putting a few miles between us so they don't sink my damn ship."

Voyager was moving backward, away from the submarine. Away from Vivian. A stoic Marshall stood at the helm.

"We need to be close enough to pick up survivors," Joe said.

He meant Vivian. She had to be alive still. She had to be.

"We can't do anything for them right now." Glascoe looked out at the superyacht towering over the waves. "Not till this is over. We're not even armed."

Technically not entirely true. They had a locker full of guns and a fire hose. But nothing that would hold off a yacht carrying who knew what and a fully armed military submarine. Joe wasn't going to win this argument on logic. Glascoe was right. But Joe didn't care.

"If by some miracle Vivian Torres pops out of that submarine, I want us to be close enough to get her out of the water before she gets blown to hamburger." Joe knew he was shouting.

Worried, Edison looked between Joe and Captain Glascoe. The dog hated conflict. Glascoe turned to face Joe and put his hands on his hips. He was taller than Joe, fitter, probably a better fighter. Joe stared him down.

Marshall froze, and the ship kept moving the wrong way. But it slowed down.

"Full speed." Glascoe roared. "You heard me."

Marshall jumped. Slowly, his hand moved toward the controls.

Joe couldn't let them abandon Vivian. He'd left her once, and he wasn't going to do it again. "We stay where we are."

Glascoe's voice was low and deadly. "I'm the captain of this vessel. I'm in command, and I'm not putting the ship or the lives of my men at risk."

"I've paid you enough to own this ship." Joe glared at him, barely noticing the wall of bright windows now. "And she's not going anywhere. We stay to pick up survivors."

Edison stood firm next to him. The hair on the scruff of his neck rose, and the dog growled. Good dog.

Glascoe started toward Joe. The man moved like a fighter. Which he was. Ex-boxer. Joe'd read his file. He'd killed people, and he wouldn't have any trouble taking out an agoraphobic programmer and his friendly dog.

Joe bent down, picked up the bow, and aimed it straight at Glascoe's chest.

Surprised, Glascoe stopped. "You're kidding."

"I've trained on this," Joe said. "I can hit a much smaller target than your heart from this distance."

"You'd have to hope you got my heart with the first shot, because you wouldn't get another." Glascoe hadn't moved, but he looked like he was calculating the distance between them.

"I can," Joe said. "How about we don't let it come to that?"

Edison growled again.

"A computer nerd with a bow?" Glascoe took a step forward. "Just like that elf in *Lord of the Rings*."

He was too close. Joe wanted to step back into the tube, but he couldn't do that. If he did, Glascoe would rush him and they would leave Vivian to her fate.

"Stop walking." Joe used his sternest voice. That voice had driven off kids who hadn't paid at the carnival when Joe was a kid, it had made other CEOs back down, and it had made homeless people leave him alone in the tunnels.

It made Glascoe charge.

Joe moved the bow a fraction down and shot Glascoe through the thigh. The arrow buried itself in the wooden console behind him. Joe pressed a button to release the fishing line from the bow and stooped to load another arrow.

Glascoe howled, but he couldn't move without pulling the arrow all the way through his leg. Marshall picked up the bloody fishing line and tied it off to a metal handrail. Glascoe couldn't move.

"You shot me!" he bellowed. "You fucking elf."

"Legolas," Joe said. "His name was Legolas."

Marshall started laughing. He laughed so hard he practically fell down.

"Cut me loose," Glascoe roared. "Get your Marine ass over here and cut me loose."

"Semper fi," Marshall said.

"Then get your faithful butt over here and cut me loose." Glascoe pressed his hands against his leg. From what

Joe could tell, he'd missed the major arteries, but blood still seeped through his fingers and dripped onto the floor.

Joe moved the bow in Marshall's direction. Marshall held up his hands and sauntered to the first aid kit on the other side of the bridge. "Just getting some supplies for that hole you made in our captain."

He took out gauze and a pair of blunt scissors, leaned under the console and pulled out a bottle of amber liquid.

Joe tensed. "What do you have there?"

"Medical and medicinal items only." Marshall returned to Glascoe's side.

"What now?" Joe asked.

"Cut me free," Glascoe said in the same breath.

"No man left behind." Marshall handed Glascoe the whiskey. "Or woman. I agree with Tesla here. We'll stay close, pick up Sergeant Torres when she arrives."

"If she arrives." Glascoe took a long pull on the whiskey, and his face relaxed a little.

"If," said Marshall. "But she's a tough lady. If anybody can get herself out of that sub, it's Vivian. I know I'd feel like an asshole if her ride weren't there to pick her up. Wouldn't you?"

Eyes fixed on Glascoe's, Joe held the bow steady.

Glascoe took another long sip of whiskey. "If you guys think there's a chance she can get out, we'll stay."

Marshall handed the captain the gauze and scissors and went back to the controls. The boat reversed its course.

Joe let out a long breath and lowered the bow.

But he didn't put it down.

Another explosion came from the water.

50

Vivian wrapped an arm around Nahal's waist and helped her forward. Nahal was too weak to move quickly, and they needed to hurry.

"Thank you," Nahal said through lips gone pale with pain.

"I've exited a submarine in an emergency suit once before." Vivian still had nightmares. "It's a pretty violent and intense experience. Are you sure you're up for that?"

Nahal took a memory stick out of her pocket and handed it to Vivian. "Here's a copy of everything for you. If we get separated or...if I don't make it to the surface, give it to Tesla. It will take some expertise to unpack it and post it where it needs to go, but he can do it."

Vivian stuffed the stick inside her bra. She didn't have any pockets. "That doesn't answer my question."

"Live or die, I want off this submarine." Nahal started walking again. "I've seen the price for disagreeing with Laila."

Vivian didn't figure now was the time to get into it. She dragged Nahal forward.

"She does not need them as she needs me. She will let them go when she is done." Nahal seemed pretty confident she knew what Laila was thinking, but Vivian wondered if she was right. But she wasn't going to argue with anything that got her away from this giant metal coffin.

They went a few steps more, and Vivian started to think they'd get through this. At the end of the corridor, women rushed back and forth, but they took no notice of her and Nahal. She looked like someone helping a companion to sick bay. In the current climate, not that unusual.

Then the sub lurched violently. Vivian's head slammed against a metal pipe. It hurt like hell, but she held on to Nahal. Short screams echoed down the corridor. Nobody had liked that moment.

"You OK?" Vivian asked Nahal.

"We were hit." Nahal looked dazed. "The *Roc* has torpedoes."

"Makes sense." Vivian touched her head. A lump the size of a duck egg was already forming. But her vision seemed fine, and she hadn't lost consciousness. Nothing to worry about.

"Torpedoes," Nahal said again.

"You stole his submarine. You came after him with it and killed his bodyguard. Prince Timgad seems like someone who knows how to take care of himself. Why wouldn't he have torpedoes?" Vivian started moving forward again, faster than before.

"How did he have time?" Nahal let herself be towed along, but she wasn't helping much.

"Money makes things happen quickly." Vivian was losing faith in Nahal's confident grasp of the situation. This was a shame because she was going to get into the escape trunk no matter what. She wasn't going to die in here.

A woman pushed by running full tilt. Blood streamed from her temple. Probably not a good sign.

Vivian dragged Nahal forward double time. It probably hurt, but Nahal didn't say anything. Vivian thought she smelled burnt plastic, but it was hard to tell over the ammonia smell the sub had all the time. Hopefully, nothing important was on fire. Although, realistically, probably every damn part of this submarine was important.

"Left," Nahal said between clenched teeth. She pointed to the left.

Vivian opened a door and stepped into a small metal room. A ladder led up to a round hatch. "Is that it?"

"The escape trunk is on the other side of that hatch."

Vivian ran through the plans of the submarine she'd studied back in her Spartan cabin on the *Voyager*. This seemed right.

She looked around for emergency suits, but the signs were in Arabic and Chinese and her limited Arabic knowledge didn't include submarine terminology. They had to be stowed in here someplace.

"Suits?" Vivian asked Nahal. "Where are the suits?"

"Never mind," said a voice from the doorway.

The voice belonged to a small woman holding a QBS-06 assault rifle like the one Vivian had retrieved from the wreckage of Tesla's sub. She'd researched it, and depressing statistics scrolled through her mind. The gun held twenty-five fléchettes. Those were needlelike projectiles designed to move through the water on a stable trajectory. But they fired just fine through air. One probably wouldn't kill her right away, unless it hit her in the heart or the head. The barrel was aimed straight at Vivian's heart. The guns were supposed to be hard to aim at a distance of over fifty yards, but since the woman was standing about ten feet away, that wasn't really going to be a problem.

"Step away from Nahal," the woman said.

Vivian looked at Nahal. She nodded, and Vivian stepped away. Maybe she could rush her, but the stranger looked like she meant business.

The gun barrel followed Vivian's movements. It was very steady. The woman didn't seem at all conflicted about using it.

"Are you trying to steal away our Nahal, Miss Torres?" she asked.

"I have to go with her, Meri," Nahal said. "I have to publish information about the prince's plan so he can't try it again if he survives, or if his allies survive. Sinking the *Roc* isn't enough."

Meri didn't seem to be impressed. "Leave after the battle is won. As planned."

"If I wait, Laila will kill this woman, and me for helping her, and the word might never get out."

"Win the battle, but lose the war." Vivian wished Meri would stop pointing that gun at her. If the submarine was hit again and tilted to the side, the gun would likely go off.

"You don't speak." Meri stiffened. "You're not one of us."

Nahal held out her hands in a pacifying gesture. "That's right. She's not one of us. She's not part of this, and she doesn't deserve to die. Why not let her go?"

"Collateral damage happens in war." Meri raised the gun slightly. She was ready to shoot.

Vivian shifted slightly.

"Like Rasha?" Nahal asked.

"Rasha was necessary!" Meri looked at Nahal. "You don't—"

Vivian dove past Nahal toward Meri. This was her one chance.

She was too close to shoot. Meri swung the gun like a club. Vivian ducked, and the butt of the rifle clanged against the metal rungs of the ladder.

Nahal cried out.

Vivian kicked low, trying to sweep Meri's knees, but the woman danced back, quick as a snake. Vivian lunged in close. She had to stay in close. Meri moved back another step and crashed into the wall.

It was like fighting inside a closet—no room to move, no room to run, no room to swing.

Meri brought the rifle up to shoot. Vivian slammed Meri's arm between the metal wall and her cast. The barrel glanced off the wall, leaving a black streak in the paint. The metal rang like a bell.

In spite of the pain, Meri didn't let go of her gun. Before she could move, Vivian grabbed the barrel with her other hand and twisted the gun. Meri's fingers bent in an unnatural way. She gasped and lost her grip. The sub pitched to the side.

Vivian yanked the gun free. She swiveled it around and punched Meri in the stomach with the stock. She wanted to smack her in the head, but kept her temper. She didn't want to kill her if she could help it.

Instead, she swept her feet out from under her.

Meri crashed to the floor with a scream.

Vivian put her foot on the back of Meri's exposed neck. "Stay down."

The sub reeled, and Vivian grabbed hold of one of the ladder's rungs to hold herself in place.

Meri writhed, and Vivian swung the rifle down and pressed the barrel against the base of her spine. "One shot here and you won't be moving so much. Maybe you won't ever move again."

Meri froze.

"Don't hurt her!" Nahal came at Vivian with fists flailing.

Vivian elbowed the tiny woman in the chest. She collapsed into the ladder.

"So long as everyone behaves, this will go fine." Vivian took the handcuffs out of her cast and slapped one on Meri's wrist. The other one she locked around the ladder's bottom rung. She eased her foot off Meri's neck.

From this position, Meri couldn't reach the corridor or the escape trunk. She might scream, but with all the screaming and excitement in the sub right now, Vivian wasn't sure anyone would notice. Best she could do.

"Suits?" Vivian kept her gun on Meri's back. No point in letting up until the last second. "The emergency suits?"

Nahal opened a locker to reveal neon yellow emergency suits. She handed one to Vivian and put on one herself. "I'm sorry, Meri."

Meri grunted. It sounded like a curse, but Vivian didn't understand it. Apparently, Nahal did, because her face hardened and she put her foot on the first rung of the ladder.

Vivian slipped into the suit on one side, then moved the gun to her other hand and put on the other side. If was a tight fit over her cast, but she was motivated. Barrel still pressed against Meri's spine, Vivian yanked up the suit's zipper.

The sub's movements had stabilized.

"Do you think the sub dove after it was hit?" Vivian asked. Seemed like a logical choice.

"No order was given." Nahal clambered up the ladder like a monkey.

Vivian was willing to chance it.

"Stay still," Vivian told Meri. "And safe journeys."

Which was more than Meri would ever wish for her.

She followed Nahal up the ladder. Her rubber boot slipped, and she caught herself with her broken arm. She stifled a curse and climbed again. She'd have to get the arm x-rayed again if she ever got back to civilization. She hadn't been following doctor's orders very much since he'd put the cast on.

Nahal was on the top rung of the ladder, struggling to open the hatch. Vivian squeezed past and opened it one-handed, glad for all her time rock-climbing. Upper-body strength was a handy thing to have.

Nahal climbed in first, Vivian after. They were jammed in so tightly it was tough to move around. As soon as Vivian was inside, she closed and sealed the hatch. She had to hope that Nahal was right about being able to work the escape trunk from this side.

She pulled on her hood and gave Nahal a thumbs-up. From now on, she'd be breathing the air in the suit. Nahal closed her hood and gave the thumbs-up signal, too. The suits were working. Nahal reached across and pressed a giant red button.

Cold water rushed into the enclosed space. Vivian gritted her teeth. Nahal buckled straps on her suit to connect to Vivian's. Whatever happened, they were going up together.

The sub bobbed, and Vivian wondered if they'd been hit again.

She turned Nahal's face toward her.

"Don't hold your breath," Vivian yelled.

Nahal pursed her lips and mimed blowing out air in a continuous stream. Apparently, she'd had the same briefing.

Great. Now the only dangers were getting trapped in this tube, running out of air before they hit the surface, being hit by a torpedo, or being pulverized by a shock wave.

All of them would be better than dying inside the submarine.

Or at least Vivian hoped so.

51

Laila grimaced when the escape trunk light lit up on the bridge. One of her crew had deserted. Or two. Only rats deserted a sinking ship. Wasn't that the metaphor?

Most of the crew were at their posts, repairing damage. The *Roc*'s last torpedo had been close, and systems were malfunctioning. Nothing they couldn't manage. The submarine was built for combat.

She glanced at Ambra. Ambra had taken over the helmsman seat since the original helmsman, Fatin, was busy with a fire extinguisher in the corner. White gas drifted around the room, and Laila coughed.

"It's out." Fatin spun, searching for flames. But the bridge was calm.

"Check the rest of the ship," Laila ordered. Fire was one of the biggest dangers on a submarine. Fire and torpedoes.

"I will." Carrying the extinguisher, Fatin left at a run.

Ambra's hands flew over the controls, trying to stabilize the craft. Ambra had stayed true. She had expected Ambra to desert her first of all, but Ambra hadn't.

"Damage report from the torpedo room." Laila didn't care about the rest of the sub. Only the weapons mattered.

"Minor." Samira spoke from the torpedo room. She, too, was coughing. "Bruises down here, a minor electrical problem. I think it won't affect launch."

"Ready next torpedoes." Laila would fire off as many torpedoes as she could.

"Readying." Samira sounded calm.

Laila wished Meri hadn't killed Rasha. Rasha had been the only member of the crew with experience aiming and firing torpedoes. She'd had valuable skills. With her death, the practice run sinking the tanker had become useless. Laila should have had more of the crew train so that it wouldn't have been a waste of time.

And lives.

"I recommend we dive," Ambra called. "We can fire at depth, and it will be harder for the *Roc*'s weapons to reach us the deeper we go."

"No." Laila had to see the yacht sink. She needed to see the prince die.

"Ready to fire!" Samira called.

Laila took a deep breath. Abandoning her mother. Faking her own death. Bullying and cajoling the women into their new roles. Sinking the *Narwhal*. Killing Rasha. Each act had led to this moment.

She could shoot and dive. The *Siren* could evade the *Roc*'s weapons and escape in the depths of the sea. The sub and the women could disappear. They could live out their lives in safety, growing old and fat and happy.

Perhaps the prince would be chastened enough to desist from his plan. Perhaps their knowledge of what he intended would be enough to prevent him no matter what. If she stopped now, she might have accomplished much.

But the prince would live.

He would find another princess and elevate her to queen.

And when he had a bad day, as he surely would, he would beat her to death as he had done with Laila's sister. As he had almost done with Laila herself.

He would never face the consequences of his actions.

He would win.

"Fire!" she ordered.

52

White water fountained higher than the *Roc*'s top deck. The explosion pushed the front of the ship up. It crashed back against the water with a terrific boom. That torpedo had found its mark.

"Oorah!" shouted Marshall.

Bob, one of the other men on the sub, laughed.

They were treating this like a giant video game. But at least they weren't running away.

Joe had set up his laptop on the bridge, back to the wall and eyes averted from the windows. He watched the sonar readout of the sub and the torpedoes in real time. In the drone footage, figures boiled out onto the *Roc*'s deck like ants whose anthill had just been damaged.

Joe glanced at the tiny green window on his screen that was dedicated to monitoring Vivian's transponder. The window was silent. If she was out there, he couldn't tell. He knew it was crazy optimism that kept him going. But crazy optimism was better than nothing.

Edison was unruffled by the explosions and yelling. He sat by Joe's side, his head in Joe's lap and his brown eyes locked on Joe's face.

"It'll be fine," Joe told him. He hoped that was true.

The *Roc* had started to take on water and list to the side. People spilled over into the ocean.

"Can we get them?" he asked Marshall.

"Let the sub stop firing first," Marshall called over his shoulder. "We won't be doing them any favors if we get sunk, too."

Joe saw the logic, but he wondered how many of those figures could swim and how many would survive long enough for his ship to reach them.

Another torpedo was loosed. Another explosion under the *Roc*, this time amidships. Water heaved the giant ship up and smashed it down against the surface of the sea like a giant hand. Smoke billowed out of a crack in the massive deck.

Joe imagined the women in the submarine must be cheering.

Except for Vivian.

The *Roc* lurched to the side and did not right herself. The massive ship was fatally wounded. She shuddered and wallowed. It was clear that she would not recover.

One red lifeboat launched from the vessel's side and splashed into the sea below. The boat was fully enclosed, so Joe couldn't even begin to guess how many people were inside. Certainly not everyone on the ship. But at least some of them.

In areas where the smoke had cleared, debris and bodies churned. Soon, the *Siren* would be satisfied with the *Roc*'s destruction. Soon, he and his men could help those bodies in the sea.

But not yet.

The *Roc* was wounded, but not yet helpless. She launched a pair of torpedoes at the *Siren*. On sonar, Joe watched them shoot through the water toward the round black submarine.

The *Siren* was already diving toward the edge of his sonar range. The torpedoes exploded deep underwater, but Joe couldn't calculate if they had been close enough to damage the submarine.

The *Siren* headed for the bottom. He couldn't tell if the sub was sinking, or if it was a cleverly controlled descent. Almost off his sonar, the sub kept falling. If Vivian was alive, she was beyond anyone's reach now.

Joe closed his eyes and bowed his head. Edison whimpered. They had lost her.

Marshall steered them toward the sinking ship. The drone captured the ship, in two pieces now, slipping down toward the bottom. She would not shoot another torpedo. The *Siren*, too, was in full flight.

All that remained was picking up the survivors. As much as Joe had ached to help them before, now he felt only numbness. The person he wanted most to survive hadn't. Vivian's survival had been a remote hope, a foolish hope, but it died hard all the same.

"The helicopter!" Marshall shouted.

The helicopter lifted off the tilting front deck. It held only the pilot and a single man in the backseat. Empty seats that could have gone to survivors surrounded him. A man ran across the deck toward the helicopter and collapsed. A second later, Joe heard the gunshot. Whoever was on board that helicopter wasn't interested in helping the others on the ship.

Joe's drone footage showed another man atop the ship. He'd climbed to the top of the topmost deck, where he yanked at the EMP device. He smashed it with a metal device. Joe brought the drone in closer. The man was trying to pry the device free with a crowbar.

But why? It was certainly heavy enough to sink him. No other lifeboats had launched, so there was no chance he'd be able to bring it to one of them. Seemingly oblivious, the man worked doggedly. Even as the ship sank underneath him, he tore wires loose, pried at the edge of the coil.

He was ready to die to remove the device from the roof. Joe admired his single-minded focus, even as he felt the man would be better off trying to find a way to get off the ship alive.

Finally, the man worked the EMP device free.

And the helicopter rose to meet him.

No longer worried about being spotted, Joe flew the drone closer to the helicopter, hovering outside the side window. The drone shuddered in the prop wash, but before it was bounced away, Joe recognized Prince Timgad sitting in the backseat. The prince had shot the man who'd tried to board. They were hundreds of miles from shore, but maybe the helicopter's range extended that far. Perhaps he would make it to safety.

The prince gesticulated to the man on the roof, and the helicopter closed in. The prince gestured for the man to throw the device, but the man shook his head. Eventually, the prince threw him a rope, and the man climbed aboard with the device tied to his back.

Joe expected them to make for the shore, but the helicopter didn't. Instead, it turned toward the lifeboat. Maybe they intended to pick up survivors and fly them to safety. Maybe the king was in there waiting.

A series of splashes stitched the water toward the red lifeboat.

The helicopter was firing on it.

"Take over!" Marshall yelled to Billy. "I'm going to the gun locker."

As if it had heard the words, the helicopter swung toward them.

Whoever was aboard that chopper clearly intended to leave no witnesses.

"Tesla! Take cover!" shouted Marshall.

Edison pushed up against Joe's leg, trying to herd him out of the exposed bridge and back into the tunnel.

"Heel," Joe said. The dog heeled.

Marshall would never get to the gun locker in time.

Joe picked up the crossbow.

He backed out of the bridge and into his makeshift tunnel. The canvas didn't provide cover against bullets, but at least the shooter in the helicopter couldn't see him.

Joe sprinted down the tube to the tent he'd set up middeck by the drones. He studied the helicopter's rotors. They spun so quickly they were blurred into a single disk shape. He recalled from a long-ago video game that it was called the rotor disk.

The man in the helicopter was firing at the *Voyager's* bridge. Joe hoped Billy was safe. He didn't want another death on his conscience.

Marshall ran full pelt from the other end of the ship, dodging Joe's canvas tunnels and tents. The helicopter gunman switched its fire to Marshall, who dove for the deck.

Joe took a deep breath. Edison whimpered.

"Sit," Joe said. "And stay."

Joe studied the helicopter. With any luck, he'd hit a main rotor blade. He pivoted so the bow and arrow and his arms were outside. Ignoring the pain in his ribs, he lined up on the middle of the rotor disk. He let the arrow fly and moved back inside before his body had time to panic.

He stepped back from the edge of the tent and watched.

His arrow flew straight for twenty (blue, black) yards, entered the rotor disk, and struck a blade. The arrow glanced off the first blade and embedded itself in the next one. The helicopter juddered, spun in a half circle, and crashed straight into the water.

Joe stared, openmouthed. He hadn't expected one arrow to be that successful.

Marshall whooped from across the deck and jogged over.

"Nice shooting, Tex!" he said. "Biggest thing I ever took out was a six-foot shark, and it fought me for hours."

"Do you think they survived the crash?" Joe didn't want to think that he had taken lives.

"Maybe." Marshall shrugged. "Most important thing is that we did."

Joe's knees went out from under him, and he sat down hard on the deck. They had survived. But not all of them. Vivian was gone. And what about the men in the helicopter? Was he a murderer?

Marshall went to the side of the boat, shouting directions up to Billy, directing him toward a group of survivors.

Joe thought about Vivian, gone, and stared at the deck. He had only a few minutes to pull it together before he had to help the victims of the shipwreck. It was time to save lives instead of taking them.

Edison grabbed his hand between his teeth and tugged. At first, Joe thought the dog was pulling him away from the light, but he quickly realized Edison was tugging him toward the bank of computer monitors Joe had set up to watch the drones and the sonar feed.

The little green window was flashing, and the monitor was beeping. Uncomprehending, Joe gaped. Even if he couldn't believe it, he knew what that sound meant.

Vivian's transponder was transmitting.

"She's up," Joe shouted. "In the water."

As incoherent as that sounded, Marshall seemed to understand, because he sprinted straight for the bridge. Joe followed through his tunnels. Holes pockmarked the tunnel. The prince had come much closer to killing him than he'd realized.

The deck moved under Joe's feet. Marshall had beat him to the bridge and was aiming for something.

Joe studied the screens. Nothing. He brought the drone down low and skimmed it across the tops of the waves.

Just because her transponder was beeping, it didn't meant that she was alive. He pushed that unwelcome thought aside and worked the drone in a circle, searching.

The drone spotted two (blue) figures in yellow emergency suits. Joe moved in closer. The front swimmer was towing the other, but awkwardly, stroking with one hand.

"Vivian!" Joe shouted.

Marshall and Billy cheered.

"Take the helm," Marshall ordered. He jogged out the door to the deck, and Joe hurried through his tunnels.

Once Joe reached the deck, he unhooked his tent from its fasteners and pushed it across to the railing where Marshall stood. Joe felt like a hamster in a ball.

But it worked.

Marshall was leaning over the side with a life ring. He tossed it down. Joe pushed up next to him and looked down at the water through the small vinyl window in the tent.

The one-armed figure grabbed the life ring and put it over the head of her companion. Not only had Vivian survived—she'd rescued someone along the way.

She fumbled with something on the other figure's suit, then waved her hand.

Marshall pulled on the life ring. Bob rushed over to help. Hand over hand, they hauled the ring and its precious cargo out of the water.

Together, the two men lifted a small body onto the deck. Marshall took off the hood. Underneath was a small woman with dark skin and short black hair. Her eyes were closed.

"She's breathing," Marshall said. "I'll see to her. You get Vivian."

Bob dropped the ring again, and Vivian put it over her head. She waved her arm and Joe and Bob lifted her up. As soon as she was close enough, she grabbed ahold of the railing and flipped herself over one-handed.

"Show off." Joe dragged her into the tent and gave her a long hug. His ribs hurt, and he didn't care.

When he finally let her go, Edison barked and licked Vivian's hand. She removed her hood and took a long breath.

"Real air smells so good," she said. "You have no idea."

"That's the last time I let you go on a mission by yourself," he said.

"I wanted to go back to the boat with you." She looked at him. "What's wrong with you?"

"Broken rib," Marshall called over his shoulder.

"How did you break your rib?" she asked.

"Puking," Marshall answered.

"Least. Glamorous. Injury. Ever," she said.

Joe couldn't stop grinning.

Vivian punched him on the shoulder. She looked relieved and happy to be alive. He couldn't blame her.

"Welcome back," he said.

A moan from the deck and Vivian went back into action. She bent over the woman she'd brought to the surface. "Nahal?"

Nahal held both hands against her chest.

"Looks like she popped some stitches," Marshall said. "I'll set up a sick bay in Tesla's cabin. You men start looking for others to rescue. Wounded first."

"I'm going back to monitor the radio," said one of guys. Joe had never learned his name. "I've put out a Mayday. The Coast Guard is sending a cutter. It should be here in five hours."

"Go back to your post," Marshall ordered.

Nahal struggled to sit up. Vivian knelt next to her.

"Take it easy," Vivian said.

"Joe Tesla?" Nahal asked.

Joe dropped to his knees next to her. "Yes?"

"Your girlfriend has a jump drive," she said. "It's got instructions on how to track down and publish information proving Prince Timgad was trying to start a war."

"Not his girlfriend," Vivian snapped.

"A war?" Joe asked.

"It lists his supporters as well. It's explosive stuff." Nahal coughed. She looked terrible. "It needs to be released now, before word of the crash gets out and the conspirators disappear like cockroaches in the light."

He could do that. "I'll bring my laptop down to the sick bay and get started."

53

A few hours later, the worst was over. Tesla and Nahal had delivered her information to WikiLeaks, *The New York Times*, *Al Jazeera*, and a dozen other media outlets. Tesla even had footage from the camera up on the bridge that showed the prince targeting the lifeboat. The prince hadn't turned up among the survivors, but even if he did, his credibility was ruined.

Vivian was fine with the idea of the prince drowned at the bottom of the sea, like he should have been when all this started, but she could tell it weighed on Tesla. She hoped he'd work through it. The guy had enough neuroses on his plate already.

At least no one was sure about what had happened to the submarine so Joe wasn't going to add that to his conscience. Nahal seemed to think they'd gotten away. Vivian wasn't sure one way or the other. Joe agreed with Nahal. Something about the trajectory of the submarine as it sank.

If it did get away, Vivian hoped the women aboard would accept their victory over Prince Timgad and stop killing. She wouldn't put it past Tesla to hunt them down again if they didn't.

She wasn't up to hunting anything right now. She was exhausted, and her arm hurt like hell. Marshall had put a splint on her damaged cast, but she'd bashed that around enough that she was pretty sure the arm would need to be reset, and she'd have to start all over with her healing. Maybe she'd have to miss Marina's party. That wouldn't be so bad.

Mostly, she wanted to lie down and sleep for a long time. But she couldn't because her cabin, in fact, all the cabins were full of wounded. There wasn't a spare bed on the ship. About fifty people had survived from the *Roc*, forty-five men and five women. A broken arm, a few gunshot wounds, concussions. The *Shining Pearl* had heard the Mayday and come to help. The *Pearl* had taken the king, who had survived unscathed, and most of the remaining royal family.

The *Voyager* had the leftovers—prostitutes and crew members. Marshall had run between them all like an ER doctor with Vivian awkwardly assisting him one-handed. But for now she was done.

Maybe she could find a place to lie down on the deck. Even a bench would do. But when she got to the deck, the benches were occupied.

She headed for one of Tesla's tents positioned near the railing. Maybe it had a chair inside that no one had claimed. She could prop her feet up on the railing and sack out. Not a bed, not a bench, but better than nothing. When she got there, Tesla and his dog were in the tent.

Tesla gestured to an empty chair. "Have a seat."

She flopped into it.

"Marshall's broken into the ship's liquor cabinet," Tesla said. "We got the short straw."

He held up a bottle of Old Crow Reserve. "Bottom shelf whiskey."

"But all ours." Tesla looked as if he'd had a few sips before she got there.

"I haven't seen that stuff since college," she said.

Tesla took a sip straight from the bottle and coughed. "Tastes like paint thinner."

He handed her the bottle, and she took a long swallow. "I've had worse."

He shook his head.

"I hear you shot Captain Glascoe. With an arrow." She couldn't even picture it.

"He wasn't following orders." Tesla didn't elaborate on those orders, but Marshall had told her.

"He's captain," she said. "You're supposed to follow *his* orders. Otherwise, it's mutiny."

Tesla shrugged. "I'm not good with chain of command issues."

Neither was she.

The ocean, dark now, tossed far below. From her position in the tent, she saw a few stars near the horizon. Nothing major, but she knew they were the first stars Tesla had seen without panicking in a long time. Mesmerized, he stared at them.

A snoring Edison was curled up at his master's feet. Like everyone else, he'd had a long day. His service-dog capabilities had been well used. He'd licked panicky people, accepted a lot of hugs and pets, and worked hard to bring everyone's anxiety level down. He'd earned a good night's sleep.

Waves slapped against the side of the boat, and they passed the bottle back and forth. A few more sips and she was going to fall asleep in her chair.

Tesla turned his chair to face hers. He looked serious, so she waited him out.

"I guess I see your point about the full-time job," he said. "No amount of pay is worth the things I've dragged you through."

"Submarines. Poison gas. Buildings falling down around me." She was pretty sure she'd missed a few disasters.

Tesla winced. "All that."

She handed him the bottle. "It could have been worse."

He took a long drink and gave the bottle back. "How?"

"It could have been boring." Tesla was never boring.

"Right now, boring seems like the best thing in the world." He smiled tiredly.

"That's not what you were saying when you were holed up in your house with your nice predictable routine. You didn't stay home and binge-watch Netflix. You hired a boat and you went out after a rogue submarine."

Even though his eyes were tired, he smiled. "Not my best idea."

"I don't know." She handed him the bottle, and he set it on the deck between them. "You know I used to be in the service, right?"

"I read your records. I wouldn't do that now that I know you, but when you first started working for me and I was worried about who had poisoned me and—"

"Right," she said. "My turn to talk."

He shut up.

"I went into the service to break out of my everyday life. To aim for something bigger than myself. I didn't join to travel the world and shoot my enemies, nothing like that. I wanted to help. I wanted to move in a sphere that was larger than my own. I wanted to make a difference in the wider world."

Edison snorted in his sleep, and they both laughed.

"Since I met you, I've been shot at, poisoned, broken my arm, been trapped in and escaped from a submarine—twice!"

Tesla sighed. "Sorry. It's not really my—"

She talked over him. "But I've also saved lives. Lives of servicemen. Lives of office workers. Lives of innocent women. Today, we might even have actually stopped a war. An entire war. You and me. And the dog and this rusty old tub."

He gestured to the debris and the discarded life jackets scattered across the deck. "It wasn't easy."

"It's not supposed to be easy." The tent shifted away from the railing, and moonlight shone against the deck and the waves. "It's supposed to be important."

She drank some more Old Crow. Her arm felt better now. Tesla didn't say anything. He was probably waiting *her* out.

She continued. "Working with you—I've been able to make a difference. I don't know why you're the target for all these crazy events, but you are. And so long as you are, I want to help. To keep you alive, of course, but also to really make a difference. So, if you're still interested, I'll take that offer."

For a long moment, neither of them spoke. She looked out at the moonlight on the water, the stars, the deep velvet blackness of the night. She smelled the salt air, still tinged with smoke, and listened to the slap of waves against the side of the boat.

"I'm still interested," he said. "Very much so."

He shook her hand, and together they looked at the faraway horizon.

ACKNOWLEDGEMENTS

As usual, I had a lot of help. Taking Joe Tesla out of New York and into the ocean required research and questions and a certain amount of making things up. I'd like to thank SJ Rozan for helping me with questions about the New York Harbor Patrol, and Christina Higgins for answering diplomatic questions diplomatically, as always. When I wanted to hijack a submarine, I knew Anderson Harp would have the details I needed, and he didn't let me down. Lieutenant Commander John C. Groves of the US Navy answered approximately a million questions about life on board submarines. He is probably now sorry his mother helped me to track him down after a few decades away. Eric Boyce had a very ready answer for my question about bringing down a helicopter with a bow and arrow on a fishing line, including a story about a helicopter destroyed by someone carrying a radio with the antenna up. Professor Milton Garces explained torpedoes and sound waves to me over coffee—he even drew diagrams. When it felt like the book was going down for the last time, James Rollins and Joshua Corin provided valuable plot advice and literary support. Cherei McCarter sent me many fascinating snippets about submarines and the underwater world, and I'm grateful for each one. My writing posse helped me whip the book into shape, again: Thank you, Kathryn Wadsworth, David Deardorff, Ben Haggard, Karen Hollinger, Judith Heath, Joyce Lamb, Kit Foster (cover artist extraordinaire), and Andrew Peterson. Finally, my Ironman husband and writer son provided unending support and love.

If, after all this help and work by so many talented people, errors slipped into the manuscript, I am completely to blame. Some people will cause trouble no matter how much you try to help them!

ABOUT THE AUTHOR

New York Times and *USA Today* bestselling author Rebecca Cantrell has published seventeen novels in over ten different languages. Her novels have won the ITW Thriller, the Macavity, and the Bruce Alexander awards. In addition, they have been nominated for the GoodReads Choice, the Barry, the RT Reviewers Choice, and the APPY awards. She lives in Hawaii with her husband, son, and a slightly deranged cat named Twinkle.

If you'd like advance notice of upcoming books, please sign up for her newsletter at http://rebeccacantrell.com/newsletter. If you'd like to see what she's up to day-to-day, you can find her on Facebook and twitter, too.

AUTHOR'S NOTES

This book took Joe Tesla out of his usual haunts and necessitated a bit of extra research. As usual, the truth was often stranger than fiction.

The submarine in the novel is based on the diesel-electric Gotland-class submarines currently in use by the Swedish navy. All the capabilities and descriptions are as accurate as I could make them, and they are capable vessels. So far as I know, none have ever gone rogue, but then again, no one would tell me if they did, would they?

Once again, Joe uses the steam tunnels under New York City to access the world above. While I don't know if the Museum of Natural History is heated by steam, the Museum of Modern Art is, so I decided it wasn't too much of a stretch to let Joe have underground access to the museum.

The small commercial drones Avi uses to film and snipe are real and have been modified to carry weapons.

Bowfishing, likewise, is a legitimate sport and YouTube has many videos of people in various states of sobriety shooting arrows at fish, both above water and under water. I was going to have Joe use a harpoon gun, but the quick and hilarious videos I found of people shooting harpoon guns above the water made me think better of it. My advice: don't do it, but if you can't resist wear safety goggles and a protective cup.

While New York has large sewage tunnels, I wasn't able to find maps to determine whether or not they had some large enough for Joe to take out his submarine. Joe bought a modified version of this submarine, with a wet exit for diving: http://tritonsubs.com/products-services/. If he was feeling extravagant, he could have gone full Captain Nemo: http://www.migaloo-submarines.com/.

My writing group had real trouble believing that Edison could actually scuba dive, but it turns out he wouldn't even be the first underwater dog. PADI (the Professional Association of Diving Instructors), the organization that certified me and many other divers, even offers scuba certification for dogs and cats: http://www.prnewswire.com/news-releases/padi-announces-pet-diver-certification-course-200855191.html . Here's a cute video of a diving dog and cat: http://www.animalplanet.com/tv-shows/animal-planet-presents/videos/most-outrageous-scuba-diving-pets/ .

Made in the USA
Middletown, DE
26 December 2017